TRANQUEB

slither
~ carnal prose by urmilla deshpande ~

Urmilla Deshpande lives in Tallahassee, a city barely visible from the air, so dense is the jungle. A perfect place for writing and for walking trails which promise the slightest danger of meeting a Florida gator, or a red wolf.

This is her third book of fiction after *A Pack of Lies* and *Kashmir Blues.* She also edited *Madhouse: True Stories of the Inmates of Hostel 4.*

slither

~

carnal prose by urmilla deshpande

TRANQUEBAR

TRANQUEBAR PRESS
An imprint of westland ltd
Venkat Towers, 165, P.H. Road, Maduravoyal, Chennai 600 095
No.38/10 (New No.5), Raghava Nagar, New Timber Yard Layout, Bangalore 560 026
Survey No. A-9, II Floor, Moula Ali Industrial Area, Moula Ali, Hyderabad 500 040
23/181, Anand Nagar, Nehru Road, Santacruz East, Mumbai 400 055
47, Brij Mohan Road, Daryaganj, New Delhi 110 002

First published in TRANQUEBAR by westland ltd 2011

10 9 8 7 6 5 4 3 2 1

ISBN: 978-93-80658-84-1

Typeset in Berylium by Mindways Design

Printed at Manipal Press Limited, Manipal.

to loves real and imagined

~

thanks

~

This book was the result of a challenge from Prita Maitra, my patient, supportive, and beloved friend and editor. These were meant to be erotic stories. But early on I came face to face with the undercurrent of carnality whose swells sometimes overflow, but often run deep, sustaining our emotions and actions covertly. This book was uncomfortable to write, but also empowering, and liberating. I experienced moments of utter fearlessness, and something like duende—when I stopped noticing myself, or even being myself, and became nothing more or less than the teller of an unknown narrator's story. It's an odd experience. When I realise I am in it, it ends, sometimes before the story is told.

Some of these stories were written while I was in Canada. Outside my sister's warm house lay a white Canadian winter. It was Christmas. I often found myself in a roomful of nieces and nephews and in-laws and sisters, typing carnal prose into my laptop while eating and drinking whatever was handed to me—perfectly timed unasked-for cups of tea or coffee (Christy), home fries (Alec), peanut brittle (Cheryl), prime rib, turkey-and-cranberry sauce, bhel, chicken curry, pizza, glasses of wine, lots of chocolate.

I am grateful that I have a list of usual suspects to thank—friends and family who are always there, to demand attention or dinner when I am immersed in a story. Tissa, Sukhi, Ashish, Saheli, thank you for being there for me in so many ways. Sheila, you thought of me as a writer almost before I did myself. You know what you mean to me.

Frank-Udo, Mithoo (with your insane humour under unimaginable circumstances), Joseph (Hellwegian of the meticulous comments), Ralf (my first-ever editor, and fawltless brother-in-law), thank you for reading my stories and pointing out the bad, and also the good. Though I don't always listen to your advice or take your criticism and praise (not just for my writing) well, doesn't mean I don't value it. I do, immensely. Bruce, you cover my work like a precious gift, thank you.

Lori, Jane, Stefan, Bakul, Boss, Fish, Dhiren, love and thanks for your good wishes, they made me smile on days when I didn't think I could.

I love you all dearly.

Who says you can't thank a place? Thank you Tallahassee, my home, St. Catharines, warm even in a snowstorm, and eternal, thunderous, Niagara Falls.

~

carnal prose

~

Slither

~

I was in love with this man once. I loved his hazy brown eyes, as he looked at his computer screen, or the TV screen, or some obscure book about the lifecycle of Amazon gingers (probably his own PhD thesis). I loved his hands, I watched them for hours, looking surreptitiously over my newspaper, as he dug, planted, watered, caressed the aggressive, suggestive flowers and spiky leaves. I watched him wash them in the greenhouse sink, he always examined his broad, muddy nails and pulled at the webbing between his long dark fingers as he waited for the tapwater to heat. Then he would hold them in the stream, softening the caked-on dirt, squirt the unscented soap onto his palms with his elbow, and entwine and unentwine them in a slow dance, covering them in a bubbly casing. I had seen snakes mating one day, on one of our ginger-finding expeditions. He had stopped me with his arm, put his hand on my mouth, and pointed. I would have gasped at the sight, but for his hand. We were alone, the rest of the team had taken a different path. We watched. I was bound to the sight by my eyes, but also my heart. They wrapped around each other like living vines, an elaborate motion of sinew and sex, they were slow, and took their time, and were fast and moved on each other in a series of strangleholds, over and over, tightening and moving like muscular liquid, time meant nothing, not to them and not to me, and I was a snake in the green shadowlight of the jungle, I was a mate, I was inseparable from the sound of my scales and the grip of my lover, and his whole body wrapped around mine so I could tell no more, which move, which touch was me and which him, and we were not one, but we were one, tied and untied, lost and found, past, present, future, and yet nothing but the flesh of our being. I remember the feeling of turning to slime when I watched them, and of despair knowing that I could never be a snake in a love knot with my snake love, not with this man, who watched dispassionately with me, nor any other. And as I watched him wash his hands, I thought of them, always, as the two hands of the same man, not his and mine, not entwined. Not now or ever snakes.

And still, I loved his hands. I wonder what it is about him that rejects me over and over. It is not that he does not touch me, or that he does not look at me. But it is not with the eyes of a lover that he sees me. It is with the eyes of a botanist. He sees my eyes, humans have two, plants none, so perhaps they do not impress him, though they are, I've been told, fine eyes. He touches my skin, but with his fingertips, not his whole hands, through my clothes, not with the delight of knowing I'm right there below that layer, but with some practical purpose—to guide me through some forest path perhaps, or stop me as he did that day to watch those snakes. He even lays with me, often enough that I would not notice his disinterest, but not often enough that I felt elevated above Amazon gingers. I suppose such a flamboyant obsession makes it hard for him to see me, a mere human female, thousands of whom pass him in the street every day. I was not one he had tramped through mud and slashed through vines for, I was not one he had finally encountered, standing in a clearing alone bathed in pale green sunlight like a fire-hued goddess of the verge, waiting there for him to take her home and make babies with her. No, I was just a garden-variety human female. Well, not garden, I suppose. Asphalt. But I loved him, and I hoped that one day he would love me. Not as he did now, but in the way of a snake.

I did not care for the gingers themselves. They looked to me like abominations, like some unnatural plastic product which had been stuck all over that otherwise luscious rainforest landscape. The flowers were hard and did not invite a second touch, the colours were without subtlety or nuance. I loved our expeditions, and everything about the forest and its people. Everything except the ginger plants. It might have been that I had no choice but to hate them, they were after all my rivals. But I didn't think so. I just did not like them, their look, their feel or anything about them. Even the smell of the gingers, some coquettish and some almost animal, put me off.

He was not always one of practical hands. Or maybe I misunderstood, or mistook his early explorations for desire. He once loved exploring me as he now did those gingers. He had once enjoyed smelling the vanilla perfume of that flower I had between my legs. He took pleasure in discovering its purple folds and in tasting its creamy nectar. He loved watching it bloom and change colour and consistency as it grew, it was a little springtime every time he gave it the attentions and ministrations of touch, and watered and fertilised it with spit or his own slime. And then eventually our ritual became just that. He would kiss me sometimes, and sometimes not even that, he would absently note with his fingertips that I had breasts, and they had nipples, he would pose between my legs for a few minutes, make a few desultory thrusts and I heard the slightly sharper intake of breath before he stopped and went to wash himself. Sometimes he would return to the bed and put his fingertips on that just-abandoned bud, and I would feel a stirring of hope, if not arousal, but that was soon stopped in its tracks by the shallow steady breathing of a sleeping man. I began to avoid the whole exercise. I began to wonder if my desire to touch and be touched was leaving me altogether, as they promise it will when ignored long enough. Sometimes it was a relief to think it would be gone and would no longer plague me, but sometimes I would wake up in a sheer terror of longing and loneliness that kept me awake all night looking at the sleeping form of the husband I had once loved and longed for, now with thoughts of suicide, murder, at least escape. Literal escape. But I ridiculed those terrors and desires into the corner, and threw the body bag of sleep over them eventually, night after night.

In daylight hours I would wonder how this had happened. He seemed quite contented with our life, he went about his work in the greenhouse, he wrote papers, he taught classes, he graded, he advised students, he was much admired and liked. One day after a particularly good dinner party, as I was washing up the good china, the panic came to me in full consciousness. It alarmed me. I frantically scraped the salmon bits off the plate. It had been a really good salmon. I used an edible ginger root that he had sneaked past customs a few years ago and grown several large plants from over the years. It had a distinct sweetness that lent itself perfectly to salmon. The guests had eaten in reverent silence. He had praised my skills too, he said that the fish had not given its life in vain, and neither had the ginger. Thinking about the salmon and the salad with candied ginger shreds and the gingery pear tart all made with different gingers did not help me at all. My heart shuddered in an awfully unrhythmic way and I put my soapy fist over it. I began to wipe the washed plates and put them in the drawers where they would stay until the next time there was a dinner party for important guests. My sexuality was treated the same way as those washed-up plates. It was put in some drawer in my husband's mind between 'Other Plants' and 'Student Papers 1981-1990'. It was taken out for special occasions. There simply weren't too many of those in the life of a botany professor and his sometime painter-slash-travel agent wife. A few anniversaries, the memory lapse of a birthday covered up with a large ribbon on a small unimportant ginger plant were not special enough occasions to take out the good china. And so it went. My heart settled down a little, into a deep sadness for myself, but also for him, for the lost opportunity, for the lost life of my physical self, the beaches of my thighs and the coves and moonlit tides of the vast kingdom of my skin and hair and breasts, a place made for cavorting, for finding the depths of lust and the shallows of peace, the place I lived.

Summer came, and with it our trip to the Himalayas. He had heard, some years ago, a friend in meteorology describe a plant to him. Apparently this one had no blooms, and there was an abundance of it in a particular spot in the forest near a village. The villagers would go to the spot and just stick a device like a giant apple corer into the ground and bring out a tube of ginger enough to last them a month. It wasn't so much that he was interested in culinary ginger, but this one intrigued him. He imagined the entire ground under the spot was a giant ginger root, and he wanted to see it. It tied in with his desire to trek in the region, and he planned for this trip as meticulously as he did everything he did.

The village was as I had expected, a beautiful, neatly laid out smattering of little houses on a small slope close to a dense forest. As soon as we got there after plane and train and bus and jeep and final stretch on our feet, we were taken to a hut that was a bit larger than the others. It was cool and dampish inside, I felt the dampness immediately as we walked in from the bone-dry air outside. It was lit only by the soft glow of persistent sunlight that made it in through the tiny perforations in one of the walls. When my eyes adjusted to the shadows, I saw a man sitting quietly cross-legged on the floor. Of course he was quiet as in he did not make a sound, but there was something quiet about his whole being. He was looking at us as we bumbled in with our heavy hiking shoes and heavy backpacks. There was nowhere to sit, so we stood, the two of us and the guide who brought us there from the jeep drop-off point, and the villager who brought us to the hut. The seated man had long dreadlocked hair, and there was an odd matte shine to his face and arms that made him look blue in the faded light. He was looking directly at my husband's shoes, and it suddenly struck me that there was an alcove outside the door with a couple of sandals in it. I stepped outside and sat on the parapet bench built in to the side of the house. I unlaced my boots and took off my socks, and left them and my backpack with the sandals.

Everyone had settled cross-legged on the floor by the time I went back in. There were some introductions in progress, and then some plans were made about seeing about the ginger grove and visiting some temple high in the hills behind us, and talk about three days hence being the second full moon that month, and something about the feeding of snakes. I noticed suddenly that the wall behind the man was hung with snake skins. Some of them were six and seven feet long, and had been looped around because the wall wasn't tall enough for them to hang straight down. There were at least forty skins there, if not more. They were also alarmingly broad. I thought they must have belonged to rat snakes, huge but harmless. I asked. I was told each and every one there was a cobra skin, and they had all been found between the rocks surrounding the village, where the snakes left them after moulting. And some in the ginger grove.

The days went by fast, walking up and down hills and valleys. The pain from walking miles and miles kept me in my hut on the third day. That night was the blue moon. Everyone in the village got ready to feed milk to the snakes. They brought out polished silvery bowls, and the children drank no milk that day, it was stored in brass buckets in the coolest part of each house till the moon rose. I had not seen a single snake in all our walking, and no moulted skins either. I wondered where all these tens of snakes that I was told would come to drink the milk would suddenly come from, on this one particular day. Nor had I seen the man we met on the first day, though he seemed to be the chief, he ran everything and all the others referred to him all the time, whether it was something he said, or some instruction of his they had to follow. When I asked our guide he said he had gone somewhere and would return that night when the moon was rising. He did not know where his chief had gone, but he seemed uninterested in finding out. If he found my constant questions annoying or surprising, he did not show it, he just stopped acknowledging them after a while. My husband had found several species of ginger that he had never seen before right around the village, and he was too ecstatic to be interested in the whereabouts of the village chief either. I was intrigued though. There was nowhere to go from the village, as far as I could see, other than the mountains that ringed us. I imagined this man walking around in the ice and snow looking for moulted snake skins. I decided to see if he was in his hut. My husband had gone to the grove of the big ginger, I was not up to the walk.

I knew the hut, it was different from the others. People ignored me as I walked toward it, the children followed me and asked for candy, but when they saw I had nothing, they ran off too. I approached the hut. I sat on the ledge bench again and took my shoes off. I knocked on the door, and waited for an answer. There was none. I pushed open the door and went in. As my eyes got used to the blue gloom inside I saw that there was no one there but me and the skins of those snakes. I stood in the middle of the room and looked around. I noticed the curtain that hung at a door on one side, and moved toward it, hoping he was there, and afraid that he really would be there. He was. He sat with his back to me, completely naked from where I stood, blue-black skin stretched over supple flesh. His vertebrae fell like a string of giant black pearls from the back of his neck down to the point of his tailbone. I could not see what he was doing, I was too afraid to move. He was cross-legged and so still that I thought he was a statue of blue flesh and blue blood. The complexity of my desire made me think it was a long time I stood there, but the speed of thought meant it was probably only minutes.

Where did desire come from? Or was it always there, buried under attempts and rejection, loss and years. All those barriers and systems of repression failed in this unknown place with this unknown being and his aura that neither conveyed nor signified anything at all. I took a step forward into the even deeper gloom of this room, where hardly any of the sunlight from the other room made it, and there were no windows or even perforations in the wall. I expected him to turn around, or to move or start at the sound of my foot on the packed mud floor. There was no movement, not even the sound of breath. I took several steps then, I was convinced he was in some kind of state where my sounds and presence did not reach him.

His eyes were closed, blue-sheened almonds resting slanted below those long dark arches of his brow bone that joined in the centre to flow down his nose and separate again into the wings of his nostrils and lose themselves in the velvet texture of his face. His mouth repeated that flaring arch of his brow, dipping deep where the arches met, a small perfectly round circle in the centre formed by the way the lips rested on each other without quite touching at that spot. I followed, with my starving eyes, the line of his chin, his throat, my gaze ran down his torso, dissecting it into two perfect halves. And then I saw something I had surely never seen before. From the intersection of heels rose a creature of his body, muscular as one of his snakes coursing between two rocks as they left their old skin behind, a single pulse flickered at its head. I turned again to slime as I looked, I was back in the forest all those years ago when I had watched the two snakes in their love dance. But I was a woman, and here was the power of manhood before me, self-possessed, self-aware, capable of great pain and great pleasure, and also oblivious. This was without a doubt the biggest, strongest, most sustained erection I had ever seen. It seemed suspended in that state by something in this man's mind, it was physical, of course, but yet also not. He was not even there in that body, and wherever he was that was causing this perfect state of manhood, was where I wanted to be.

I did not perfectly understand my own thoughts, but I stood there, unable to take my eyes or mind or body

away from that man being a man and nothing else, and
I have never wanted anything so much as union with that
maleness. Nothing more, nothing less. I wanted to surround
his strength and power with the softest, slimiest flesh I had,
and be with him in that expanse of raw, basic, utter life. I
imagined slipping slowly down on him, feeling that sweet
pulse inside me, and then, with my legs around his body,
feeling nothing but our own living, our existence, and the
existence of the world. I wanted to know where his mind
was, where he was travelling, what he saw and whom he
was with, that made this beast stand before me without any
physical reason to sustain its life.

When I left the hut, it was almost dark. The moon would
rise any minute, and I waited with all the other people, men,
women, children. The moon began to rise, we couldn't see
it yet, but a serpentine vein of white began to creep along
the edge of the hills, moving slowly along until it suddenly
got lost in the wash of blue white moonlight as the moon's
curve appeared gently from behind the hill in front of us.
I sighed, and my husband standing beside me asked where
I had been, he had been looking for me. He didn't wait
for my answer, he began to tell me about the amazing size
and depth of the ginger root. I hushed him after a while,
not with any heat, just gently, so I could watch the moon
in silence, as everyone else was doing.

As soon as the whole disc became visible, there was a
lot of activity. Everyone disappeared for a few minutes and
returned with the little bowls which they placed around the
open courtyard. Then they just sat down and waited. I sat
too, three quarters of an hour, perhaps, but there was nothing.

I had no memory of any thought or decision of what I was going to do, but I was standing outside the main hut again, outside his hut, taking off my shoes again. I went inside. He was there, and there were seven small children with him. He smiled at me, slanting his eyes even more, and asked me to sit. Then he explained to us how we would call to the snakes, how we would sing, and they would know that the milk was there for them. He told us all not to be afraid, because the snakes would not do anything to harm us on that day, but also that they would not come as long as they could taste our fear on the moonlight. Then he gave the children his silver bowl and asked them to put it in the right hand corner of the courtyard farthest away from the village. And then they all ran out. We sat there, face to face, and though he was fully clothed, I could think of nothing but his closed eyes, and the creature that lay sleeping against his thigh. He laughed, startling me. He offered me a cup of milk that sat next to him. I took it, and took a small sip. He motioned me to drink the whole cup, but he didn't need to. It was creamy and went down smoothly leaving a faint aroma of flowers in my throat. Then he stood up and began to walk toward the door. I wanted to follow him, but I could not. I heard him laugh again as he closed the door behind him. I noticed another cup of the milk in a bowl right where he had given me the one I drank from. It had a pinkish tinge to it, and I leaned forward to take a sniff. I found I kept leaning forward, and couldn't stop. And then I knew what he had given me, or what he had done to me. My vision was different somehow. I could see everything, but I felt I could see it with my eyes and some other sense as well. I felt the earth below my ribs, and I heard, or felt, I had no words to form thoughts of my sensations, footsteps everywhere. I went to the door, though I knew he had closed it. But it was as good as open to me, I just went through what must have been a huge gap between the door and the floor. I went out into the moonlit courtyard, and I saw so many bowls of milk, and I saw at each of them beautiful beings glowing in the cobalt light, their scales making a soft shirring as they moved about, their black tongues flickering like flames savouring the dry air smoky from the small fire someone had lit at one end of the courtyard. I saw a familiar leg, dark and covered in curls, and I brushed along the skin. He did not move, or notice what to me was a definite and not abrupt touch. I could not smile, but I felt a smile inside my new self. I went to one of the bowls, but I knew I should not drink. I knew my spell would be broken if I even touched that milk.

The darkness called me, I could hear soft sounds of insects and birds in the short grass. I scrubbed myself along the rocks, and it felt good. I stopped on a smooth rock and tasted the air again and again. And then I tasted his smell on the night air. It came to me, clear and strong, and I was ready for him. And he appeared beside me, his scales delineated, a precise pattern of iron and night, silver and water, blue as the depth of the ocean. I was ready for him.

This was everything I thought it would be and more. I knew there would be touch. I did not know that it was not just surface touch. The kneading and muscularity of the way we moved on each other went deep into the layers of my body, down to the bone. The skin that I thought would not feel anything sent repeated shivers and tingles up and down my long leanness, the scales rippling the wrong way when he slid his on mine, tugging at each nerve ending in a crisp and staccato prickling, and then as it got almost unpleasant, smoothing out again with the movement the other way. There seemed to be no purpose to our ceaseless mutual motion but pleasure, there was no need or urgency about it. We just went on and on climbing, rubbing, knotting and weaving, holding and lengthening and shortening and gnashing and jerking, standing almost on our tail points in moments of ecstatic oneness where I could not tell where he began and I ended and I ended and he began. I had not understood at all when I had seen those other two in the jungle in another life what it meant to be this way, I did not understand the nature of touch when it belongs to two and not just one. I did not understand the nature of coupling, and how there was no separation between the two units of the couple in those moments. And they were not just moments, they were hours. I could see him, I could hear him, I could feel him, and I could smell-taste him with a flick of my tongue, and every time I sizzled my tongue I could feel and taste the metallic electricity we had made like a blue cloud on the air around us.

And finally he lay along my full length and gripped me, and I felt him within me, and then he grew and grew, and I knew the power of that maleness finally, I had longed for it since I was born that first time, lifetimes and lifetimes ago, and I had been this same me, and he had tried to show me then, how it could be, and how it was meant to be, life, love, and the making of new life.

He stayed with me till my eggs were laid, and hatched, and a year went by like the flow of water over the stones in the river. When it was that time of year again, he led me to a place that was not familiar to me anymore. And I followed him because I trusted him, and I found myself in a place full of heavy footsteps and moonlight like that first night we had been together. He led me to a place where there was drink for us. And I knew what it was. It was the milk, it was the night of the snake, it was the night I could return to the life I had known before, one that had faded every day from my senses. I left him and turned away into the dark places that I knew, the rocks, the leaves, the cities below the earth that were damp and cool and away from the dry air. I knew he would be back for me. We were one, he and I, I was his lover.

I came out into the morning sun, and began my search for a place where I could thrust off this old skin, it had grown too small on me. I found it, a place of spiky leaves and a smell that I knew very well, where a huge root lay below the earth. I would smell of it for a long time. I found two rocks and began to move and writhe between them. It would soon be off me, that skin, laying there in the ginger grove, abandoned like an unwanted life.

~

d U I

~

What purpose has coincidence? A car travels at a low speed of twenty miles per hour: a woman, driving home from seeing her only childhood friend dying of cancer in a hospital. She pauses at a bar in an attempt to numb but does not even come close to blunting her sorrow and her horror. The car moves listlessly through an almost green light, scrapes another car and startles its very alert driver, comes to a hard halt at a wall. The woman immediately jumps out of the car, and immediately thereafter realises that she has succeeded in numbing her extremities if not her brain, with her injudicious application of whiskey sours. She sags against the car, and then crumples gently to the macadam. The driver of the other car has neither sadness nor alcohol to impede his slower but steadier walk across the street to the car that hit his. He is slightly shaken by the impact, of course, but recovers enough to walk over to her and sits down by her on the warm ground. The concrete is warm because it is high summer, and there is not enough night nor lower temperatures during the night to cool the concrete. He sits down by her and says nothing. She leans her head on his shoulder. Seen from a distance, they could be a couple very much in love, but very much in sadness. Or they could be a brother and a sister, or close friends. The sadness, though, is clear in their postures. They are to one side of a perfect circle of yellow brightness from the street lamp right above them. Seconds, minutes pass, and a passerby would pass by, there is nothing more to see here. To the two people who came together though, this is a momentous moment. They will recall and retell it many times through their lives. Whether they understand the importance of this incident, or whether they create it, is unimportant, perhaps. But in either case, they are reluctant to speak those first words to each other. She is the one who takes her hand from her lap and puts it around his shoulders, and strokes his ear and his hair, which, cut very short and close to his scalp, is a brilliant blond pelt. She brings her hand to her face when she feels a sticky dampness on him, and then shows it to him. Still, they are reluctant to bring words into the moment, as if somehow sound would break not just the still silence of their existence, but the sense of future that is fast building between them. Words would start the lies. So they do not use any yet. He looks at her hand dark with blood from his head, and then finally turns to look at her, full in the face. It is a little face surrounded by short black curls of hair, now slightly wilted from the gathering sweat on her skin. The sweat gives a pleasant dewiness to her, and her eucalyptus leaf shaped eyes of indeterminate colour are half closed, throwing long shadows of spiky eyelashes on her freckled cheek. Her mouth is too large for her narrow-chinned face, it only works toward constructing a symmetric beauty because of the weight and importance of her eyebrows. They arch darkly inward from her temples not pausing in their march and creating a small confusion of direction among the tiny hairs as they collide above her small nose. He forgets himself and speaks to her. She corrects his assumption that they are her father's eyebrows. Having spoken, they must now acknowledge things of little consequence, such as the little accident, his bleeding wound, insurance, her drunkenness.

What purpose has coincidence? To dam two streams into a single flow, to stroke an eager cock, suck a succulent nipple, arch the long back of a long torso in the moment of the end of the scene? And then?

His car stands scraped and abandoned at the scene of their incident. They are in her apartment because it is closer, and because his head is bleeding. She cleans the cut and removes a sliver of plastic from it with one of her several eyebrow tweezers, she puts a solution on the wound which she tells him will dry into a second skin on his temple and stay on till it heals, she makes kava tea, to calm him down she says, but really it is for her. They sit for a while, and the adrenaline and alcohol dissipates, to be replaced by the hormones and pheromones of arousal. The cock is stroked and the nipples sucked, the long back arched in the moment of the end of the scene.

If we think of coincidence, or this particular coincidence at least, as an explosion, a detonation, then, as with any explosion, there is a shock wave. In this case of ours, this wave moves through time, not space. The time of the lives of these two people. The shock wave throws up the dust and carcasses of creatures long dead, it shakes loose fragments of childhood that float up into their days and their nights distorting their view and visibility. Old experiences hang in their new moments and influence their every move, and obscure their possibilities. Clarity is impossible. He touches her mouth with the back of his hand, she feels the back of her father's hand, the soft inside of her lips collapsing on the hard outside of her teeth, she tastes the blood on her tongue, she decides to turn away from the memory and toward this man and his caress. But it isn't that simple is it, and she returns again and again to the tortured heat of those nights she hides under her bed smelling dust, she curls her toes as she is dragged out by her arms, she crosses those bruised arms and soft thighs against the anger and shame her father feels for her, for trespasses she does not understand, she returns to the city of her birth and the house of her father with every human touch, even this one. She never thinks it will be different. But still, he reaches for her, still, over and over, he thinks he will make contact with her skin and her lips one day, and not her memories.

What purpose has coincidence? To return us to another explosion, another shock wave? We have a sense of time and future and past and present, we have a sense that a shock wave moves the time of our lives and the space of our being, that it has a beginning, a middle, an end. The shock waves are still strong in their lives, this couple in the lamplight, though they rapidly weaken, unable almost, to withstand, to obscure the impact of older, stronger detonations. The area of its reach is limited. Limited in itself, but also by them.

She is not yet a woman, he not yet a man. They are still just creatures of flesh, living in the sweet aftermath of their collision. They sometimes fulfil the roles of their physical bodies, but usually not. She cooks well, but he is better at it. She burns the dinner sometimes, and he rescues it, he has the skill to do so, disguising the smoke with honey and lemon, or emphasising it with paprika and cumin. She cuts her fingers sometimes, his highly sharpened German knives make deep gashes that deliver copious bloodflows, and he, because he is motherly, exclaims and fusses and puts the distraught smeared finger in his mouth. And because he is himself, the colour and taste and smell of the blood lead him elsewhere, to other blood, and he kneels before her on the kitchen floor, her bleeding finger held above her head, her knees threaten to give up, her dinner is half done, her man is lost to her and in her in some ancient bonding ritual of drinking her blood whenever and wherever he finds it. Her arm is tired and she thrusts her finger into his mouth, and he receives it, with all the other flows.

Coincidence leads them to this place, of gentle blood and gentle love. They are not particularly man and woman, not yet. Just two beings connected by lips and tongue and labia and blood and breath, until he, the man, and she, the woman, arrive at the point where it ends. In these moments they are even less man and woman, but these moments are too soon fewer and farther between. Is there pleasure in the second or third, or fifteenth time in the stroking of that eager cock or sucking that succulent nipple? When does it end, the pleasure, or does it wane and wane, the pleasure and the eagerness and the succulence, all of them, without the hand, the mouth, the cock, the nipple noticing, until it is ended? When the reach of the detonation of the coincidence ends, something else takes over. Memory returns, and all his efforts of touch, all his contact with her skin and her nerves, all his success with her heart and her love, all his knowledge of her sweetest places, the shyness of her mouth, the aggression of her fingers, the weakness of her thighs, the surrender of her cunt, the guilt of her eyes, it is all useless against the force of memory. Her body loses control, her mind retakes it, and their life retreats from love forms to reality. They don't find time to lay in their bed all morning, doing nothing but breathing, arms and legs wound in each other, waiting for a lazy sleepy cock to wake up and crow. Instead, they spring out of bed each day to make coffee, run a few miles, dress, she kisses him goodbye sometimes as she heads for the door, the car, the job, life. She begins to feel his love fade, even though it does not fade. She begins to fantasise about pain, because that is what she does, she had just stopped for a time while he touched her. She begins to be who she always was, before the collision. A woman.

He stays home, her home because it was closer and his head was bleeding, remember. He stays there and writes articles, and tries to finish his book. He waters plants, he grows tomatoes and he cooks her beautiful dinners most days, and he opens the bottle of wine before she is home, so he can pour her a glass as she comes in the door. He tries to kiss her in more than just a welcoming way, but she is tired, or on her cell phone, or needs to answer an email that she didn't finish at work. She enjoys his dinners, but she goes back to work straight after, and then sleeps, some nights with clothes on, and some nights without any physical contact with him.

And then, all they are left with are the roles, of man, and woman, and so they play them, with more and more rehearsal, better and better, and the story of the meeting and the mating is just a story, and the pleasure is gone, and finally the man is a man, the woman is a woman, each unloved, unstroked, unfucked, cohabitant, coincident.

She comes home from work one day, and he is gone. They have had years together. But there is only that one collision, and it has lost all its energy a long time ago. There is nothing more to keep it alive, and she knows it. There is sadness, but not very much. The eager cock was stroked, the succulent nipple sucked, the back arched in the moment at the end of the scene. That was really the end of the scene. Everything else was just scripture.

~

Isis

~

The house is in a part of the city I had never been to. There is almost no part of the city I have not been to, but this subdivision was so hidden that I never even knew it existed. The first time I went there, the taxi driver was as surprised as I was. He was sceptical and shook his head when I read out directions. We were both familiar with the road up to and the area around the docks. I had done a big story about the security of the city's shoreline, and the dockyards were a big part of it. The instructions called for us to drive along the high wall near the commercial fish market, and make a right turn. From where we were it looked as if the road ended at the wall. It wasn't till we were right up against it that we saw the road. We turned right, and the taxi driver was still shaking his head, endlessly grumbling about the road surface and the trauma to his tyres. The taxi was so decrepit that I could not imagine the tyres needed this much concern lavished upon them, but I didn't say anything to encourage him. The rough grey Arabian Sea was to our left, and a long barbed-wire fence to our right, discomfiting signs were hung on it at regular intervals telling us we would be shot if we crossed or even attempted to breach the fence. I assume it was protecting armed forces land. It was topped with razor wire, and I didn't see any normal person attempting a vault. That was a job for the very person I was on my way to meet. She would have done it, back in the day, dressed in her pointy bra and high-heeled boots. The fence cornered at the end of its territory, and there was a little forest for a few hundred yards. The road ended abruptly at a large yellow colonial house. I was back in her time. It wasn't the only time I would feel that way. Whenever I was there, I entered a bubble of her time which had persisted, or floated into mine. It wasn't the way it looked or smelled, it was where she took me. It wasn't old times, it was her time.

Except for the very bald tyres chewing small stones as the taxi drove around the fountain in front of the house on its way out, there was no sound but the sea breeze in the leaves. I stood there, confused and enchanted. At the centre of the fountain was a larger-than-life statue of the great woman I was here to meet, modelled after *Venus de Milo*. Water ran quietly down her hair and naked breasts, and the once white marble nipples and the curves of her waist and wide hips were now dressed in a bright green velvet of moss. She was so familiar to me, but I doubt any of my contemporaries could have identified her from a photograph, let alone a corroded marble statue. The face, looking up at the sun, did not have as much moss on it as her body did.

Her nose tilted up, she had a classically bow-shaped upper lip, dipping deep in the centre, steeply angled to meet the plump lower one. This statue was made in her younger days, when she was still had both of her eyes.

That summer I had been down to my grandparents' home to de-stress after a difficult book project. I loved spending time with them. Most of my childhood we had lived together. Then my grandfather decided to retire to his own childhood home, a four-hundred-year-old ancestral house in a lovely little seaside village. The long walks through coconut farms and rice paddies to the endless virgin beaches, the exhausting but exhilarating swims, the dark women I encountered along the way, the ganja a neighbour grew under his mango trees, all added up to one of the best summers of my life. One of my last afternoons there, I asked my grandfather to show me his collection of old movie posters of Isis. I hadn't understood when I was younger, but his infatuation-bordering-on-obsession with her had been a family joke for years. I made sure I brought up the subject without a hint of mockery in my voice. He smiled in a way I had never seen him smile before. At lunch, he told my grandmother he would be pulling out some trunks. To show me some things, he said. But she knew.

'Oh sure, it's that woman again. Isis, the Egyptian goddess. I was so jealous of her, you would never believe. And I tell you, she was way beyond the women you have nowadays, let alone the way we were back then. She would drink, and smoke, and even kiss her heroes, and she wore the most outrageous clothes, oh dear.'

'All that was after she lost her eye,' my grandfather said. Good writer that I am, I sat there quietly, waiting for the story to develop. 'Before that, she acted in a lot of quite good movies for about five years. She was half Egyptian, and half English. Yes, her father was a British officer, and he had married a Coptic woman when he was stationed in Egypt, and he brought them with him when he was posted here. That's why she chose that for her screen name, Isis, like the Egyptian goddess.'

My grandmother raised her eyebrows and rolled her eyes to her ornate ceiling and the fan that swirled gently above us. I ate my lunch. The food tasted so good there, everything was fresh and homegrown, or grown by a neighbour, and the fragrant rice you can't get anywhere else on the planet. It grows near the mango trees, and smells of mango blossoms.

'That Isis' my grandmother said, 'he was so in love with her, he could hardly stand it. It was probably more painful for him to love her than it was for me to be jealous.' She laughed as she said it, but I thought caught a whiff of an old and long held bitterness. They had had five children, in quick succession. I had the wicked thought that my grandfather's lust for Isis might have helped, he might have fantasised about her as he lay upon my grandmother. Well of course he lay upon her, they only fucked in the missionary position back in my grandparents' time. Unless, of course, it was Isis doing the fucking. She would probably be on top. She was incredibly beautiful, there was no doubt about that. She had dark, dark eyes, they glowed and sulked and looked at you like shining black coals. She looked as if she could eat you up, but also demanded that you eat her up. She was beautiful. I could see why my grandfather had been utterly enthralled.

After dinner we sat on planter's chairs in the veranda, my grandmother and I sipped rum and soda. My grandfather lifted his very watery whiskey to his lips and said, 'She was, by far, the most intriguing woman of her time.' I glanced at my grandmother. This time I did not sense the same bitterness as she smiled.

'Ajoba,' I said, 'you only had black and white films back then right?'

'Yes,' he said, 'fortunately. Because she would have been truly unbearable in colour.' He turned to his wife. 'I am sorry, my dear Malati, but you know I couldn't help the way I felt. It was a boyish infatuation gone mad. But here we are, darling, five children and seven grandchildren later. It was really harmless after all, wasn't it?'

'Yes,' she said, and patted his arm, genuinely forgiving. She had forgiven him a long time ago, if at all there was anything to forgive. I had always thought of these two as the best couple in the world, ever since I was old enough to understand about relationships.

After his wife went to bed, my grandfather told me a lot about Isis, punctuated by how beautiful and glorious and stunning and unmatched in every way she was by any other woman living or dead or who would ever live and die. But in the end his stories of her life intrigued me too. He told me how she had started as an extra, and worked her way up to the movie star she became, and there were no good rumours about how she did it. It wasn't sex, he said, more that she was dangerous, they said she threatened people with bodily harm, and even death. They said she had even killed people, and that's why people were afraid of her threats.

'When did she die?' I asked him.

'Oh, she's not dead, she lives in your city,' he said. 'She was much younger than me, and I'm still here,' he said laughing. And that's when the idea came to me, that I could do a book. I spoke to him about it. He was thrilled and touched by my interest in a woman who was, in some ways, the love of his life. He felt deeply she should have been an icon of feminism, the way she protected herself, the way she never had bodyguards, lovers or husbands do it for her. She was, except for one brief marriage, a strong single woman who would have been admired today, but never got her due back then, because, he said, though he loved his wife, women like my grandmother despised Isis. Isis threatened their safe existence somehow. 'I think,' he said, 'other women thought they would be expected to be like her—sexual creatures.' He was embarrassed that he had said that to me, his grandson. I grinned at him. 'I've done that, Ajoba,' I said, and we laughed.

I knew that my lovely agent would find me a publisher eventually, but I thought maybe I did not have all that long to wait. There was no harm in starting the process. And I got the editor of my magazine to call and make an appointment with her for me. He did. For three weeks later.

I watched as many of her movies as I could. What amazed me most of all was her ability to be intimate. No matter who the leading man, and there were many, and I didn't really pay attention to them, she made me feel like I was present in a room where she and the hero were about to embark on a long and lovely afternoon, or evening, or night of carnal delights. There were only long and suggestive song sequences, of course, no actual sex scene was even suggested in the films of that era any more than there is any real sex in films today. Still, while watching, I would feel at first romantic, and then aroused, and then angry and a little sick watching Isis smoulder at some man as he lip-synched to her of her incomparable beauty. At times when she was alone in a scene, she seemed about to look straight at me, and invite me into the room with her, or into the garden where she waited for her lover—me. And the number of times I stared into those eyes willing them to look at me while I slowly caressed my hard self, the number of times I spoke her name, I began to think I was a bit insane. I have access to no end of porn, I could get myself off watching anything and anyone I chose. And yet here I was, getting aroused to the point of nonsense by a movie star who was so old that I thought she was dead. It made no sense. Except, she was a goddess of an ancient time.

As I stood there gazing at the fountain, a small grey tabby kitten walked casually down the wide steps of her house, and I saw that the door was ajar. I adjusted my computer bag and walked up the stairs. I pushed the door open a little, and peered in. I expected exactly what anyone would. Velvet drapes, chandeliers, heavy carved tables and coffee tables cluttered with old things made of jade and china and brass, a sense of old decadence, the kind layered with musk and must and dust and impending death. Gloom, of course, the light would be restrained by those same musty dusty velvet drapes. An old houseboy, one who had been with the household since bygone days, sinister, made more so by his dyed black Dali-esque moustache. And though I was expecting all this, I thought that it would be kind of a disappointment for me, to have to write about musty drapes and sinister servants in the house of an aging movie star of a bygone era. Too much kitsch and cliché. I retracted my head from the gap in the open door, because other than a large screen, I could see nothing. I knocked on the door, and waited. Nothing happened, and then I noticed a small nipple-like doorbell. I pushed it hard. I did not hear it ring inside the house, but a few seconds later the door opened abruptly.

There she stood, herself, not much of an aging movie star of a bygone era, more of a Sofia Loren with smaller breasts, all cleavage and sophistication, a faint smell of cardamom with notes of a lemony freshness, an almost indiscernible aura of cigarette smoke, fitter than most women my age, said the strong brown legs and feet in plain leather flip-flops under a her short purple dress. She wore an eye patch made from a maroon crocheted flower on one eye, but the other was made up in a smoky deep purple, muted enough for daytime. She smiled at me. She was smaller than I thought she would be, but she wasn't tiny. Her hair was dyed, of course, but not a hideous jet black. It was loosely tied back. There were lighter streaks in it that must be the white or grey. She was neither of nor in a bygone era. She was now.

She smiled and nodded at me, and turned and walked inside. I followed her in. The house was not what I expected, and I was pleased, and disappointed. It was impeccably neat and clean, there was no must or dust or clutter anywhere. The surfaces were all natural, wood and stone, nothing plastic or metal, but nothing old either. And light lived in the large living room, and it was not restrained. Inside, still smiling, she held out her hand to me, and took mine in a firm, rather manly grip. I've always liked it when women have a manly grip. I feel like I can trust them in a pinch. I hadn't heard her voice yet.

'Vishram,' she said. 'Nice to meet you, what will you have to drink?' Her voice was a product of cigarettes and talking too much. More velvet in her throat than in the room, with just a touch of mould. If I closed my eyes, that voice could transport me into that musty, gloomy room I had wanted to be in. Her phone rang, and she said 'Oh excuse me a minute, I really have to take this, it's from Belgium.' I would have preferred to stare at her as she spoke, but I did not, there would be plenty of time for that. A ridiculously large disarray of flowers in what looked like a fish bowl sat on the main coffee table, there was a large colourful canvas on one wall, and the other was covered in framed posters many of which I had seen before in my grandfather's house. I put my bag down and sat on the couch. It was a deep-pile royal blue velvet. I smiled to myself. Velvet.

She finished her conversation, it had been only a few seconds, and a young woman came in to ask what we would have. I said tea. She just nodded.

'Thank you so much for seeing me,' I said to her. 'I hope we can talk a little while?'

'Oh yes,' she said, 'I have all day, no appointments today. As long as you like.' She looked right into my eyes when she spoke, with her single eye. What an eye it was. There were creases around it, of course. But it was that sulky smouldering eye with its missing twin which had felled my poor grandfather. We talked. Or rather, she talked. She stuck to the general rather than the personal, more about the days and the studios and the way things were run, the movies in which she was a typical heroine, unhappy at the start, happy at the end, in love, riding or sailing or running away into yet another sunset after defeating whatever troubles and despairs were scripted for her. It was the first meeting, and we had to talk about all that before we got to her. I wanted to know who she was, then and now, what she had done and been through, what she had felt, when she was making each of those men feel like he was the only one.

I had to walk to the main road when I left, and it was a walk I would come to enjoy every time I went to see her. It was solitary and refreshing, and the fact that it was in a busy part of the city made it even better somehow.

She called me herself as she had promised me she would, and offered me an excellent dinner. She was dressed in a floor length black jersey dress which looked like it was a very long t-shirt. Gold snakes sat on her wrists, and gold coins in her ears. Elegant, and as always, simple. More Nefertiti today than Isis. The dinner was elegant and simple too, the woman from the last time served us. A Moroccan chicken dish with rice and roasted vegetables, giant white beans in a spinach sauce. And dessert—baklava she said she had made herself, with Turkish coffee. After dinner, we sat in the living room with glasses of brandy. The room was quite different at night. Lamps glowed in corners, a huge cut-out leather shade from a floor lamp threw strange shadows on the wall and parts of the ceiling, and, on her face.

She began to talk after her brandy was all gone. She poured herself a second. And she took her hair down in a single fluid action that sent it tumbling down her shoulders. I was a little breathless, but also quite relaxed from the brandy. I noticed that she had a very smooth cleavage, for a woman her age. I thought about how it would feel. As I looked, I noticed an almost invisible gold chain around her neck. She played with it a little, and then pulled it out of her dress. A small gold ankh hung from it. Of course. She was Isis. I wondered how she might react if I did reach out and touch her. She smiled at me. She positioned herself so her good eye was closer to me. I was uncomfortable suddenly. She could see my thoughts as surely as if they were in a bubble over my head. Flustered, I mumbled some inane question that turned out to be a good one.

'I made mistakes,' she said. 'I was young, and I was not like anything any of the men had seen in this country. I had to be careful. They wanted me, some very badly, if you don't mind my being so blunt,' and she paused for a response from me, so I spoke. 'I think that would be great, if you were as blunt as possible. I want to know every detail, especially the ones where you would need to be blunt.' She laughed, then, and said, as if I had challenged her, 'Well, I'll be blunt, then, let's see how you like that!'

Men she encountered in her line of work, young and old, reacted to her in ways that were predictable, but also unpredictable, she said. She worked mostly for one studio. The studios themselves were dark and strange places, dimly lit corridors and tiny rows of rooms except for the massive shooting areas. Even those, once the lights were off, were mazes of backdrops and forests of movie lights, which to her, in the gloom, were large-headed creatures on thin three-legged bodies. She was a few weeks into her first major role. She described it to me as if we were walking through that corridor together. I had been with her through the day, which had gone well, she had settled into it, being in front of a camera came easily to her. They never needed more than three takes for her to get it perfect. She was perfect. At the end of the day she went to her make-up room to degrease and change before the studio car took her home. I was there with her in the room, standing in the shadows, watching. There was a knock on the door. She was fully dressed, so she opened it. The cameraman, Rehman, stood outside, asking if he could speak to her. She invited him in, and he sat on the plastic covered sofa. I watched him as he watched her as she took off her makeup with cream and pieces of cotton she dropped one by one onto her dressing table. He kept watching her, saying nothing at all. She couldn't see him very well, the lights around her mirror illuminated her, but the reflection of the room was dark. She could feel him staring at her though. She was puzzled. Why would he be staring at her now, when that was what he had done all day anyway? I shrugged. I could stare at her all day, watching her take off her makeup, undo her hairdo, take off her clothes. She asked him what it was he wanted to speak about. He said nothing, and then suddenly, he came right up behind her, and put his arms around her and began to kiss and suck her nuzzle her neck. She was pleased, and even a little flattered. She was new, and he was a veteran cameraman. She said he should wait a little, till she was done. But he said he could not. I felt his need to touch her. He said he had waited all day, and all week, and from the first moment he had seen her, and he could not wait another second. To her complete horror, he literally tore off his own shirt, and began to undo his trousers, looking at her with wide eyes the whole time. She stood up and backed up against the wall, right next to where I stood. He was between her and the door. She was terribly aroused by this time, not by the man, she said, but by the fact that he was so desperate, for her. I could see that. I could see her mouth open, and little breaths rasped from her. She thought about it then. She decided she would let him have something. Something small. She smiled at him. I could see her, her eyes, full of invitation, as she stood against the wall, one arm up over her head, the other playing with the edge of her blouse, pulling it down to reveal her breast slightly. I put my hand over my trousers to hide how I felt. The man emitted a groan and fell upon her, sucking her neck, both his hands upon her breasts, pushing his naked penis against her thighs, and she let him, and she began to whisper and moan, and egg him on, recognising he was out of control, he was pent up for days, he was close to exploding. She put her hands on his naked bottom and pulled him toward her, pushing into him at the same time. He groaned horribly and ejaculated all over her skirt. She wanted to laugh, she said, not from contempt, just delight, just at the discovery of her own power. But she did not. She rubbed the top of his head which was buried in her breasts, and asked him if he wanted a drink.

She refilled my drink for me. I watched her as she poured it. Her good eye was toward me, and in profile, with that sweep of hair and uptilted nose, I saw the woman my grandfather saw. I would let her lead me into studios and bedrooms. I would watch her and be there wherever she went, and whatever she did. I knew I would be there when it happened, when she lost her eye. She would take me there. I just had to be patient.

She came and sat down and gave me my drink. A little closer that she had been before, I thought. She sat with her legs tucked up under her, elbow on the back of the couch. Her hands were very strong. Feminine, long fingered, with long nails. Not grown long, but long on the nail bed itself. She wore a ring on her little finger, a small silver signet ring with a dull gold surface where the insignia would be. Her neck was long and also strong, and her skin didn't hang in folds, but rather, was attractively creased around the eyes. I wanted so much to take the patch off her eye, and see her whole face, whatever it was under that patch, which was a black and gold tapestry this time, I was somehow sure she would be beautiful to me. My fading erection began to squirm again.

After that first time, the cameraman came whenever he could to her room. It was not very different the following times, she wasn't sure whether his tendency to ejaculate on her clothes was a problem he had, or if it was because he worked himself into a frenzy when he was watching her from behind the camera every day. I could see his trouble. She did nothing to prevent either his visits or his ejaculatory habit. She said perhaps she even encouraged it, she seduced him and made love to him when they shot all day, and when he arrived in her room, she made it very hard for him to contain himself. She would rub against him and moan and whimper how she wanted him, and that was that. She said she never had to undress, let alone let him penetrate her, and the most he saw of her body was a nipple which she intentionally showed him once. This made him act so insane, clutching at himself and groaning and staring wildly at it, that she decided it was probably best not to do that. He was a married man, she said, married to the daughter of one of the studio owners. She thought she would store this fact for a time when she might need it.

It was late when I left. I walked the two or so miles to the main road, past the trees and the fence, I walked on the sea side of the road. I didn't think about a time when I would be done with this project. Or she would be done with me. Usually I thought about the end of a project with relief. But now this thought filled me with emptiness. My grandfather's descriptions and exuberance about a woman who had obviously been the lust of his life, and perhaps still was, had raised expectations in me which were bound be disappointed. I was seeing the faded, aged, musty, dusty version of his Isis. But I was not disappointed. She took me to her other self, Isis, young and sweet, and I desired her. I couldn't wait to see her again, but she said it could only be in two weeks, she was going to Belgium, to meet someone. That bothered me too. Whom would she be meet in Belgium? A lover, at this age? Then I was ashamed. I would be her lover, if only I had the nerve. Of course it was a lover. My thoughts had brought me to the main road. I got into one of the taxis there and dozed all the way home. Back in my bed I dreamed of a closed door which

I opened, Isis sat on a blue velvet couch in a small make-up room, in a black lace dress with her arm up, staring at me with her smoke eyes, and when she slowly pulled her dress down and showed me her nipple, like a young boy I came in my sheets. I woke up for a few moments and then went back to sleep thinking how absurd that I was made crazy horny by my grandfather's heart-throb.

Two weeks later I was back at the house. The atmosphere was very different from the last time I was there. She wore a denim shirt over her faded jeans, and a denim patch on her eye. She had sandwiches and lemonade for us, and the huge dining table was laid out with photographs. All the photographs we were looking at were pre-patch. In spite of my decision to let her lead our conversation, I saw the opportunity to ask her about the eye. We looked at the photos, one by one. I put aside the ones I wanted for the book. Isis in front of the pyramids. With her mother, a plump Cleopatra, and even in the blurry old photograph I could see the hair, dark and long, and the child beside her, looking at the world darkly. Strange things, photographs. Whatever might have happened before and after, the moment I was looking at was probably nothing like it looked to me. Isis was not plotting the destruction of the cameraman, nor of me, as she stood there in a simple cotton dress with no breasts and huge knobby knees. It was an odd thought, her as destroyer, but I pursued it in my head as she showed me a series of her glamour shots, the ones which appeared in publicity about her. They were classic backlit Hollywood type portraits, and her expertly and exquisitely lined eyes stared out at me, aggressively beckoning. I would have followed her anywhere.

'What happened to that cameraman? Is he in any of these photos?' I asked. She laughed. 'Yes, we'll find those, they are not among this lot. What happened. Rehman died. A light fell on his head from above, and he died instantly. Poor man. And his poor family. One of his sons came to see me after he died.' She smiled. It was a funny little smile, almost malicious. But I was imagining things, of course. I was letting my own guilt make me nervous. Not that I had anything to be guilty about, but I felt something. Something that made me squirm. Something like guilt, but was just discomfort really, about my own preoccupation with her. And the fact that she knew exactly how I felt. She stood up and came around where I was sitting, leaned over me from behind, and shuffled through another pile of photographs. And then, there it was, a clipping from the *Times* with a photograph of her holding up her hand against the flashbulbs as she got into a car, she wore a dark dress, her hair was severely pulled back, there were what looked like huge diamonds in her ears. She had a very stylish black patch on her eye. There it was, my moment. Questions collided upon each other in my head. She was too close to me, and I could smell her perfume. Cardamom and lemon leaves. I closed my eyes, and she was that young dark angel standing there. I kept my eyes closed, trying to sort through and find the right words, trying to stop my heart from being too loud, so loud that she would hear it.

'Ah,' she said, with her rattlesnake voice, 'that's the first photograph in the press of me like that. After the eye.' I sighed. She had said it, now she would tell me the rest.

She didn't. She told me about her affair with another man. A big actor, I knew him, I'd seen him in three of the films I watched, and even my colleagues would know his name. He was a big man, tall and imposing, handsome, of course, in the style of the time, but in a brutal, cruel way. He was not in love with her, in fact, she said, she did not interest him at all. He was in love with a small, thin, fair actress who had played a second lead with her in two films he was also in. That woman, Anusaya Devi, hated him. She would tell Isis how he disgusted her. And they hatched a plot for him to fall in love with Isis. They tried all sorts of silly girlish tricks, to no avail. His affections seemed immovable. And then one day, Isis saw it. She was checking her makeup right before a shot. An assistant held her mirror, and as she peered at her own beautiful face, she noticed him standing behind her, looking intently at her reflection. She pretended not to notice, and called for the lipstick. And as he watched, she put some on her already perfect mouth, handed it to the waiting boy, and then smeared it a little with a finger. He had not taken his eyes off her.

She kept her eyes on him all day, and saw that he watched her, but only when she was not looking. He did his scenes with her expertly and his passion was convincing, I had seen it, and he had convinced me. But he detached immediately after the director said cut, and made no other conversations or banter. Later, after packup was called, she picked her trailing and rather dramatic costume up off the floor and walked to her makeup room, dismissing the entourage saying she would remove her makeup herself. She did that sometimes, and they were used to it. She called for a tea, and left her room unlocked. She was sure Rehman would come in that day. She waited, but no one came. She stepped out of her room to see if anyone was about in the corridor, but there was no one. She tiptoed to her hero's room the next door from hers, and knocked. There was no answer, so she stepped in. There was no one there. She looked around. There was a poster of their last film together on the wall. She noticed a shiny patch in the middle of it, and went to touch it when she realised it was perfectly round. She poked it, and the piece fell out and her finger went right through the wall. She looked through the hole into her own vacant room.

The next day after packup, she went back to her room and let the makeup assistant take her makeup off. She drank her tea. When everyone was gone, she locked her door, and, with her back to the peephole, she slowly stepped out of her skirt. I watched her, I was there with her as she told me. I didn't know what she would do next. She took off her blouse, and stood there completely naked for a few moments, just rubbing her own breasts and belly as if to relieve her skin from a whole day of heavy and ornately embroidered clothing. I wanted to do that for her, rub her belly and breasts, make her nipples rise. She did not turn around, she put her day clothes on and walked out to her waiting car. She had never stood there naked before, she had always changed in the adjoining bathroom, which was not adjacent to his room, so she knew that was the first time, if he had been watching, that he had seen her bare bottom. She knew he was there, she said. She felt his presence, she could almost hear him breathing, touching himself. I felt it too. I saw the single eye pressed against the hole, looking. I knew what he was doing on the other side of the wall.

'Oh, I don't blame the poor prick, it was a magnificent bottom, many told me so. I knew, because I saw it on film too.'

'On film?' I asked her, not knowing what she meant. 'We made other films, not just the ones released to the public. Private films. Would you like to see them, Vishram?' I was breathless. I wanted so much to see them, but I couldn't say that to her. I didn't need to. She knew she had me. She did. I nodded.

She gave me a stack of videotapes as I was leaving, and on my long walk by the ocean I thought with some irritation that the story of her eye had been evaded again. But, what I carried in my computer bag was the antidote to my irritation for the next few days before I saw her again. She walked me to her door to say goodbye. She walked out with me into the darkness and stood right next to the fountain. She sat on its edge and leaned back and looked at the sky, like another statue of herself. I stepped close to her and looked down at her. She was beautiful, her age be damned. I couldn't live my life knowing I had let the moment pass. I kissed her on her mouth. She kissed me back, and then, as I began to get more ardent, she laughed and stood up. I thought the moment was over. I thought everything was over. But this was Isis. You never could tell. 'Would you like to come back inside?' she asked. I nodded yes again. It was not because she was old and I didn't want to hurt her. It wasn't that I didn't want to make her angry and lose my book project. I just plain wanted her. I wanted to fuck Isis, goddess of magic and fertility. I didn't care how old she was, she was a goddess. She could have been nine thousand years old, I still wanted to fuck her. She was more beautiful than Sofia Loren, and not as old. I wanted her.

'Yes,' she said. 'And you will. But first I'll tell you what happened to Rehman.' We went back into the house, and she took me upstairs to her bedroom. There it was, the place of velvet and chandeliers and a huge bed. Symbols and artefacts of her childhood home were everywhere. They looked real, not the sort sold outside the pyramids, or on the streets of Cairo. She sat me down. She undressed as I watched. She wore high-waisted panties in a dark blue, and a matching bra, her waist was small and her body was muscled in a way people who have been active all their lives are. She poured us another glass of brandy from a bottle from her rolltop desk, and sat down beside me.

'That man, Ubaid,' she said, 'I knew I had him. The next day I did not go to work, I told them I was unwell. I knew he would come looking for me, I knew I had inflamed him.'

He arrived by noon, he drove there, to that very house, straight from the studios, which were almost an hour away. He knocked on the door. As instructed, the watchmen told him Madam was unwell and was lying down. Ubaid said he would wait. He sat in his car sweating. I stood up and walked over to the window. I could see the fountain there below me. Ubaid sat there looking at the ocean. Wanting her. Thinking about her bare bottom, which I would see soon enough. I listened to her telling the story. She was not laughing at him, but she was cruel, in her own way. Two hours later she sent the cook to call him into the house, and had him sit a while on the couch, where he was given refreshments. Then she went downstairs. He stood up, solicitous and worried about her, he said nothing at all about waiting there for hours.

'He was shaking from nervousness and desire, I could have done to him what I had done to Rehman. But he was important, and besides, I wanted him. I wanted to unleash his real self, that confident man, that role he played as my hero in the movies. I leaned on him. That's all it took. He was huge and strong, and I couldn't wait to see him naked. I knew there would be a huge piece of meat on him, his hands, his lips, his feet, everything pointed to that. He carried me up the stairs and put me gently on the bed. How more classic can this get? I had this scene in two of my films.' she laughed. I left my view of the ocean and went back to the bed where Ubaid lay. She leaned back against her cushions. Her robe opened exposing her left breast. She did not cover it. He looked at her for a moment, into those charcoal eyes, and he fell upon her as Rehman had done. She could feel the expected monster in his pants grinding and pushing at her, and she made him stop. She really wanted that thing inside her, she said, and put her hand casually on mine. I gasped. I wanted to fall upon her too, but I didn't. I listened, as she stroked me. She made him undress. She had a Belgian device, she said, that they had inserted for her, and back then there was no fear of other infections. He took off his underwear, she was delighted. I was awestruck. It was a monster, and she was going to have it, as often and as much as she wanted. He told her there was just one way for him to get it in her.

He turned her over and pushed it in. I watched the sheer pleasure on her face, and her hand stroked me harder through my pants. The idea of her naked bottom right there in his hands proved too much for Ubaid, and a few thrusts later he was screaming and shouting and spewing into her in copious amounts. His shouting brought the servants up, and they stood at the doorway in horror when they saw their Madam on all fours and this man pounding and screaming like a demon. Isis was stroking me to point of no return, she had my zip down and was bending forward to lick me and take me in her mouth. I stopped her. I took her panties off and turned her over. And then, her naked bottom in my hands, Isis, goddess of magic and all things beautiful, nine thousand years of floods on the Nile, oh Isis, Osiris and Horus forgive me, I hope I lasted longer than poor Ubaid, but I was soon screaming and shouting my own delight, and, for joy, so was she.

The tapes were everything pornography should be and is not. The mystery, the beauty, the photography, it was overpowering. I didn't have the urge to get off and get away from it, I wanted to sit, and watch for hours, and let my arousal build and build with the people whose images I was seeing before me. I saw her, young Isis, I saw her in strangely realistic Egyptian clothes—because they were vintage now, they became believably antique. I saw her as the goddess Isis, with a sun on her head, and wings she held out to both her sides. It was a pity, I thought, that she had stopped being this Isis. After she began to wear her patch, she did a different kind of role. She became a different kind of Isis, a kind of crazed avenger-woman character. In those films she lured men into strange sexual traps, and then as they were about to have her or one of her sisters, she would kill and mutilate them in bizarre ways. It became a series, and although the first one or two did well at box office, there was a quick decline. Sure, she wore tight rubbery garments with deadly pointed killer breasts that could put an eye out, if I could say that in this particular context. And she smoked those long cigarettes in cigarette holders, and drank down whiskey faster than you could say King Tut. She was imbued with a dark power that was fascinating. But the story grew old. How many times after all could you watch a woman almost fuck a man she had lured quite viciously into a bedroom or train compartment or in one case a haunted mansion, and then kill him just as viciously, with a single blow to the head when he was expecting a kiss, or a decapitation when he was on his knees asking her to marry him, he was dead without even a blowjob to show for it. Men didn't want to watch their onetime sweetheart turn into a monster, and the women of my grandmother's era didn't care much for her blatant sexuality. It made everyone uncomfortable.

The best thing about the tapes were that they had no voices. The soundtrack was an eerie quasi Egyptian sound, scratchy, but perfect. No, that was not the best thing about the tapes, but I was glad for it. Moaning and sex talk would have spoilt it all, as it often does. Also, the transfer from medium to medium had deteriorated the quality in a way that added rather than took away from the effect of a secret camera, professional, but hidden from the protagonists. The tapes were numbered, and I watched them in order.

Every single one of them aroused me gently and carefully, and I was almost sad when I did the inevitable. There was no narrative in the few I had seen, usually it was Isis the Egyptian queen goddess consorting and cavorting with her beloved husband Osiris. They had sex in different positions, and on different Egyptian-looking sets, and in every one, Osiris was a played by a different man.

It was late at night when I came home from work, ate my dinner, and got myself a glass of beer. I popped the tape into the borrowed video machine and waited for my erectification to commence. The man in the story this time was a handsome moustached man, and he wore the usual headdress and robe of Osiris. He sat on a throne of the kind you see in ancient Egyptian scrolls and paintings, more a golden chair than a big puffy throne. The music began as Isis walked toward him, this time stark naked except for her sun and cow-horn headdress, and a giant ankh around her neck, hanging between her beautiful sloping black and white breasts. She sat on her husband's lap, and he began to fondle her breasts and kiss her neck. He was soon highly aroused, and, so was I. He kissed her and kissed her, and began to slip his hands between her thighs. She parted her thighs to show his penis, which stood between them. She held it between her thighs and stroked it as he kissed her neck. She brought his hands down onto his own penis and they began to stroke together, she rubbing against him, both of them obviously enjoying it. Finally she turned around and climbed upon him, and lowered herself on him, quite forcefully, and I, was bestowed the view of that magnificent bottom. As she moved up and down on him, his hands were in her hair. As they moved together faster and faster, I did too, I was the man on the chair, I was Osiris this time, I was coming hard as they both were on screen. As I cursed and got up to get a towel or something to clean up my couch yet again, the camera went to a close-up of the man's face. I paused it involuntarily. It was, without a doubt, in post-orgasmic splendour, flickering on pause, my own grandfather. I stood there in my own ungainly post-orgasmic splendour, my mouth open and my limp dick hanging next to my hand with the remote. I began to laugh. How the hell, I thought, had the old fox managed that?

I called him. I didn't know how I would ask him. When he answered the phone I said, 'Ajoba, if you tell me how you ended up as Osiris, I'll tell you how she lost her eye.' There was dead silence for so long I was about to ask if he was still there. Then he said, as if it was the most normal thing in the world, 'Do you know how she lost her eye?'

'No,' I said, 'but is that a deal?'

'It's a deal,' he said, and hung up.

I was to see her in a week, I would be done with all the videos by then, and I had to ask her about her eye. My agent had come back to me with a book deal. Even more reason I had to know where her eye went and why. I wanted to know, apart from books and pornograndfathers.

The last videotape was a little strange. It was darker, the whole atmosphere. I recognised the actor who played Osiris at once this time, it was Ubaid, her lover. I was soon to be regaled by his monster member. She was right, its presence made it the third actor on the set. And this was by far the most explicit video from among those I had seen, maybe because she and Ubaid were actually lovers. Ubaid was not overwhelmed by Isis anymore. He kept it up for long periods of time, stopping when he was close to letting go and moving to something different. At one point, she sat on the throne and he knelt in front of her. This was the only cunnilingus I had seen on these films thus far. She was obviously in heaven, her beautiful neck thrown back and her legs flung across the arms of the throne, so far apart that she looked like she was flying, she held her wing props out behind her. She was beautiful. She was so very beautiful. I was feeling my own pleasure in spite of myself, and though I had resolved to just watch and not react I couldn't help it, I unzipped my pants. And then a man in normal pants and a shirt walked into the scene. Ubaid continued doing what he was doing, but her face took on a strange darkness. She didn't stop Ubaid, in fact he seemed to have no idea another man was standing right behind him. The camera focussed on the other man's face. It was distraught and tearful. It was Rehman, the original cameraman. I recognised him at once from the photographs. Isis pushed Ubaid's head down and put her legs around his neck. Rehman continued to stand there looking horrified. She seemed to have a spasm, jerking her hips more and more and finally raising her face toward the ceiling, her mouth open in a scream. And then she thrust Ubaid aside, and he was thoroughly surprised to see a man standing there right behind him. She pushed him aside and said something to Rehman. He took a step toward her. Then he picked up a spear from next to the throne and began to strike her with it, using it like a stick. Ubaid, huge and imposing, stood there confused, his huge penis hanging heavily in front of him, not doing anything. Isis held up her hands, she seemed to be shouting at Rehman. He began to jab the spear at her, still crying. Even though I knew what was going to happen, I flinched when it did. As the music played, Rehman spiked her in her eye. I could not tear my eyes away from the film, and watched, as Isis, my beloved Isis, blood streaming from her ruined eye, snatched the spear from him. She seemed to grow tall and bigger than them both. Rehman seemed horrified by what he had done. He fell to his knees, staring at her face. Ubaid stepped forward at last, to deliver a blow to him, but Isis held up her hand to stop him. She put the spear at his heart. He did nothing now but look at her face, terrifying in its anger and blood. She leaned as hard as she could and pushed it into his chest. I know this was real, I saw a stain appear on his shirt. I saw him fall over. Just before the film ran out, I saw her face. I loved her.

I saw her again, just once. She smiled at me sweetly when I returned the tapes to her. I didn't tell her my grandfather was in one of them. I didn't say much at all. We went through more photographs and she talked quietly and simply and quite without fervour about feminism and how hard it was for her to be who she was forty years ago. It was a great interview, and I told her I would make it the centrepiece of my book. She said she was going to Belgium again, and she kissed me goodbye on my mouth, she was too tired to walk me out that day. And then she said, 'You know, when Ubaid was about to hit Rehman, I stopped him. I knew that I never wanted any man to be my saviour or protector. Not Rehman, not Ubaid, and not even Osiris himself. I am the goddess Isis. Who can protect me?' That's all she ever said on the subject of the eye.

I sent my grandfather a copy I had made of the tape. He called me back and told me how he came to be on the video. He found out that he could have sex with the great Isis, but it would cost him a lot, and he would have to give permission for it to be filmed. Two cameras, and he would never be told what to do or how. He would not even see the cameras. They weren't afraid of the internet in those days, he told me, nor diseases, and he was happy to pay a great deal of money to sleep with Isis. He didn't think his grandson would get hold of the film. 'Damn, I didn't think I would have a grandson!' he said, laughing. 'It was the best time I ever had. And I mean ever. She was beautiful, and she made me happy.'

'I know, Ajoba,' I said.

She didn't come back from Belgium. She had gone there for treatment for an advanced cancer. She had left me all her tapes and photographs.

'Keep what you want, and give the rest to the film archives,' she told me on the phone. 'Make me look good, in your book, yes? And take care of yourself, sweet boy.'

I will. Because Isis told me to.

~

Beyond the Pale

~

Shweta drew her dupatta over her face to cover her nose. She fixated on the tracks silvery below her, feeling her eyes caught in a stare, but really her irises shimmered back and forth at high speed to the periphery of her vision and back. It was very early in the morning so it wasn't too crowded. Her journey across town was the opposite way from most people. She lived downtown and worked in one of those 'li'-ending suburbs, so far out that it was barely considered part of the city, so her ride was never too crowded anyway. The winter cold smothered the city with an intricate hanging particulate composed of a million slow and fast acting poisons. Warming fires in the track-side slums were kept alive by garbage and newsprint and anything that would burn. She could smell things she knew she shouldn't allow into her nose or lungs, things that evoked the military, industry, pharmaceuticals, petroleum, heavy metals, things with weight and no intent which would surely kill her and everyone alive today. There were defecating men and boys squatting along the tracks. They didn't offend her as they used to. She didn't notice the faeces piled up below them, nor their contribution to the air. She hung in a trance as the train shuddered and lurched its way to her destination. Her day would be quiet, she worked in the library of a technical college, while she earned her own degree there. After she graduated she would look for a job closer to home, but there were a couple of years to go still. She thought about her husband. She always thought about her husband. If she had passed him in the street, she would have turned her head to look at him, and kept on looking till he was out of sight. His boxy bleached white homespun shirts and white hard starched pants, the fine leather chappals, and even if it wasn't his meticulous dress, his meticulous face would draw her eyes, as it did every passing stranger's. He was a blue stone Buddha statue come to life and wandering the soiled streets of the city, floating just off the grimy surface, untouched by the thickness of the dissatisfaction and misery around him. Men forgot, for a moment, when they looked at him. They forgot their bedbug infested mattresses, shit-smeared toilets, the fingernail of soap that wouldn't conjure up a cleaning lather anymore, the daily wage that wouldn't fit a new bar into its meagre bounds, they didn't remember the whiff of sourness from their wife's underarm as they turned quickly away and pressed their hands on her unwelcoming breasts and squirted a small guilty ejaculate into the thick condom, and then quickly, before they could see her disgust in the neighbour's light coming in through the barred window, turned away. Women forgot, the hair oil, the boredom, the pointless coupling, the slight prickly movement of the IUD, endless chopping of endless onions, the onion aura that had become their signature scent, they forgot themselves, and the small hardness of their existence. His face somehow conjured up the delight in voices of small children eating guavas, and a moment of all the work in the world done, and sweet gingered sugarcane juice quenching and cooling the throat, and a lungful of beedie on a cold night, and the actual spasm of release, that moment of being nothing. He did that to people. He did that to her too. Made her forget herself. She watched him, when he wasn't looking at her. She imagined them not married, them strangers on a bus, or in the street. She imagined him bestowing his look on her. Just his look, nothing else. A passing glance of universal caring, blessing, not meant for her, just his look, as it passed over the world, passed over her. She watched him when he wasn't aware of her, she looked at his hands from under her eyelids, the long, elegant brown fingers, the long nail beds, wrinkles precisely on the knuckles and nowhere else, she looked at his blank palms, three dark lines and nothing more, no confusion of thought or crosshatches of desperation on those hands, just like his face, untouched by wanton emotion or desire. This was the man she saw when they were to be married, this calm, benign, viceless face, and she, like the rest of the world, mistook the workmanship of the mask for benevolence in the man. He made her forget herself. He made her forget, when she looked at his dark heavily lashed eyes, that only hint to the aggression in him, that she was small, thin, weak breasted, barren, ugly in every way a woman could be ugly. He made her forget that her hair was lank and formless and colourless, her eyes, pink tinged and lost in black plastic frames and thick prescription dark glasses, could not stand the daylight, her skin, shades of white, covered in a shiny blonde down, sickened her, because it sickened him. She forgot herself when she looked at him. Her schooldays fell away, those days of taunts and derision, insults about her white-cunt, English-pig, but which were still validating, they were still acknowledging of her. Better those words than the fearfilled avoidance that sometimes took their place. When she looked at her husband, she forgot her frantic and forever search for colour in herself, her eternal prayer to the mirror to reflect back something other than paleness. She imagined herself as him, when she looked at him, imagined herself as dark, dark with the blue darkness of a god, her lips deep jamun stained, her eyes, as his, shuttered with shades of thunder and coal, so rich with pigment, so saturated that it seemed it would rub off, she wished it would rub off onto her, she would forget her own translucence, opalescence, dead milk-cream-yogurt whiteness. Until he looked back at her.

And then the rattling train invaded her senses, and she hurtled down that tunnel of his disdain and loathing, she was scraped and gouged and yet contained forever in the cage of his contempt, mutilated even more than she already was from birth, by his hatred. There was a time when he was curious about her body, about the total lack of colour on her. He was curious, and fascinated. There was a time when she mistook his curiosity for attraction, and it was a kind of attraction, but not the kind she thought it was, and the fascination for devotion, because he was exquisitely fascinated by her. She thought wrong, but she responded to it, his searching, exploring, his examination of every inch, every pore of her achromatic flesh. He wanted to find colour in her too, she supposed, just like she herself did. He wanted her, when it first began. He had left marriage too late, and was too old for most, but she was almost as grateful as her parents when his mother broached the subject. They were married within weeks. He had consummated the marriage on that first night, in the dark, but the real journey began later, when his mother returned south to her hometown, and left them alone in his flat, in his bed. That very first night they were alone, he came back from the station, ate his dinner, and took her by her wrist to the bed and told her to lie down. He turned on all the lights in the room. Then he took off all her clothes himself, and though she was afraid, she said nothing, she lay motionless except for her breathing, drenched in anticipation and clenched in a sticky fever. He looked at her everywhere, lifting her arms, turning her this way and that. He looked at her eyes, her mouth, inside her mouth, as she had done too, all her life, the mirror showing her what she was. He looked at her small breasts, nipples, navel, ears, back, searching. She knew he would never find it, she was devoid of colour. And then he opened her legs and looked there, and she knew what he would see, she had looked at herself with small mirrors and large, ones with magnification and in all manner of rooms, and lighting conditions. He would see the white clitoris, almost transparent, the veins clear through the skin, the only colour in her was her blood. He would see the slickspace below, the same colourless shade as the substance that oozed from her because he was looking. He would see the hairs like threads of transparent plastic that curled all over her front and down the crack and around her white anus like the inside of a computer terminal. She thought of the day she had opened up a broken toaster to try and fix it, and she had cried out in horror when she found a cockroach inside it, as colourless and detailed as herself. She understood then what she had invoked all her life, for just a second. She had felt it. Revulsion. It was much greater than if it had been a normal dark insect with its thorned legs. It was an appalling whiteness. An all-encompassing flaw. Emptiness. She had smashed it to a pulp, and cried her heart out. And so he examined her, every night. And then every night, just like the first, he would abruptly release his indigo penis from its constraining fabric, hold it in his hand, and quickly turn off the light before engorging her with it, and hurtling in an out of her until he had one of his violent, screaming orgasms that frightened her in their intensity, he screamed hoarsely every time and clutched at the sheets around her head. She tried to hold him that first night, and she moved a little, to participate, and he had stopped her with a harsh growl, forbidding her from touching him, ever. And it happened every night, until one day, even though she tried to stop him, he parted her milk thighs and found the colour of her womanness, just as she had found it that first time when she was fifteen. It had delighted her, that smear of perfect red seeping out of her, she stayed in the bathroom a long time with her legs apart and a mirror propped up in front of her, watching herself produce a colour, not just any colour, the colour of life. He was not delighted by it. He turned her roughly on her back and pulled her up in a face-down foetal crouch. Then he tried to grind the dark thing into her anus, first pushing and then thrusting, but he could not. She tried not to make a sound, but the pain escaped from her in a high wail of entreaty. He left her for a moment and returned with something cold that he applied to her behind, shoving it in with his fingers. Perhaps it was the scream that drew out his submerged malevolence, if she had stayed silent, she thought, this would have been a momentary incident, a failed attempt, done before she knew it. After her menses was done, he returned to his usual practice. And so it was, for a year. And one day, it changed. He stopped looking at her or touching her the way he used to. His touch now was only violent, he used his hands, his beautiful hands, dark against her blanched flesh. He would drag her against a wall, or throw her on the bed, he would rip off her clothes, he would hit her and kick her, but never hard enough to break skin, and then at some point he would become aroused, and masturbate. At first he went into the bathroom, but by and by he just stood over her as she lay on the floor or the bed, making no eye contact, ignoring her presence as the other children sometimes did when she was a little girl, and he would relieve himself, screaming in an agony of anger and horror. His revulsion had eclipsed his fascination. Still, she thought, it was her he sought out for this. And, by the end of the week, she was painted in all the hues of bruise from ink to marigold, from iris to sky, his fingers and palms and the soles of his feet left rainbows upon her breasts and hips and ribs and shoulders and arms and thighs. She admired them, and tracked their progress from birth to death, coloured flowers blooming and living and dying on the incandescent garden of her skin. He wanted her. She was the object of his desire. His desire, like everything else about him, was different from any other man's desire. And when she understood that, she was satisfied. She was in pain, but happy.

As the train left the city for cleaner tracks and the green smell of trees, Shweta readjusted her dupatta and wrapped it neatly around her ash-blonde hair, and swung the ends over her shoulders. She had dressed in a blue flowered kurta which enhanced the blue tinge in her eyes and skin. She had put on mascara that morning, not black, but an ocean blue. She had read somewhere that blues were good for people like her. And today was the day visiting professors were coming from a university in the American North. She had looked forward to this all week, she knew she would enjoy the activities and festivities and special events. She would meet the four professors, and she would enjoy the fact that they would not react to her any differently than they did to anyone else. She had experienced this before, when the Norwegians came, and when the South Africans came. She found her fears of meeting new people were simply unwarranted when the new people were from outside. She had never left the country, but she wondered if there were so many freaks in these countries that people had stopped noticing, or if they had internalised difference as diversity to such an extent that even she would not only be accepted, but unnoticed. The idea thrilled her. She imagined walking into shops she had never been in before—something she never did—and talking to people normally the first time she met them. It was an irony that didn't escape her, that a colleague from the Delhi office was considered fair and therefore beautiful, but she was a freak. Too fair. And it was this fairest of fair skin of hers, after all, that got her this husband, so beautiful, and his fascination for her. He would come back to her, and touch her as he used to. Her thoughts slowed with the slowing beat of the slowing train. But did she want him to? Touch her any other way than the way he did? Are two people closer than when one can cause the other pain, know a person well enough to cause pain? And derive such deep pleasure from that pain as to arrive at the pinnacle of pleasure through it? He would never find anyone like her, ever. Not in the world he inhabited, of a quiet back office, a world of rows and columns of numbers. He would never find someone he could despise as he did her. It was special and unique, their love. She would do whatever it took to be his victim. For him to be her master. For him to be a god, he needed her by his side, and in his bed. For him to be a god, she had to be his goddess, white shadow to his shadow darkness. The two of them were like the gods her grandmother prayed to. They were gods, and not like other mortals.

Professor Wyeth, Joan, was a woman with hair the colour of the polished copper pots and lingams in Shweta's grandmother's prayer room. It was cut shoulder length. There were spots and dots and smudges all over her skin, on her face and nose, and the tops of her breasts which were two lovely little pillows disappearing into an emerald green t-shirt. She could not keep her eyes off this woman, and the woman seemed just as taken by her. Shweta was delighted when she was elected to show Joan around the library, and they were still on the tour at lunch time. Joan said she didn't have to go back to the others, so Shweta invited her to sample the lunch buffet in the college cafeteria. They stood in line with large metal trays. Joan watched Shweta, and served herself exactly and only what she did. And then, as they sat at a corner table eating hot parathas and what she referred to as green goo, yellow goo and orange goo—aloo palak, daal, and chicken do piazza—thoroughly loving every bite, they became friends. Joan told her about her life back home in Syracuse, the snow, the lake effect, her hiking addiction, her little girl, her father who was a writer of self-help books. Shweta told Joan about her husband. There wasn't, and had never been anything else in her life worth talking about. Him, and her search for colour. And Joan wouldn't understand the latter at all.

They finished lunch, and when they went back to the conference room, someone had bolted the door from the inside. It was a mistake, of course, but they could hear the first post-lunch speaker being introduced, and didn't want to hammer on the door. Joan asked to use the restroom. Shweta knew by now that it was a toilet she needed. While Joan was inside the stall, Shweta washed her hands again to remove the smell of the chicken that clung to her fingers, and then pushed her sleeve up to check on the colours of her arm. Joan walked out just then. She took a sharp audible breath. Shweta covered up the arm, but it was done. Joan had seen her skin, mottled with old and new blue fingerprints, where his colour had rubbed off onto her. She wondered if she should retract her offer to show Joan the city, and to take her shopping that weekend, and her promise to introduce Joan to him, her beautiful husband. She couldn't find the words or the opportunity.

The day went by in a blur of excitement and delight, and Shweta realised she need not have worried at all about her friend's reaction. Joan was gentle and quiet and willing to have a good time, finding joy even when things when wrong. When the dish she ordered at lunch was too spicy and her face turned bright red, she laughed, wiping tears and eating pieces of what the waiter called boiled ice—meaning it was made of boiled water so it wouldn't make her sick. When they couldn't find the perfect shade of green to complement her red hair, Joan bought a black silk scarf saying it would make her fatty sister look good. She was lovely, and Shweta loved being with her. They were freaks, the pair of them, and it was easier to be one of a pair. And then, too soon, it was evening, and they took a taxi to the restaurant where they were to meet him. Shweta was quiet the whole way, and as the taxi slowed to a stop, Joan reached for her hand and squeezed it. Shweta didn't understand the gesture. She detected sympathy, and was puzzled, even angered by it. Joan would soon see him, her husband, and she would feel what everyone felt when they saw him. Belief in higher beings that walk among us. And Joan would see that Shweta needed no sympathy from anyone. That she was to be envied, not pitied, for she, the white freak, the transparent bug, she, and no other woman, shared this man's life. And she shared his bed. She brought him to the end of all his feelings, to the bottom of all his dreams, to the completion of all his wants. She owned his orgasms. She was the one complicit in his carnality. There would be no need for anything but envy to be felt for her, about her. And then there he was, and Shweta tore her eyes away from him to look at her friend. Yes, Joan's eyes were upon him. And her eyes were glazed in the way everyone's eyes glazed when they encountered him.

Joan clutched Shweta's arm suddenly, and tilted her chin, to show him to her. Shweta looked at him again, through this foreign stranger's eyes. Through this red-headed woman's forest green eyes. He sat there, by the window, looking out at the world, tall, dark, and so beautiful, the late evening sunlight almost unable to light up his darkness. She wanted to run to him there and then and kneel before him and make him look at her, she wanted to arouse his disgust and hatred from the root of his precious being, she wanted that dark part of him to rise there and then and demand her, her and no one else, and against his wish, he would have to have her. She remembered Joan, who was still waiting there in suspended motion, with her mouth slightly open. She forgot herself, as everyone else did. She was probably thinking about giving herself to him. She was imagining herself at his feet, naked and open, Shweta thought. She took Joan's hand and led her to the table. And introduced them. Joan was at a loss, she had not realised that the man she was looking at was Shweta's husband. Her face was hard to read, but the evening went well. He was, as always, charming, and attentive, but never in a focused way. Joan felt his benevolence upon her, a warm light on a dark day. She smiled and smiled, and if anyone had asked her what was said that day, she could not have told of anything but the calm in the eyes and the smile on the lips of a man she would never forget.

It was two years before Shweta saw Joan again. She ran into her unexpectedly on the steps of the university auditorium. It was an awkward moment, made worse by the bitter Syracuse cold. Shweta knew firsthand now what the lake effect was. She had seen it those past two winters.

She would never forget her first snow. It was a short walk across dead lawns which, she had been told, would return in the spring, from the restaurant to her little second-floor apartment. She enjoyed walking under the tall street lights, there were three dark steps from one circle of light to the next. Upstairs, she closed the curtains against the light right outside her window, and went to sleep. When she drew the curtains the next morning, she thought her whiteness had infected the world. Every last colour had vanished. The cracked black street, the distant red university buildings, the usually cobalt sky, the yellow windowsill, everything, near and far, everywhere her eyes could reach, was white. Snow had taken the world. She had smiled. She had felt at home, one with the white landscape.

Joan Wyeth had made it possible for her to be there. She had helped her apply, she had told her how to get finance, how a graduate student got work, she had done it all for her. And Shweta was grateful. Even though Joan had never understood her, she had meant well. Maybe it was she who didn't understand Joan, she sometimes thought. But it didn't matter now. Her husband was gone. He was dead, and it didn't matter anymore. She thought of those days sometimes, but not often, after he died, and the police came, and though she was never arrested or charged or taken to court, she felt a shudder of fear when she thought about it. She did not often think of the actual day. That was too much for her.

'I want a divorce,' he had said into the darkening spiral of her mind. She did not go back to those moments at all, if she could help it. 'Are you listening,' he said again, and she was listening, but she did not understand. She began to take off her sari, she was wearing a sari that day. She took the pallu off her shoulder, letting it fall to the ground. If only he could see her naked, she thought, he would stop saying those words. 'Stop doing that,' he said, taking a step toward her. 'You have a job, a life. I need to get away from this. It isn't right. I want a divorce. Please stop doing that,' he said, as she unbuttoned her blouse and removed it, a statue carved from a hunk of blue white marble, her feet still unfinished, covered in the heap of sari. She was still, waiting, naked, finally listening. He kept his eyes on hers, looking onto their colourless depths for the first time in their life together. 'I can't go on like this, you understand? I am hurting you, and you are unhappy, and it is wrong,' he said. She wasn't unhappy, she said to him, of course she wasn't, if that was what he wanted, it was her privilege to give it to him, he could have her any way he wanted, she was his wife, after all, she said to him, tears of relief and love began to flow from her. He thought she was unhappy, that's why he wanted to leave her. For her own good. How wrong was he, she thought, now everything would be fine. Forever. She began to step toward him, so she could put her arms around him, so she could give herself to him once again. Maybe this time, now, finally, they could kiss, and he could take her to their bed, and he could just lay on her as a man, and she a woman, now that he knew. And then his words: 'Stay away from me, don't do that to yourself. Don't you understand? I don't want to feel this way about you. I met someone else, a woman, a normal woman, you know what I mean? I want to be with her. I want a divorce. I want to be free from this—abomination.' And then she saw all the colours of the rainbow in her eyes and in her head, and she took the two steps forward and threw herself at him. He fell. He hit his head against the wall. He never stood up or walked or spoke again. He never touched her again.

When she met Joan at the airport that day she arrived, she was surprised at the reception. Joan enveloped her in a hug. Later, when they arrived and she was settled in her apartment, they had talked. Joan approached the subject as she was getting ready to leave. 'You poor girl, you poor girl, what you've been through... I can't imagine... but you know I understand. I would have done the same thing, if I had half the guts you did. That bastard, I saw what he did to you... it was self defence, I know.' And Shweta asked her, 'What do you mean, Joan? What he did to me?'

'I saw your arms, and the bruises. I know how that is.'

'That's not it, Joan. He was my husband, I was his wife. That was how he showed his love. That's not what hurt me at all.'

'What then?' Joan asked, clearly puzzled. 'What made you—do what you did?' Shweta had tried to explain to her friend, but she hadn't understood. Joan had only stared at her in shock, and then stood up and walked out. They had never spoken again, till that cold morning on the auditorium steps. Shweta was the puzzled one at the end of it. She had told her friend the truth, she didn't know what else she could have told her.

'It was another woman. He had another woman. He wanted a divorce, Joan, he wanted to leave me. For another woman. That's why I did it.'

~

'O Johnny, let's play'

~

In spite of the heat, my toes were beginning to freeze. No shoes were ever good enough to keep the monsoon wet out. I was wearing gumboots that day, and I had tucked my trousers into them neatly, and my long raincoat covered the tops of the boots. But still, somehow, the water got in, soaked my socks, and my toes were cold and probably beginning to become waterlogged. I knew how they would look when I took my socks off. My skin is a terrible colour to begin with. I am considered fair, and therefore handsome, but the paste colour that runs in my family is close to hideous. I know you think I digress. But, I'm just telling you how it was, you know, that day. Middle of the monsoons, you begin to feel every day will forever be rainy, and it was the middle of the monsoons. I hated sitting in the bus on rainy days. It was just another part of a poor childhood that was so like everyone else's and therefore not really poor enough to complain about and certainly not poor enough to be traumatised by. It was like everyone else's, just uncomfortable enough to be, well, uncomfortable. Itchy sweaters, wet socks, just enough food in the lunch box that one was not hungry, but not enough that one was happy, no major achievements at math or science, no accidents, injuries, or windfalls. That sort of thing. And then there was Madan. Madan was different. Yes, I told you I'd get to the point. And here it is then. It's not easy, but that's what I'm here for, so today, Madan. The day he and I met. Which is why I started telling you about the monsoon. One of the school buses had broken down, and our bus, after picking up everyone on our route, took a detour to pick up all the stranded kids from the broken-down bus. Without lifting his eyes off the slush we had tracked in onto bus floor, covered in his funny little grey plastic raincoat that he had worn over his clothes and his huge heavy backpack, looking like a small sad hunchback, Madan took the two steps into the bus with some effort. All our backpacks were heavy, but he was small, so it was heavier on him. The seat next to me was the only available one, and he took it. He said nothing to me the whole way to school, in fact he didn't lift his eyes off the brown sludge of the bus floor the whole way to school. I could not even see his face, the raincoat hood shielded all but a little sliver of his profile from me. I could see his hands, clutching the rough strap of his water bottle, twisting it and digging at it with his nails. I watched his hands and fingers all the way to school. He got off the bus with me, of course, and he walked into the school building with me, and he stopped next to me, right inside the entrance where other busloads of boys and girls had collected to take off their raincoats, shake the water off, fold them into small bundles, push them into plastic envelopes and stash them in backpacks. It was a wet and uncomfortable and crowded operation, but we all did it, squabbling and laughing. Madan spoke to no one. He was done at the same time as I was, and we walked side by side down the long corridor to our classroom. The strange part was, he walked into my class. There were about sixty students in my class, but still, it surprised me that I had never noticed Madan. He sat in the front row by the window, as far away from me as he could be. I was in the back row, diagonally across the room from him. Still, I just couldn't understand how I had missed a whole person. It bothered me somehow that I might never have noticed him if he hadn't got on the bus with me. I kept glancing at him all day. He had got under the thin carapace that protected me from the minor daily discomforts of my existence. I got to know the back of him, the way his hair shaped itself around the side of his right ear, leaving a strip of bare skin. I noticed that the top of his collar where the white shirt touched the skin of his neck was dark, unwashed. It occurred to me that my mother would never let me wear the same shirt twice, and this one seemed to have been worn for a week. I watched him all morning on and off, when I could, and at lunchtime, I don't know to this day why, I waited till he was ready and then followed him to his lunchtime tree, and sat down next to him. He did not open his lunch box. I opened mine, it was a two-storey steel box, I knew there would be four chapattis in the upper half, and some kind of vegetable in the bottom one, and on some days, a small bowl of yogurt or maybe pickled mangoes, or even something sweet if was after Diwali or Ganpati or someone's birthday. I began to

eat, I had green peas. There was no little treat today, but the
food was my usual home food, my mother's cooking. Hot
and available at times when I needed it. I ate, not speaking
to him. But he did not open his box. I was almost done
with one chapatti, and he just sat.

'Aren't you going to eat?' I asked him, and those were
my first words to him.

He said nothing, but he did open his box. There were
two biscuits in it. I didn't know what to do, but suddenly I
felt like closing my box. I couldn't make such a large gesture,
so I turned away from him slightly, and I had trouble putting
my next bite in my mouth. I could see those biscuits from
the corner of my eye. The corners of his lunch box had
crumbs in them of a different colour, I think they did not
belong to the biscuits that currently occupied the box. I took
a few more bites, but turned more and more away from him
as I did, and finally I could not eat anymore. I sat there
for a while, and I could hear him scrape the biscuit on his
teeth, sawing it so that the dust fell into his mouth. I knew
exactly what he was doing, we all did it for fun. I knew he
was doing it to make the biscuit last longer. I don't know
why I did it, but I opened up one of my remaining two
chapattis on my palm, and scooped half of the peas into the
centre, in a long fat line. Then I added a little more, so I
had less than half left, rolled it up, and handed it to him. I
did the same with what I had left. We ate in silence. When
we were done eating, he gave me his last biscuit. I ate it. It
tasted old. Then we closed up our boxes, gathered ourselves
up, and, as the bell rang to signal the end of lunch break,
we walked back to our class, and to our seats.

If what Madan and I had was a friendship, then that was the beginning of it. You must understand, I find this hard to talk about. You must understand, this was the beginning of my emotional life, Madan was. I never felt before him, I did not feel myself. In more than one way. I tell you because you asked, because I must, but I don't find it easy to put it in words, let alone go back there. I know I must talk about it all now. For me, and also for Johnny.

The next day I woke up early, after laying in my bed and listening to my uncle snore and thinking about Madan. I went to the kitchen where my mother was making the chapattis and asked her if she could give me one or two extra. She laughed, and shook the rolling pin at me. I told her it wasn't for me. She asked, but I said no more to her. Then I put my bag on the seat next to me so no one would sit there, but the bus didn't go that way, and I sat alone with my bag for company all the way to school.

He was not in his seat, so I asked the boy who sat next to him where he was. He said he didn't know, but he said Madan missed school a lot, he was probably sick again. I tried asking more questions, but the boy just didn't know any more than what he had already told me. My mother was annoyed with me when she unpacked my lunch box for washing. I was unable to eat the extra chapattis she had given me. I didn't say anything when she kvetched at me, and my uncle told her to stop, and she did. He smiled at me, and I forgave him for keeping me awake with his snoring.

He and I shared a room, his room, actually. It had been his room all his life, and then my father—his older brother—married, and brought home his wife, and had me.

He was very nice to me, he was the big brother I did not have, a father figure kinder than my father, I suppose, an uncle figure. He never married. I remember times when they brought girls to show him, and there would be a sort of mild electricity in the house, my mother would make two or three special little foods, one fried, like bhajjis or batata wadas, and one pohe or upma type thing, and one sweet. Then, after the girl and her family had left, my uncle and I would sit at the table and finish all the leftover food, and there would be a lot because prospective bride families hardly ever ate anything, and he would tell me the things he did not like about the girl. There were individual characteristics about some of them—a fat upper arm in one, or a plump chin, and in one he did not like the way her hair hung in front of her ears like sideburns, I remember this one because I began to notice it after that, and I don't like it myself, to this day, but some things, like the tiny hands and high voices, he universally disliked. My mother heard him once, and complained to my father, who looked out from behind his newspaper and said to his brother, 'Don't fill the boy's head with your filth.' He said it mildly, as if he was following my mother's instructions. And my uncle continued his discourse about women being fleshy and tiny in the wrong places. Later at night, laying in bed in the dark, he told me about the more disgusting aspects of women, how they had holes where we didn't, and how they oozed blood and terrible bodily things from there which got stuck in the hair that surrounded those holes, and how their breasts were squishy and utterly contemptible things, useful for feeding babies and nothing else, and how their soft snail-like flesh had an old garlic smell which got stronger as they grew older, and was impossible to smother with all the sandalwood and jasmine they poured upon themselves. I stood behind my mother waiting for my lunch box one day when I saw two rolls of snail-like flesh hanging below her saree blouse, the two layers of flesh stuck together by a scum of sweat. I searched for garlic, but there was nothing, just the burning wheat smell of fresh chapattis on hot iron. I wheedled an extra chapatti from her, but there just wasn't enough of the yellow potato.

Madan was in school that day. He was already sitting at his desk with a book open when I walked into the room. I felt an uncomfortable tightness in my throat and chest and other parts that I did not comprehend then, when I saw his chair occupied, after being disappointed so many times that I had almost given up looking for him. He did not look up from his book, and I did not know if he noticed my presence or cared if I was there or not. I was unreasonably elated. And I was disproportionately relieved that I had a chapatti for him. I would give him all the potato, I thought then, and spent the whole two hours of class before lunch thinking about how we would eat lunch together. We had an English class right before lunch, and the poetry teacher had his once weekly class. Most of the students except for one of the girls hated this class. That day, Joshi Sir read a poem out loud. It did not make any sense to me, it seemed to be about a woman talking to her beloved whose name was Johnny. I know it well now of course, and it's why I call Jonathan Johnny even though he hates it, but that day all I could think about was the lunch bell and my extra chapatti. It seems a strange poem to read out loud to thirteen- and fourteen-year-olds, but I have stopped questioning it. It just fits with everything else that happened. It makes sense now, in hindsight.

When the lunch bell rang he did not speak to me, but we walked together to the tree. He opened his lunch box and there was nothing in it, not even the crumbs, so I scooped up the potatoes and put them in there, and we ate the chapattis from my box and the potatoes from his. Our hands touched occasionally when we scooped at the same time, and I felt things I cannot describe even to this day. I know what it is, I have read about it and heard it described and seen it enacted in movies and I hear it in music and poetry, I know what it is. But I did not know what it was then, all I could do was feel it. I would have done anything for Madan, and I would have done anything to be with him. We spoke after lunch that day, as we were washing our hands. I said I would take his bus home, and walk home from his stop. I knew it was a short distance, from the day his bus had broken down. He said okay. We met after school, and sat together on the front seats of the bus, not saying much. We got off at his stop. It was a short walk to his house, and the only thing he said to me was that I must not speak to him as we approached, and I must keep walking past once he went into his house. We didn't question these things, as children. We accepted how things were, the rules adults made. I had a reasonable life, as I said, I had enough discomfort but it never elevated to pain or fell to the level of becoming actual pleasure. I assumed everyone's life was more or less like mine. I did not have the imagination to gauge how much more or less like mine his life was. I walked on as he walked into a little house with an overgrown garden. Not even a garden, just weeds and what might once have been intentionally planted rose bushes on either side of the metal gate. I did not speak with him or acknowledge him, and though I very much wanted to, I did not turn back to look. I had a sense that if I did not follow his softly spoken but very specific instructions, I may not see him again.

I have not described Madan to you. I have never described him to anyone. He is a feeling in my memory more than a picture. But I want you to feel my feelings, so I will try to describe him to you. He was like warm water in a stream, on a hot day, but in a cool place, like when the water flows over rocks, or under trees. It comes there warm from the sun, and makes the cool place warm. He was pale, but not like I am pale, I am pale without translucence. The light seemed to come from the inside of his skin, and his eyes. His hair shone, though it was always dirty. He smelled, of unwashed adolescence. I know that smell, I smell it now on my own students, but his was sad. It was not this carefree smell of underwear worn for a week out of laziness. It was sadness, it was a smell that weighed upon him. I saw him washing his neck in the school hand-washing sink once, hurriedly, trying to get it as clean as he could in the few seconds he had before the bell summoned him somewhere. I felt that day, for the first time in my fourteen-and-a-half years, tears at the back of my throat, bitter with sadness for another person. Madan woke me. He made me a person. He made me feel, human.

When I lay in my bed listening to my uncle snore after he had masturbated into his sheets, I thought about

Madan, and wondered if I could somehow bring him home and run some hot water for him so he could take a bath. The thought of him taking a bath was the first time my feelings about him begin to become solid and real. They began to coalesce into my flesh, and I put my hand down and followed my uncle's example and stroked myself with my teeth clenched and eyes shut tight.

He was not at school the next day, nor the one after. The next day was Friday, and I knew that if he did not come on Friday I would have to wait till Monday. I was distracted and upset all evening, causing my father to cuff me in the head twice, and my mother to start a long lecture about grades and mathematics and the upcoming final exam. Madan was not at his desk on Friday, and I wondered if it would be okay to walk into the headmaster's office and ask him if he knew of anything. I promised myself I would do it at lunchtime. Although I spent the rest of the morning thinking about that act of bravery, or perhaps because I overthought it, I could not go through with it. I ate my lunch with a few other boys, and miserably went through the rest of the day. I have to say, at this point my discomfort did elevate to the point of becoming pain. I felt pain. I felt desperate. I had to see him.

I took Madan's bus instead of my own. I got off at the stop before his house. If you see my hands tremble at this point it is because I wish I had not. But now that I have come this far in the story, I might as well tell you the rest.

I got off at the stop before his house. I walked slowly toward his house, remembering what he had said about me talking to him or acknowledging him. I stopped at the fence of the house just before his and loitered, as schoolboys do. No one passing by paid me much attention. A few schoolchildren passed by, laughing and chattering, and soon disappeared into their houses. I knew they would come out to play on the street sooner or later, and I was not sure what to do next. There was a small wilderness between the Madan's house and the one I stood in front of. I looked up and down the street, and slipped into the bushes and tall weeds. I went right up to the barbed-wire fence surrounding Madan's property and carefully climbed over. I did tear my khaki uniform pants, but didn't know it then. I saw a window at the back of the house. I put my backpack down against the wall and climbed onto it to get a view of the inside. I don't know what I thought I would see there, I know what I was hoping to see. A glimpse of Madan. Just a glimpse at least. I hoped he would see me, and come out and talk to me. I did not expect to see what I saw. The room I was looking into was a bathroom. I saw Madan completely naked, standing at a table of some sort, his thin translucent body bent over, his head down on his bent arm, as if he had got tired in the midst of bathing and put his head down to take a rest. His face was turned to me. His eyes were closed. I could see only part of the room, and I did not dare move, my legs wobbled on my backpack, it felt unsteady against the wall. I did not dare move. I had a sick dark feeling that there was something here I did not understand. I was afraid, and I was moved in a way I did not understand. I could not take my eyes away from Madan's nakedness. Though I could not see him entirely, this was enough for me, this was enough to make me want to grind myself against the wall, tottering on my backpack. I clutched the windowsill with my left hand and shoved my right into the waistband of my uniform pants, and I clenched my teeth, and kept my eyes open. I could see the curve of his small body, I could see his ribs, and if I stood a little taller, I would see more. I fell.

It must have been hours later when I awoke, and I thought I had died. I could see electric wires crisscrossing over me, some straggly leaves of a tree, and sky, a dark sky, through it all. I knew immediately where I was. I stood up, and without looking in at the window again, I picked up my bag and sneaked out of the gate. I walked till I was past Madan's house, and then I ran, till my legs hurt, till my lungs hurt, all the way home.

My mother and uncle were so pleased to see me that I did not get into trouble. It was late enough that their anger had dissipated into a frantic worry. My father had not returned from work, so they had not decided what to do yet, but conversations about the police had already taken place. I was dispatched to the bathroom, and as soon as I came out and explained my bus breakdown and my tripping and falling on my walk home, and how I woke up and realised how late it was and then how I ran home. My mother patted my back. My uncle hugged me. I ate dinner and went to bed without doing my homework. All I could think of was Madan, naked in the bathroom. All I wanted was for morning to come, so I could go to school, so I could see him again.

This is hard for me to tell you, but now it is also hard for me to stop. So many years have gone by, and so much has happened to cover up my feelings and memories. So many habits have put layer over layer on this core of all my experiences, but still, as I speak to you, I uncover, I undress myself, and I want to know it too, who I was and who I am and what it all did to me. I want to know who Madan was. Who he was in my world, even if I never know who he was in his own.

I went to school the next day, and he was there. There were blue shadows under his eyes. We had to wait until lunch, but as soon as we sat down, he gave me his little lunch box. There was nothing in it. I took it, and I gave him mine. He tried to open it, but his hands shook. I opened it and gave it to him. He looked at me once, and I nodded yes. He ate everything in it. Then he drank my water, and only then he talked to me.

'Will you come to my house?' he asked me. 'We can do the homework together, and we can play outside after that, we can climb the guava tree in my garden.'

I said yes, I would come after school, but the next day, because I had to ask my father. 'No, today, come today,' he said to me. I thought about telling him I had been there the day before, but something stopped me. I did not know if he would understand, but I also had a feeling he would. I said I would try to go over to his house, after going home first. I knew I had to go home first, after the previous day's episode. I was in a terrible state of waiting, anticipation. I did not want there to be any time between seeing him and seeing him again. I wished to stick those times together, delete the moments between.

I went home, and my uncle was the only one there. I told him I was going to play with a boy down the street, from my class, and he smiled and waved me out. I did not ask where my parents were, I knew his permission was not good enough, but I took it. I ran all the way to Madan's house. I stood on the front doorstep. I rang the doorbell. I waited. After five minutes I started looking in through the windows. The second window I looked into showed me once again what I did not want to see, what I do not want to remember again, what I want gone from my mind, from my body, because it lives everywhere. I did not know, you understand, what I was looking at. I did not understand. I saw the man, a man dressed in a shirt and nothing else, his trousers were around his ankles on the floor. I saw my Madan, but I also did not see him, I just knew he was there. I saw the man's face, his expression, I heard the groan coming out of his throat, I saw his hands somewhere below him, I could not see them. I was overwhelmed with a kind of shuddering feeling that I know now, I know what it is now, it is the birth and death of my sexuality. I did not know, what I was seeing, I did not. I cry now because I understand it now, this violent need to bring myself to a kind of death, I cannot help it, how I feel when I think of that. I am back in that place, I am torn to shreds of pure desire, it is desire, but it is like a torture, I want to be that man, or I want to be in Madan's place, that poor little soul, that poor thin beautiful boy who ate my lunch and who touched my hand, and who wanted to be my friend.

Forgive me, for the tears, I could not help myself. I am better now, I can tell you the rest of the story. Madan never came to school again. When I went to the headmaster two days after, they went to the house to look for him. Madan was found dead in his father's bathroom. There was no one else there. I was never told what it was, this story. When I went back to India this summer for my mother's funeral, I visited the place again. I asked a neighbour, but they did not know who I was talking about. I decided to dig into it until I knew what it was, the story of my first love.

How can a boy of fourteen understand what rape is, when he sees it, when he has never seen it before? Even Madan himself did not comprehend what was being done to him, all he did was try to find a way to express his pain, his fear, simply by asking me to come over to his house. I could have done something that day, to help him, if I had understood. But I did not. I was lost in my own lust, my own ugly lust for a boy who was being raped, and killed. Murdered by his own father. He was hungry, and tired, and afraid.

But you know, he was not unloved. Madan was not unloved. Whatever his life was, he was not unloved.

Thank you for listening. It has taken months for us to reach this point. Months of your patience, your questions, your silence. You can call Johnny in now, and I will tell him, that now I can start to love him too. And one of these days, we will read an eulogy for Madan, Johnny and I, and put him to rest. Madan, he was really my Johnny, wasn't he?

Wait, listen a minute... I think this is how it goes: O the valley in the summer where I and my John, beside the deep river would walk on and on... While the flowers at our feet and the birds up above argued so sweetly on reciprocal love... I leaned on his shoulder, 'O Johnny, let's play'...But he frowned like thunder and he went away.

～

The title of this story and the lines he quotes are from the poem Johnny *by W. H. Auden*

Rhumb – line

~

The director was making Samir wait. Usually, when he came in to the bank, the secretary took him straight into the beautiful ground-floor office with bay windows that opened out onto a wild rose garden. He didn't bother to pick up the latest issue of *Wired* magazine that lay on the table in front of him, he didn't think it would be very long before he was summoned to see her. He enjoyed his monthly meeting with her. She was a very stylish woman, and their short meetings, which ended in Samir collecting his cheque, were always interesting, and pleasurable. She was a little old for him perhaps, but Samir often wondered what she would be like in a more intimate situation. He always thought about inviting her out, but the same forbidding thing about her that interested him stopped him from asking.

When the secretary finally came out to escort him in, he realised that he could have read at least one article entirely if not the whole magazine, almost three quarters of an hour had gone by. When he walked into the room, he was surprised to see someone there he had never seen before. An older man sat at Ms Selva's desk, in her red leather chair. He got up and shook Samir's hand, and explained that he was just there temporarily.

'Don't worry,' he said, 'she'll be back soon, she's just gone up to head office for a training session—she's doing the training, as you know, she's one of our best. We'd have her up there permanently, but she likes it here.' Samir, surprised at his own relief, moved around the desk to sit down. The light flooding in from the bay windows shone onto his face, and the old man stopped halfway as he was sitting down.

'I know you, don't I?' he said, clearly puzzled. Samir didn't forget faces. He had never seen this one before. But, he knew this routine.

'No,' he said, slowly to the old man. 'I've not met you before, Mr Kohl. I would remember you if I had.'

Mr Kohl continued to stare at him, until the moment became uncomfortable. Samir sat and waited. He wondered, for the thousandth time, with more than a little irritation, if he had the sort of commonplace face that was always mistaken for someone else's. This had happened to him since he was a little boy. He was adopted, and he didn't look like his mother and father, and he was in the minority with his very dark brown skin in the predominantly white scientific community that dominated the university town. He had grown up there, so people knew him, and now, since many of them had known him since he was a small boy, he didn't get much of this here. But strangers were another story. All he had to do was go to the city for a meeting, stop at a restaurant for lunch, and take the train back home, and he would have at least one incident of the kind he was going through with the bank director. Random strangers would tell him he looked familiar, sometimes insist they knew him, or had met him, and once or twice people had become upset when he said he didn't know them and had never met them before in his life. Mr Kohl seemed to be on the verge of it. He wondered what to do. He once thought this was a common experience, but now he knew it was not so.

'Do you have a twin brother? Or a cousin or uncle who looks a lot like you?'

'I don't know, Mr Kohl,' Samir answered, a bit tiredly. And then it struck him, and he wondered why he'd been such a fool.

'I don't know, you know, I might have a brother, or I might be one of quintuplets!' he said, smiling broadly. 'I was adopted, and for all I know, there may be many of my siblings walking around who were given up for adoption to many different couples, and you may have met one of them?'

As he walked back to the department with his monthly cheque in his pocket, he thought about what he had said, and wondered if it might not even be true. Not quintuplets, though the amount of times he had had this experience it might well be quintuplets, but maybe there was a twin at least, living somewhere close by. As he walked past the endless glass walls of the Jenny—what they all affectionately called the gene labs—he thought about it. His mother and father were long gone, so he couldn't ask them but he thought seriously about going to the authorities, whoever they were, to find out. He hardly ever wondered who his birth parents were, if he did it was nothing but a passing thought. He thought often about his mother and father, whom he had loved and who had loved him and cared for him and let him want for nothing, even after they were both gone. He missed them terribly. Not constantly, but there were still times when he felt the sharp pain of their absence.

The types of encounters he had with the bank director was not the only thing Samir was confused and irritated about. There was the thing with women. He didn't have any problem starting a relationship. He was charming and sweet and sensitive and understanding and accommodating and easy to please. He was well endowed in body and bank. He not only made a reasonably good salary, he had the research grant, and on top of all that, there was the fat cheque from the trust fund every month. There was just nothing wrong with him that he could see. He was beginning to think there was a conspiracy. He said as much to Enoch, and he was laughing as he said it, but there was enough seriousness in his voice that his roommate was concerned, and offered Samir the name of a certain professor Sturgeon in the wellness department who would see him privately. He declined the offer as he always did. Enoch, and Ronny too, made this suggestion regularly. Samir was beginning to wonder if he should go talk to the professor. He was beginning to feel resentful about his poor luck with women. He looked himself in the wall sized mirror left behind by the previous couple who had occupied the apartment, a couple from the small but very prestigious Eng. Lit. department. Samir and his two roommates were very glad for their predecessors. They had inherited a meticulously clean, beautifully painted space with an abundance of mirrors that brought light into what might have been a dingy and depressing place. The two women, who were lovers and colleagues, and had published extensively together, had dealt cheaply and artistically with what was probably the apartment's only flaw. The windows were all on one side, and it may once have been bright, but a very tall building had grown slowly up that side and plunged them into gloom. The two women had made a good effort with paint and the mirrors, but they weren't satisfied with their accomplishment, and they left. Not having seen what the place was like before the gloom, the new renters couldn't believe their luck.

The mirror showed Samir a very tall but not too tall, very dark but not light-absorbing dark, very well dressed but not uncomfortably metro, and, even if he said so himself, a very good-looking thirty-six-year-old scientist. Pale green eyes in the dark face somehow alluded to his maker's sense of humour, it took away from the severity of his good looks, made him accessible. He took great pains to make himself accessible too. He made himself very accessible. He was ridiculously good-looking, but he didn't let that be a hindrance to anyone. He was always friendly and helpful and full of disarming self-deprecation, sometimes to the point of goofiness. He was brilliant at his work, and he never flaunted that, and he didn't flaunt his money either. He didn't care for male company in his bed, but he was beginning to think about it seriously. He simply wanted a relationship that involved friendship and closeness and sex. He had almost stopped caring about the sex of this imaginary partner. He was tempted to ask Enoch if he could just sleep with him, just so he could have his leg over a body that he felt love for. He did love Enoch after all, they had been together a long time, they had lived together and run together and drunk too much and plunged clogged toilets and hiked and been sick together. It was a thought. Enoch didn't ever have a girlfriend for longer than two days. And Enoch was magnificent. An Ivoirian father and Irish mother had come together to create a thing of beauty. Samir had seen him naked many times, and he had looked and admired often. He began to lose himself in this fantasy about his long-time friend. Maybe, Samir thought, Enoch would agree to let him sleep with him. Naked. He was certain that if he ever talked about it, Enoch would offer him the fish professor's number yet again. And maybe he would offer to move out. And maybe he, like everyone else, would disappear, leave him forever. It was odd, this whole history with women. It occurred to him that maybe it was physical, maybe there was something he did in bed that was really really wrong. He didn't like the idea, but he had narrowed it down to that. He thought about the last time he had been with a woman.

She was a little shy, Sharon, but, because of how he was, approachable, she approached him for help on her project. He always made time for people, and it was not only attractive women, he thought. There was fat Maggie, and she didn't count among the unattractive, she was very beautiful, but really, he didn't even think about how a person looked or what he might get out of them, he genuinely cared and liked to help, men and women, if he possibly could. Sharon took him out to lunch the afternoon her paper came back to her from her very difficult professor with a note saying it had been accepted for the journal she intended it for. Lunch. It could have been a long lunch, they had meant it to be a long lunch, but by the time they had had their first glass of wine and a few breadsticks they were ready to go to his place. It was closer than her place. He was always careful not to push himself on anyone, he was even more careful after his last few episodes. Sharon showed her eagerness more than he did, she kept saying she could not believe that she was actually going home with him. He worried that she had had too much wine, that she wasn't herself, that she was not entirely in control maybe. She undressed him right in front of the mirror wall in the foyer. She undressed him carefully, piece by piece, and though he had only seven pieces of clothing on, she took almost fifteen minutes to take them all off. She left his boxers for the end, and took him into what she thought was the bedroom, to do the rest. It was the kitchen, and they laughed. He took her into the bedroom and admired her beautiful hair falling in waves to her shoulders, the light from one of the mirrors made it shine, and he loved that he could see her front and back at the same time because of the huge mirror on the opposite wall from his headboard. She was soft and plump, and he was happy to lie back and watch her as she undressed, not as slowly as she had undressed him. Her breasts were very white, and very large, and he couldn't wait to have them in his hands. She left the bra on, and her black panties, and smiled at him the whole time, and came and lay down in the bed beside him, stroking his happy erection, she was in no hurry, and nor was he. They had kissed a lot, and he

felt warm thinking about her. He could even feel movement
in himself, in his body and his mind when he played back
that first time with her. It got even better the next time,
Sharon was abundant in her body and soul, and she gave of
herself easily and with great joy. She loved being with him,
he was sure of it. And he loved being with her. She liked
the conventional, it was true. She did not like it when he
tried to go anywhere below waist level with his fingers or
mouth, and he stopped as soon as he sensed her discomfort,
so that could not have been why she disappeared one fine
day. No. He had been most gentle with her, just as she
liked. He had always been on top, he had not tried to force
any of the things he would have liked, and he was sure she
was always pleased when she left. Always was too big a
word to use for their four or five encounters, even though
they lasted a few days each time. It wasn't erotic or exotic,
but they enjoyed each other. He wondered if she had been
hurt somehow, if he had conveyed boredom, if that was at
the root of her disappearance from his life. He was sure he
had not done anything wrong. In fact he was beginning to
have a really odd feeling about all this. He wondered if he
should really ask Enoch for that number of professor trout
in the wellness department. But then, Sharon and he had
not been in love, and they were not very intense in either
their lovemaking or their conversation. Maybe she was the
one who had got bored. Maybe she wanted something more.
Maybe, he thought, he should have pushed a little more,
maybe he should have been a little rough with her, tried to
get her to let him touch her lovely plump pussy. She had
been the one to undress him that first time, so maybe there

was something wild in her that he didn't catch on to. He gave up. He was just going around in circles that made no sense. He would never know why Sharon left, and he may as well leave it alone. But then there were others.

He thought about Russi then, the absolutely stunning Serbian girl. She wasn't a girl, she was a woman, but she was so tiny that he thought of her as a girl. He told her so, and she laughed at him and said, 'I'll show you, Samir,' and she had done all the things that Sharon would not do. She loved getting him impossibly hard. She would lean with her back against him and drive him crazy by feeling and touching herself so he could see all of it in the mirror in front of them. When he couldn't take it anymore, and she knew exactly how hard he was because she could feel him against her ass, she would jump on him and ride the hell out of him, looking in his eyes the whole time. He missed her. She was smart and crazy and utterly sexual, and intense in every way. He was nearly in love with her, at least as a bedmate. And then, inexplicably, like every other woman he had ever liked, taken out to a meal, a movie, a coffee at the Jenny cafeteria, kissed, fucked, and almost started a relationship with, Russi said she had been offered a job thousands of miles away, one that was just too good to even consider not taking, and she was gone. He couldn't trace her, or Sharon either.

Enoch, and Ronnie, their other roommate, told Samir over and over, that other than his constant irritation of being mistaken for someone else, and his strange obsession about disappearing women, he had a great life. He always had had a great life. Everything was perfect. He had a perfect childhood, right there in that town, among the very smart, smartest of all his own parents. They had adopted him right after he was born, and he knew he was lucky. His mother worked in the Jenny lab, only the most prestigious and powerful gene and microbiology department in the country if not the whole world. The place was funded partly by his father's money. That's how they had met, his mother and father. She was a student there, one of the very few smart enough to get a full ride at Jenny. She was the star of the university by the time he came along, she was a legend in her time by the time she died. She was called the Professor telomere. It had to do with the lengths of DNA strands in clones. It wasn't his subject. He did know basically what it was about, but his thing was physics. The biology of living things just did not interest him. Even though his mother had built the first ice bear to be seen in the wild in four decades. He was proud, unbearably proud of her, and in awe, but biology just didn't make him tick. His mother was always proud of him too, but he thought she might have been disappointed in his lack of interest in her field. She was a little obsessive too, about his health. Every six months the check-ups, the prodding and poking, the blood tests. Still, his parents loved him. She may have been that way because he was an only child, and one she could not have herself, for whatever reason. It was ironic, that the woman who transformed cloning, who changed the course of religious and political thinking on the subject, who, with her work in bioethics committees changed laws and got funds flowing to areas which had nearly died out, could not have her own child. She was older than his friends' parents, much older. People who didn't know them, though there were not too many of those, thought his parents were his grandparents. He had minded sometimes, but usually not. Enoch and Ronny reminded Samir that he had had the best parents in the world, all the money he would ever need, an amazing education, everything and anything at all. He had no cause to complain. A few disappearing women were hardly worth fretting about. And how many times had he heard from every one of his friends and colleagues and professors that one line? 'One day she'll come along, Samir, you'll see.' They all seemed very certain, but he was tired of it. One of these days, he would propose marriage to Enoch.

And then, she did come along. Jamima. What happened to him when he saw her was inexplicable and unbelievable to him. He went to the bank, for his monthly collection. She stood in Ms Selva's rose garden. She was with someone, a man in a suit. Samir could not see his face, but if he had, he would not have noticed. He felt as if his heart had stopped. She stood there, her head slightly tilted, listening as the man spoke. Her hair covered half her face from where Samir could see her. He did not know what to do. His thoughts were berserk inside his head, and he was in a kind of pain and fear that he could not bear. Ms Selva noticed his distraction, she couldn't not have. He was unable to answer her questions or sign the usual papers. She asked him if he was alright, and he knew he was not. He was afraid. His heart started up, and would not slow down. He had a sense of certainty, and yet, though he felt that she would be his, surely that woman would be his, he was so afraid that this, this love, this fulfilment, this piece of his heart and soul would be ripped from him.

Ms Selva smiled at him. And then somehow he knew. What he was afraid of was real. There was something, or someone manipulating him, his life, time, and if he did not do something about it, he would lose her. Forever. He stood up and walked out into Ms Selva's rose garden, walked up to Jamima, looked into her dark brown eyes, and held out his hand to her.

She took it, and smiled at him as if she had known him all her life, as though she was expecting him, as if she was looking into his life, his soul, through his eyes, as if she knew his past and his present and his future, and they were all hers. He was afraid.

Jamima did not disappear, but nor did he see her again until a week later, a long unbearable week. She called him finally, one dark rainy night, as he tried to sleep, tossing and turning in his sheets, hating the mirrors in the room for throwing even the tiniest sliver of light into each other so that they became a nightmare of stars glinting on the periphery of his vision, keeping him awake, driving him mad. But he knew, it was she who kept him awake, the fear. If she called him, if he saw her, if he touched her, if he loved her, and he knew he already did, then he would lose her. And then she called.

'Samir?' softly, as if she had said his name a million billion times, as if she had said nothing ever but his name, as if she had thought about nothing but him, Samir, the luckiest little boy in all the world. They ate on the terrace of her apartment. It was an odd place, the apartment, it was decorated in an older style, but not old enough to be vintage. It looked like it might be her parents' or grandparents' apartment, too grown-up, too sophisticated for a thirty-something woman. He found out she was barely twenty-eight. She didn't drink any of the wine she served him. 'Maybe in a few weeks,' she said, and through their conversation it seemed to him she had been ill, but he didn't want to probe. He didn't want to do anything at all, he felt sick. And yet, he wanted to consume her. The thought shocked him. He wanted her, he realised, so badly that he felt sick. He loved her so much that his head hurt. He was out of control, and the fear would not leave him.

She helped him, somehow. She seemed to understand, and he did not know why. They did go to her bed, that night. And it was a strange and lovely night. And at the end of it, Samir was more afraid than he had ever been, more than he could remember. She kissed his hands, his wrists. She followed the lines on his palms with her fingers, but with her eyes closed. She kissed his face, and his eyes, and she ran her fingers hard through his hair, and she felt the scape of his skull. She kissed his neck, and his earlobes, and then she placed her mouth carefully on his mouth. He did not move, he did not speak, and he did not respond except with his heartbeat. He did not dare, lest she disappear right there before his eyes. She gazed at him, and he saw in her eyes a look that he had seen in his mother's eyes, but yet there was such a love and such a lust in her that he almost let his fear go. And she smiled at him again, and put her hands on his face and kissed him, and then he did let it go. He tasted her, her lips, inside her opening mouth, her tongue, his hands, released from their fear, they had their own places to find, and she placed her hands upon his and took him everywhere, his hands saw all of her in the enveloping darkness that slowly settled around their bed, all her secrets that she didn't want to keep were his, they were all his, her softness, her breasts. 'Samir,' she said, 'my love, my love, I lost you, and found you, and here you are,' and he lost himself, he was in places he had never been before, but she showed him, deep places, swamps of desire and oceans of old lust, he consumed her, and she him, they lost themselves in each other, and searched to find themselves again, in lips, in inhalations and expressions and moves like waves, he swam in and out of her, they were barely conscious and yet certain of each other. They burned, they were lovers. They could not stop, they were soft, and sweet, and kissed and loved, and then they were hard, and clawed and scratched and cried, and tore away all the skins and doors and reflections until they arrived at that place of surrender, and of one sleep, one being together in one dream, where neither knew which was which.

The morning came burning into the room, and Samir's fears fell on him as he watched his love sleeping, her nipples awake from the slight chill in the breeze, her legs spread wide, one across him, so he could see her open nakedness and the slime of their togetherness ooze from her. He moved her leg off him gently and slid down to drink her, slowly with his tongue, he knew she awoke, and he felt her hands again in his hair, feeling his scalp, pushing him, opening herself more, lifting her hips grinding him down, sighing, sighing his name, again, as if she had said it all her life, as if she had said nothing else, and then her orgasm, no his, it was his, he thought. She was his. And as she trembled and quivered in the dying waves of her pleasure, he began to sob. He fell, and she held him, but she could not contain his fear, nor could she tell him who he was, because he had lost himself.

The old man was quite familiar to Samir. He had just never known his name. He was an old friend of his parents, and Samir remembered him from back then. For once, he was the one who said it to a stranger. 'I have met you before, Professor.' And the professor smiled, and said, 'I've met you before too, Samir,' and smiled an inscrutable but very kind smile. Jamima sat on a couch just outside the professor's office door. Only after assurances from both Professor Sturgeon and Jamima did Samir agree to leave her there while he went inside. The professor spent thirty minutes with Samir, and could keep him no longer, he became nervous and upset. He had to check on Jamima twice during that time, to make sure she was still there. The professor sighed and let him go.

As he watched the two of them leave hand in hand, he went and stood at his window and lit his cigar. He was too old not to smoke, he thought again, he was too old not to pleasure himself in the ways that he still could. He saw them come out from under the building, not hand in hand but even closer now, she had her arm around his shoulders, and he had his around her waist. Even from up there the professor could see his desperate grip. The professor smiled. Time would heal Samir, he knew that. He knew she wasn't going anywhere, the beautiful Jamima. He knew they were together till death parted them. Again.

It was a long story, was Jamima's. This was only the luckiest girl in the world, and the most beautiful. Her mama was beautiful, her daddy was rich. Wasn't that the song? And then the beautiful Jamima fell in love, the professor remembered her and her green-eyed lover walking hand in hand everywhere on campus and all over town. Their love had no shame, he remembered thinking. He saw them once, as he sat behind them at a movie. They kissed, they stroked each other, the professor heard every gasp and giggle clearly as the boy brought her to pleasure right there, with his fingers, and the professor even heard her say, in a breathless whisper, 'Push it right in baby, yes, oh, I love you', he was younger himself then, and the sounds of their love and his imagination in the flickering light from the screen had done things to him that made him ashamed then, but now he only smiled. And then the wedding, she wore a saree, a green one that reflected in her husband's eyes, making them even greener. He had given them a pair of bicycles as a wedding present. They had loved the gift, they had laughed and she had hugged him, and he remembered again that he had been privy, even if secretly, to the delicate gasp of her orgasm. She was a beautiful creature. And her Samir was too. He was smart and gentle and loved her. And then they found out the flaw in the perfect story. He was sick. The cancer that lived and grew in him would kill him within six months of their wedding day. Jamima was heartbroken, she did not want to live. She became despondent, and suicidal, and there was nothing anyone could do. The professor visited Samir once in the hospital, and it was close to his last day. She sat there on his bed, and her life was draining out of her as she watched her love fade away. She just looked at the professor helplessly and said nothing, she was out of words, and out of tears. And again the professor remembered that lovely whisper of their love, and his heart broke for her, for them, but there was nothing anyone could do for them, for her, sweet Jamima.

What was the song again? Your daddy's rich and your ma is good-looking. Well they didn't sing the part about her ma being the smartest woman in the world. Professor telomere. She couldn't let her baby girl, her one and only child, be unhappy for the rest of her life, could she now? She did her magic trick. She quite literally, made a new Samir for her Jamima. Daddy's money, an endless stream of it, was poured into getting him right. The professor heard whispers from the Jenny lab students and researchers that over a hundred Samirs had gone wrong, and over a thousand messy embryos and disfigured foetuses were thrown away in those first years. They had no end of genetic material, he heard that Samir's body, some said there were more than one, was stored in a suspension unit developed for the space programme, for deep space travel, until he was out of any danger. Jamima's daddy was able to get it there on loan. Samir was brought out into the world, their new adopted child. There was nothing at all wrong with this new Samir, he was perfect. Which, in fact, his progenitor was not.

And Jamima, sweet and beautiful Jamima, who got what she wanted, always, realised that she would grow old while her Samir, a little boy, grew up. She prevailed yet again on her smart ma and her rich daddy to suspend her in time to wait for her lover, her chosen life-mate, to catch up with her. The professor had heard that in the process of perfecting the unit, seven or eight volunteers were brought in. Not many outside the labs knew where they went or what happened to them. But Jamima was placed in the unit only after it was deemed safe enough. Her ma and daddy were gone when she was woken from her hypersleep. They couldn't have known, the professor thought, that when they put her in, that they would never see their beloved girl alive again. And ma and daddy took care of her Samir. They kept him for her. They never let him want for anything, they never let him stray from her. When they knew they were not long for the world, they called him, the professor, their old and trusted friend. They told him what they needed him to do. And he had kept an eye on Samir, many eyes on Samir, just as they had instructed. He didn't do it just for the money, he had told himself through the years. All those women, sent away in ways he did not even know, all those people, all that suffering, he saw it all through because he understood to some degree how those two people felt about their one and only daughter. He understood because he felt it himself. He loved her more than any living creature on the earth, and he had waited all the years of Samir's life to see her smile again, to see her in love again, to see her be loved again.

The professor knew that finally, after all those years, after all that had happened, she would be happy, with her man. Samir was made for her after all. He was made for her.

~

Wet

~

I am thirteen years old and I am a virgin. I do not know what that means, because I do not yet know what it means to not be a virgin. This word, this idea, is only a negative. It is a label, indicative of what I have not done, of what I have not experienced, of what has not been done to me, of what I have not done with someone. Is there another word quite like it? For any other not being, not doing? I suppose there is. Barren—never had children. Spinster—never married. But those are so negative. Compared to virgin. Which becomes negative too, as you grow older, as your virginity grows older and staler, and along with those other things becomes a label that defines you in a way you perhaps did not intend yourself to be defined—barren, spinster, virgin. But I go too far. I'm not there yet. I am thirteen years old, and I am a virgin. No, I do not know what that means, but I am soon to find out. I find out two very important things in my life on this day.

I live in a village not very far from a smallish town in western Maharashtra. Not on the coast, and not even close to it. There are not too many bodies of water here where we live, and it does not rain very much either. It is barren harsh land, the land my father owns, and all the land around us as far as the eye can see, and as far as I have ever travelled. This is drought land from primitive times. The mountains to our west stand as a barrier between us and the rain clouds from the Arabian Sea. The wind blows incessantly across the plain and it has blown away all the soil around us almost down to the rock. We grow crops on the remaining thin layer of dirt. Hardy crops of grain that need little water, dry crops that are made into dry meals. There are two bodies of water I know well. One is the canal that divides the village. All villages are divided into the two communities, ours is no different. This canal sometimes has water flowing through it. Sometimes when it rains on that faraway river, the overflow feeds our canal, and I am reminded of what moving water looks and sounds like. It is rare, and happens once every three or four years. Otherwise, the rest of the time, the canal is a dry gulch between the two sides of the village.

The other body of water I know very well is the well on my side of the divide. It is full this time of year because the water table is high. Nandu and I go to the well for a walk. It is a longish walk, but not too long, so we are allowed to go on days when we don't have school. Nandu is fourteen. She has breasts. She asks me if I want to swim in the well. It is a huge well, a big square of green water, and deep at any time of year. It is full, so I will have to climb down fewer steps to get to the water. I am not yet ready to throw myself off the edge like the little boys do, I am afraid I will hit my head on one of the many steps. I am happy that Nandu wants to swim, but she says I should go ahead and she will join me later. I am puzzled, I ask her what she will do while I swim. She smiles at me mysteriously and pushes me to the edge. I go down the steps on the well wall, down to the water's edge. I undress there, I take off my long blue cotton skirt, but leave my blouse and panties on. I take a breath and enter the dark water. It is warm, a little warmer than my skin, so I almost don't feel it at all. It is kind to me, it holds me sweetly on its surface. I float on my back and look up at the sky. I swim laps around the perimeter, touching the walls, the old stone and the moss. This is the only place I have ever seen moss. I am here for a long time, because time stops when I am in this well, when I am in water. I go into its green depth, but not too deep, it is murky. I am tired, but more hungry than tired. So I come out and air dry myself for a while before I put my skirt back on. I tie the drawstring tight and shake out my hair. Little drops fall everywhere, and almost immediately my hair begins to dry as the dry air sucks the water out of it.

Nandu has not returned, so I will go and look for her. There is no sight of her around the well, so I walk a little distance toward home when I hear a sound in some dry bushes and turn toward them. I hear a sound like an animal. I go to investigate. I see them. Like everyone who has seen that for the first time, I am confused. There is my friend, on the ground, her face is as I have never seen it before. I have known her since I was born, and I have never seen this look on her before. I do not recognise it as fear or pain, but it could have been either. I do not know the look of pleasure, so that thought does not cross my mind. Her blouse is pushed up over her breasts. Her skirt is pushed up over her legs. Her legs are spread impossibly wide. There is a boy upon her, between her legs, making jumpy movements. His hand is full of one her breasts. I make a sound myself, and he stops moving and springs up quickly. Before he pulls his shorts up I see a shimmering, quavering, rapidly diminishing bolt of veined flesh. My friend is confused, and turns her head to follow his alarmed eyes. She makes contact with my eyes and tries to tell him that it will be okay, that I am her friend. He looks at me apologetically, and beseechingly, and then walks away rapidly and does not look back. I know the boy. He lives on the other side of the canal from us. The wrong side of the divide.

I am now aghast and confused. We do not, and never have, touched anyone from the other side of the canal. And this was more than touch. It was, though I did not know it then, penetration. Nandu and I talk all afternoon, until someone from home is sent to bring us back. I find out two things that afternoon, both about myself. One is that the water and I love each other. The other is that I am a virgin.

~

I am fifteen years old. I am still a virgin. I am in a school in the big city. My teachers convince my big rich father that his daughter must go to school. The village school ends at the eighth grade, and my father thinks I must marry his best friend's son. The son says he will not marry a girl without an education even if she is a virgin. My father agrees to send me to school until the tenth grade. The best part of the school is its swimming programme. The public pool is part of the school grounds. We have a strange coach who yells and yells at the other girls. He sits on a high referee's chair at the edge of the water. He never yells at me. He tells me that the water loves me. But I already know that. I live with the older sister of my father. He is not happy about this at all. I find it strange that my aunt locks me into my bedroom at night and slips the key to me under the door. She tells me every day that I must never give the key to anyone but her at any time after sunrise. I also have to wait for the secret words. She tells me these words the first night I am in my room, and never again.

I do well at school. I learn English. I swim every day. The swimming coach calls me to his office one day. There is a very pale person sitting there in a chair. I think it is a woman but I am not sure. My coach tells me the name of the person is Susan. I cannot tell from the name if it is a woman. Then coach tells me I must change into my swimming clothes and meet them at the pool. I walk through the little wooden gate to the pool. Susan is standing there with a small clock in her hand. I have seen she is a woman now because I see her toenails, and they are bright red. She smiles at me and calls me dear girl. She tells me I must signal her when I feel ready, and then jump into the water and swim to the other side and back as fast as I can. I nod, and I jump in. I swim to the other side and back as fast as I can, but it's not as fast as I ever have. I know I have swum much faster than that. But I am heavy with batate-pohe from the school canteen, and it weighs me down. When I get out of the pool Susan is looking at me, shaking her head and smiling. She tells me I am going to Florida.

That is also the day my aunt tells me that Nandu is dead in the village well. Not our well, the one on the other side of the canal. She is pregnant. But dead. I give my aunt the key of my room as I leave. I ask her why. She tells me that if she had not locked me in my room each and every night, I would not be able to say: I am sixteen years old and I am a virgin. I am going to America with Susan.

~

I am seventeen years old and I am standing on a pedestal with my two best friends. I have a silver medal for my high school. The three of us are now officially the fastest swimmers in the district. We take every medal for our school. I look at the cluster of boys in our swim team and they are so beautiful, like young land dolphins. The pool is where I am happiest. Our pool is huge, and the house where I live with Susan and four other students from different parts of the world has a pool too. That pool is not as big as the ones we swim competitions in, and not even as big as the school pool. But it is my favourite pool. It is surrounded by big old trees such as I have never seen before. I tell Susan that there is more water in her little pool that there is in my whole village, in all the villages where I come from. She smiles and calls me dear girl. I tell Susan that my father is a rich man, but I never had my own room or my own bed, and I certainly did not swim in a pool like hers. I can see the pool from my bedroom window. I am on the upper floor, and when Susan brings me into my room and sees the look on my face she says at once that I must not jump from the window into the pool. I promise her I will not. I will take the medals to Susan and she will smile and say dear girl, as she has always done.

When Susan and I come in from the car that brings us from the airport, she puts our things away and immediately takes me shopping. I have never seen shops like this, and I have never seen clothes like this. But most of all the swimming clothes thrill me. Susan buys me many many swimming clothes. She makes me try them on in little trying on rooms, and she stands outside. I am unable to figure out the ones that are worn in two pieces and she has to come in and help me. She laughs when I am embarrassed. On the way home I get a sharp pain in my abdomen and clutch myself. She is concerned, and when I step out of the car she turns me around to face her and asks me if I know what menstruation is. I tell her I know. I ask her for a sanitary napkin. She gives me some, and they are soft and wonderful and stick to the crotch of my brand new panties. I thank her very much and tell her that they are the best thing I have ever worn. I tell her we had rags of old clothes at home, and that they would soak through quickly and we would have to change many many times a day. I begin to cry as I tell her this and I tell her that I remember my friend Nandu. I tell Susan what happened to her and Susan is very angry. She tells me this will not happen to me because I never have to go back there. I ask her if I can take the next days off from swimming, and she explains to me that I must wear a tampon. She says she will show me in the afternoon after we have rested.

Susan makes me lie down on the bed with my legs apart. She holds a little white wad of cotton in her hand. She tells me it will not hurt, and then she touches me between my legs and I feel her pulling something apart some more. She tells me to sit up and watch. I do. I see the white wad disappearing inside me. There is string hanging out. I laugh, and she laughs too. Then she looks at the string and laughs some more. She says she has seen it so often that she had forgotten how funny it was. We go downstairs and drink orange juice.

When I show Susan the medals she has tears in her eyes. Everyone in the house is excited. One of the boys won a bronze. We don't have long. The Olympic trials are in a month. Susan is throwing a party to celebrate that day's victories. Susan's friends are here too, and the house is filled with music and dancing and people of many ages and colours. One of the girls who lives with us is from Australia, and one is from Germany. The Kenyan boy is not a swimmer, he is a runner, and there is a Russian who is a basketball player, and Susan does not coach them, but they live with us. They are all happy that night. The Russian boy is very beautiful. I have never seen eyes or hair that colour before, and I stare at him a lot. I know I should not, somehow, but I do. He brings me drinks every now and then, he talks with the other girls, and I do not think he likes me much, but he comes over to talk and give me a drink. He asks if I will go upstairs with him, and I do. We go to his room, which is on a different floor from mine. I see the pool from his window too. There are people all around it. He seems a little shaky, and he lays down on the bed. He pats the bed and asks me to lie beside him. I do. He smells very nice, of smoke and beer. Susan does not allow her trainees to smoke, but he is not one of hers. I put my head on his arm. He turns over so he is looking at me. He looks into my eyes with his slanted blue ones. Then he comes very close so I feel cross-eyed trying to look at him, and close my eyes for a moment. I open them quickly again, and he puts his mouth on mine. I feel warm and happy. I open my mouth a little so he can put his tongue in. He is like a gentle stream, flowing over me with his hands. I imitate him. I run my hands over his face, through his hair, I slip them under his shirt and feel his back, I bring them to the front and feel his nipples as he feels mine. He laughs. I tell him it all feels nice. Then he pushes up my shirt and looks at my breasts. He smiles at me. He puts his lips on one of my nipples and that feels nice too. I am breathing evenly, as if I am in the water. It feels as if I am in the water. He is like a gentle river, getting slowly less gentle as the falling rain of desire swells him and makes him more and more turbulent. He flows over me and under me and I wrap myself around him and him around me and he is waves and I am the swimmer and I flow with his current and I am not afraid. He undresses me and I undress him, and there is that bolt again, of flesh and pulse. I have not seen that since Nandu by the well, in the bushes. I understand the look on her face. I say it to my boy kneeling beside me. I say I am seventeen years old and I am a virgin. I say it because I know this is the last time I will be able to say it. I say it because I want to open that door and walk through it and never look back. I have no desire to be a virgin. But he does not understand. I see again the flesh that would take my virginity from me diminish and his face lose its glow and become a little sad. He says to me that he cannot do what he wants to do so much. I try to tell him that it is what I want too, that I only said what I said because I had to. But he only looks at me sadly and lies down. We sleep, naked and entwined, until Susan knocks on the door the next morning.

She calls me outside and asks if I have any protection. I tell her I feel very protected in her house, and she laughs. Dear girl, she says, and explains to me that I need protection of a different sort. She takes me to her side of the house and gives me a box. She takes out a packet and tears it open. Then she takes out a skin from within. I am shocked, and she laughs. She asks if she should be concerned, and I tell her that our boy did not want a virgin. She is surprised and somehow sad. She tells me he is a good boy, and she tells me she is glad. But my boy does not ask me to come to his bed again. He is always nice to me, though. And there is something different about everyone in the house after that. I have a lot of protection suddenly. My girlfriends never leave me alone in public. The boys are courteous, but not as familiar as they used to be. Susan and my Russian have given me so much protection that I do not need the skins she gave me anymore.

~

I am nineteen. Yes, I am a virgin. I am in college. I have a swimming scholarship. I want to be a doctor but there is no time to finish the courses and prerequisites that I need. And the training is hard and every day. Training also means training out of the water. I go to the gym, use the treadmill, eat so many meals each day that I feel I am eating all the time, but all this is going somewhere that I want to go. The new college year has scattered all of us. I am still with Susan in her house, but many of the others are gone. My Ruski has left, and most of the girls too. My best friend is still with me, she and I will have some of the same classes, and we will train together. Although college is in the same town as I have always lived, it feels different now. My friend and I share a car, Susan's old car. We have our own money. I get paid to swim. I get paid to wait tables at the lovely restaurant across the street from the athletic centre. I am in love with one of the cooks. He is a graduate student, he has a year left, and then he'll be gone. I want him to be the one.

I am one of five who stay back to clean up after closing, for the extra cash. Juan Carlos the cook stays back too. He doesn't help clean up, but he does hang around in the outdoor seating area, smoking clove cigarettes. I dare not take even a drag of a cigarette, though I have always wanted to try it. I don't, I might lose a tenth of a second. That night, what I was hoping for happens. Everyone else has left, I go to the bathroom to pee, and when I come out, Juan Carlos is the only one left. He smiles at me. I feel the familiar feeling of anticipation and delight, the feeling I get still, before I jump in the water. Every single time I know how it will be, it is a feeling I don't remember not having, I must have been born with it. I know that having sex will be this way too, for me, I can feel it. I have my condoms in my bag, I have replaced them every month since that first time Susan gave them to me. Juan Carlos is sitting there, his legs crossed at the thighs. His thighs are huge, and I know I want their weight on mine. I go and sit next to him. Really next to him, with the side of my leg stuck to the side of his. I breathe in as he exhales, and get a lungful of clove. He stubs it out on the ground somewhat to my dismay, because I swept the floor myself, but I forgive him instantly when he puts his huge hand on the back of my head and his scrubby face on my neck and breathes the clove essence into my skin and hair and mouth. I know my response to this, and it is instant. I swing my leg over his and climb onto his muscular lap, I wrap my arms and legs around him. He grabs the sides of my thighs, and squeezes. I close my eyes and just feel. I hope for more but try not to move too fast into those thoughts. He moves faster than I do. He slides his fingers over my thigh and into my panties from the back. He finds a flood of joy and desire there too, and moans into my neck, still biting and sandpapering my face. I love the feeling. He reaches down and unzips his pants. It's there for me, all I have to do is one move, all I have to do is lift myself up a little and slam down on him, and it will be done. I stand up a little. My bag falls to the ground. I remember the condoms. I get off him and kneel on the ground. I rummage in the bag. I find it. I am in a hurry. So is he. I stand up while tearing at the package.

There is a white light shining in my eyes. He is leaning over me. He does not look aroused, only worried. There

is a pain. I lift my hand to the source of the pain and he
tells me not to touch it. I have a bruise and a swelling like
a small tomato on my head. I was in too much of a hurry.
There is a bag of frozen corn in his hand. A car door slams.
My friend has forgotten her wallet and has come back for it.
Juan Carlos explains to her that I hit my head on the table
while standing up. He puts my arm around his shoulder
and walks me to the car. He gets in the passenger seat in
front. They tuck me into my bed. When I come back to
work three days later I see them kissing, Juan Carlos and
my friend. I am sorry it isn't me he is kissing. I am sorry
his huge thighs won't weigh me down.

~

I have three Olympic silver medals and a bronze, I am the
swimming coach at one of the premier swimming schools in
the country, I am on the committee that decides who gets
swimming scholarships, I get to travel all over the country
and all over the world, I have my own car, bank account,
citizenship, a huge long delicious life I could not have
predicted. I have been to that village I came from. There
is hardly anything or anyone there. Most people have left
for the city. There is a house there that I am told was my
father's house, and it looks small and old and dusty, and a
few goats scrabble about in the dry bushes around it. I ask
the driver who brought me here to wait for me. I go for a
long walk. I find the well I once swam in. It is dry but for
a small patch of green algae sludge at the bottom. It is still
a magnificent building, if it can be called a building, since

it goes down into the earth rather than grows above it. The stone steps all around it are old, and the sunlight enhances their complex geometry. I sit on the edge for a while. Nandu laughs behind me. I do not turn to look, I know she is only in my mind, in the mind of the child of this village who still lives in me. Nandu is dead and gone, and has been for a long long time. She did not die a virgin. The look on her face still haunts me, the look of completion, of being filled. I still think it will happen one day, but I have doubts. It has become too big a thing now, not a simple little thing that anyone could have. I am forty-seven years old, and it is not a virtue anymore, if ever it was. I wish suddenly, sitting there, that that boy from across the village would come there now, and I could be that wet girl on the dry ground below him, happy then, and now long dead.

On the way back, I stop to meet my aunt. Her husband has died some years ago, the one who might have robbed my then precious virginity. I would have given it to him free, this day, but he would have been too old to care or want it. My aunt tells me how Susan returned to the village and got adoption papers signed by my father, and how easily he did it. He assumed, my aunt says, that in America I was past that point when he could marry me to anyone even for a large dowry. I laugh when she says this. When I leave, I know I will never see her, nor this country, ever again.

~

The sun was working hard that day. Maybe that was why there was no one else in the pool. I did a few warm-up arm swings, gently, because my joints were not what they used to be, and stepped down the steps, holding the metal of the ladder carefully. It was warm from the sun, and the water, when I got in, was very warm too. I knew it was terrible for my skin to swim at that time of day, but I loved the living reflections that ran and jumped and played on the floor of the pool. I watched them as I did my laps. I looked up occasionally at the clock, but I didn't really need to. In the water my body and mind really immersed in time. I wondered, not for the first time, why we humans had ever crawled out of the primordial lake. It must have been a threat that sent us out into the dryness of the world outside water. I thought I should have gills by now. I had the urge to pee, and almost did. It was something I hardly ever did, and I didn't that day either. I stroked to the edge and hauled myself out, feeling my muscles and bones grow heavy with every inch they came out of the water. I wrapped my old towel around myself and pulled the goggles down so they sat around my neck. And then I heard his voice.

'You've been swimming without stopping for almost forty-five minutes,' he said.

My eyes were a bit blurry still, but I saw crinkles at the edges of dark blue eyes in a lean brown face.

'I've been watching you the whole time,' he said, unselfconsciously, without a hint of apology.

'And?' I said, not knowing what else to say, and bursting from bladder pressure.

'And, would you like a cup of coffee? Or lunch, I guess you want some food now, after that marathon swim?'

'I have to pee,' I said. I was desperate. I walked, almost

ran to the changing rooms. I peed, I showered, I took my time rinsing out my suit and conditioning and combing my hair. I didn't think I would find him there when I finally walked out. But he was right there, and he knew me, even though I knew I looked quite different in my clothes and without my swim cap and goggles on.

'Lunch?' he asked without preamble. I laughed.

We went to the restaurant across the road from the pool, where I had once waited tables. Where I had once almost had the cook. I ordered a beer, I was thirsty and dehydrated from the swim, and tired and a little breathless, but I think that was from the man. He got a Negro Modelo too. I was grateful for the chips and salsa, I was starving. It was after half the beer and all of the big bowl of chips that I was able to concentrate. I took a closer look at my companion.

'Okay?' he asked. I was embarrassed for staring. We hadn't said much to each other except to discuss what to order. There somehow didn't seem much to say. We ate, again mostly in silence, I paid and he let me, protesting, but only a little, that he had invited me to eat. He said, 'I'll get the next one.' It didn't occur to me till later, much later, that we had both assumed there would be a next one.

I brought him home with me. I parked the car outside, I didn't want him to come into my house for the first time through the garage door. We made it into the living room. He saw my medals and cups and assorted swimming hardware all over the room, between the books on the shelf, on a coffee table, even on the floor. I put my arms around him. He was only a little taller than my six feet, maybe even not. He didn't respond as I expected. He pushed my swim dress up and put his hand right into my panties, right there between my legs. His palm skidded smoothly over skin smooth from years of waxing and found gelatinous goop there. I did not stop him, I just moved my legs apart and let him feel. He sighed deeply and followed the suction in with his finger. He stopped at my sharp intake of breath. I had to tell him, I felt. I had to tell him this would be the very first time. I didn't tell him. I let him do what he was doing. He slid his finger in a little more, grinding himself against me as he did, pulling my face against his with his other hand gripping my skull, his fingers through my hair. I moved on his finger, loving the complete lack of friction. I must have been moaning in his ear, he must have sensed my delight, too much of it. He stopped and looked at me. I took his slippery hand and led him to my bed. I took the dress off, but left the panties on. I still didn't say anything. I lay on the bed and watched as he took his shirt off, and then his shorts, and then his undies, and I watched as he held in his hand what would be my bolt of flesh, and I watched as he got on the bed on top of me. He rubbed against the wet fabric of my white cotton panties. He didn't do anything more. He didn't kiss me, or touch any other part of me. He just looked at me a few moments, and then pulled the panties off. His eyes were even darker in my dark bedroom, the afternoon light barely made it through the curtains. Then he pulled my legs up in his arms, and, his eyes locked on mine, slowly, carefully, and yet forcefully, impaled me.

I am fifty years old today.

～

Xen

~

The banister was old and smooth and warm as she ran her hand down to the bottom of the sweep of stairs, and then pushed the gold-flecked glass doors and stepped out into the street. She was almost instantly overwhelmed by the alienness of her surroundings, and yet, the sounds were not so different from those she heard the streets of home. She stood there for a few moments, wondering which way she should go, or if she should go at all. She looked around, taking in the faces, she was struck by how attractive every man, woman, and child she saw was, how vividly coloured, how differently dressed from what she was used to. She noticed too, the feeling of opulence that came off the women, all wearing gold, like at home, and she remembered that the Spanish valued their gold as much as they did at home. She didn't know how long she stood there, and then remembered that she had promised herself a meal and a glass of wine that day, after staying indoors out of nervousness for so many.

She took a few steps to her right, and then, on impulse, turned around and began to walk the other way, towards the bridge, where she could see the river, and the dome of the great mosque-church. She turned towards the church, and began to walk along the cobbles, avoiding the huge piles of horse manure, even that smell could not quell her fluttering pulse. What if she couldn't find her way back home, she thought, but kept walking anyway. She saw a row of little bars, and began to worry about which one she should go into. She decided it would be the third on her left after she had passed the next one. But when she came up to the next one, she saw a little gate, and a courtyard beyond it that she would have missed altogether had the gate been shut. She quickly went inside and sat at one of the wrought iron tables. No one came for a long time, and she began to think no one would, when suddenly, as if a bell had gone off, people began to stream in and sit down at the tables around her. The place filled with chatter and laughter. A waiter came out and threw down menus at all the tables, bottles of sherry and glasses of red wine, bowls of enormous olives and chunks of cheese and ham came out on huge trays, and she began to get very nervous all over again. She stopped looking around, stopped enjoying herself, and stared at the menu, thinking she would have her order ready before the waiter came to her table.

'¿Puedo sentarme yo aquí?'

She looked up, startled. She found herself looking into a chaotic face with aggressive black hair, and his eyes, because he was standing up against the blue Mediterranean sky, looked like holes in his head.

'Si, si,' she said,

He smiled. 'Thanks. I am in a bit of a hurry, and saw you, and figured you wouldn't mind. You're the new attaché's wife eh?'

She was so relieved to hear a familiar language that she did something she never did. She reached out and touched his arm, drawing it back almost as soon as she touched the dark hair on it.

'Yes, we got here two weeks ago, and I've been too scared to venture beyond the house...'

He laughed. She looked again at his eyes, seeing that he was looking away from her for the waiter. They were a clear blue, fringed with dark smoky lashes. She was fascinated. This was one colour that did not occur at all in India, as far as she knew. There were greys, greens, of course browns and hazels. But not this cold, clear, cloudless blue. No doubt in the blueness. No adulteration by any other hue. She suddenly wondered what it would be like to look into those eyes from even closer. She shook her head, thinking she must have gone a bit mad from the smell of the orange trees. He looked back at her, and she looked down.

'So what do you want?' he asked her.

'Want?' she was alarmed by his question, and it puzzled him.

'To eat? And maybe a drink? It's the least I can do, buy you lunch, when you let a stranger sit at your table.'

'Oh. Yes. No, it's okay, I was going anyway... ' she began to push her chair back, wishing she had not worn that silly dress, that she was back in her sari, back in her room, back...

He put his hand on hers, and she knew then that there was something very wrong with her responses that day.

'Hey, sit down. Your husband won't be pleased if I don't look after you. Have a glass of sherry, it's really lovely.'

The waiter came to their table just then, and he ordered in his obviously Irish-accented Spanish, and she laughed, and when the man was gone, she regained some of her lost composure and asked him his name.

'I'm Gabe Hallam,' he said, 'and you?'

'Saroj.'

'Sa- ? I don't mean to be rude, but can I call you Sara? I'm just not good with foreign sounds.'

She wondered why he had to call her anything, she didn't think they would ever meet again. But she nodded.

The sherry was crisp and cold and smelled of fresh bread at the same time. She had two glasses, and the ragout he had ordered for them both, with hunks of dark bread and a salad with leaves she had never seen before. He told her about the church, how it was a mosque when the Moors were there, about the river, muddy and in a turmoil, about his home. She listened, not saying much, watching his eyes, the expanse of his gestures, his laugh, his voice, everything about him was big and aggressive. He was nothing like Viren, her husband of a mere year, she hadn't known any other man, nor been alone with any other, so he was her only comparison.

'I thought you were in a hurry,' she said into a lull in the conversation.

'I was. But... would you like to walk down to the river?'

'Yes,' she said, and he paid the bill, and took her hand in his, and walked her out. He started to let go of her hand when they were on the street, but she held on with the slightest pressure. He stopped, and looked down at her, puzzled again, and then walked on, saying nothing.

He didn't stop, didn't say anything, until they were at a small building with an ornate stoop. He pulled a small flower off the bush there, cupped it in his hands, and held it to her for her to smell.

'Close your eyes and take a deep breath,' he said softly.

She did, and reeled from the heavy sweetness of the fragrance. She didn't open her eyes.

'Will you come upstairs with me?'

'Yes,' she said, with the outbreath, releasing the perfume from her lungs, ready for the first and only love of her life.

As she lay in his crumpled cotton sheets later and watched him, naked, huge, too big for her in every way, she wondered who and what she was, and a sort of restrained panic began to fill up her lungs, and she began to breathe rapidly. He came and lay beside her, stroking her from her breasts to her thighs, touching her with a familiarity and disdain for shame that she had never seen or even thought possible.

'You're so bloody small,' he said, 'did I hurt you?'

She shook her head, not daring to move in case he stopped doing what he was doing, his hands were definitely moving her legs apart, he was actually putting his hands, his fingers in places she had not even touched herself. He pushed her legs apart and got up and knelt in front of her. She was speechless and breathless and hopeless and faithless, and he was tasting the sweat and slime he had made in her, and she tried to stop him and herself, and instead found herself opening up and giving him more and more, and found herself in a sheer panic and confusion and delight of convulsions from something she simply had not felt before. She thought she was surely dying, and put her hands in his strong black hair and moaned from her very soul, as if it were the first and last and only sound she would ever make.

He lay quietly for a while, and then slid up and looked at her, propped up on his elbow.

He said, laughing slightly, 'Has no one ever been here before?'

~

From *Kashmir blues* *(Westland/Tranquebar June 2010)*

Cosmic Latte

~

How did I end up here? Let me start at the front, and maybe on the way to the back I will figure it out. Or maybe I should start right here and go back to the front, and maybe then I will figure it out. I have a feeling I won't figure it out no matter which end is up. How does a guy like me, who dropped out of school and then dropped out of community college and then dropped out of art school and then sold paintings propped up around my van in the park, and occasionally sold some pretty good weed from a source in Florida, a guy like me, who had unsavoury friends in the eyes of the law, who was a misfit and a walking dysfunctional, but still, made a decent living, or at any rate enough to keep me in gas and paints and sometimes even a meal of lengua and barbacoa tacos from the Mexicans' van parked next to mine, and they were such good tacos too, I haven't eaten for five hours and could do with a plateful of those right now with the crazy hot salsa, how did I, fostered and never adopted and never at ease anywhere on the planet or at least not in the sixteen places I have been, how the fuck did I end up here, in this eight-point-seven by nine-point-four concrete box with a toilet seat stuck in the wall and nowhere to look but the too-near walls?

I was in a bed this very morning, watching a sleeping woman's skin as it changed slowly from a pure Bronze to a perfectly saturated American Rose, light coming in through hideous Magenta curtains created that strange redness, I took out my moleskine notebook and made a note. Of course I would paint her, and I would remember when I began to paint her but still, I am meticulous about some things. Such as colour. Pretty much that. I am meticulous about colour. I would paint her, if I got out of this Asparagus Grey cement box. I would paint her Bronze skin turning American Rose, not usually a pleasant colour, and not one I have ever used before, but that's how it was, and I would paint those hideous Magenta curtains Magenta, I wouldn't change a thing, I would paint her breasts slightly sagging, pleasantly sagging, I thought of how they moved in my hands when I stood behind her in front of her bathroom mirror, we rattled the bottles and jars out of place, and her breasts swayed uncomfortably as I fucked her, so she took my hands off her hips and made me hold them, and they moved in the cages of my fingers, because I didn't clutch them hard like she wanted me to. She laughed, but it was such a sad laugh. She wore rows of minute jet beads like shiny mustard seeds around her neck, with a pendant of two little twenty-two carat gold bowls. I could tell, this was a purer gold than I was used to seeing. She said it was a noose. I would paint that too, as it nestled between those womanly breasts. Her breasts, they had heft, they had experience. There is something about breasts like that, the ones which have been in the world awhile, they have known the teeth and hands of men and children, and the cold of mammogram plates, I went with a girlfriend once, her breasts were flattened vertically and horizontally, one by one, she said they hurt, but not terribly, I took care of them and consoled them later anyway, breasts which had known many bras, uncomfortable ones, those first-time cheap trainers and then later padded ones if the breasts don't grow beyond trainer size, and the uplifting ones that make breasts look unreal, like noses on carnival clowns, this woman's breasts, I could have lived with them a long time, they had so much to tell me. They didn't stand up arrogantly like young stupid breasts, hers brushed her chest, and I had found that under-the-breasts place important, the fears and rejections of the day collected there, and she didn't even know it. But, as usual, I've lost track. Breasts will do that to a painter.

So before I was fucking her, I was talking to her, hoping her interest in my paintings would today become cash. For months she came to the park, three, four times a week, she sat on a bench with a book, sometimes she brought a laptop and typed, sometimes she just sat on the grass on a yoga mat and watched the park crowd do their thing, smokers, yoga class of four, dog walkers, squirrel feeders, kissers, there were a lot of kissers, and a lot of variety among the kissers, men and men, men and women, women and women, some you couldn't tell, and then she would look away. I watched her as she watched them, and she always looked away, not in embarrassment or disgust, but sadness, always sadness. She would look at my paintings, and I guessed even then she didn't know what to make of them, she probably would have looked away if I hadn't been watching her, she probably didn't want to hurt my feelings by looking away. She didn't know it, but it was hard to hurt my feelings. I expected the worst most of the time, so my feelings were not in any place that could be reached let alone hurt. An old lady had yelled at me about displaying my paintings that morning, and I had seen her smile as she watched me being admonished like a schoolboy, sad, but still, it was definitely a smile, it was the old lady's umbrella-shaking, so classic as if we were in a movie, and her words, 'You filthy perverts, filthy perverts ruining my walk and the whole city!' She was right, the old lady. But my paintings were not so bad. There were actual women attached to the body parts, and they were women I loved, and painted with love, and I think it did come through. I think what got the old woman so mad may have been recognition of my anger. It was this woman I definitely did not love. This painting was an act of violence against her. I could have been one of those kids who shot their fosterparent sixteen times, it was either that, or this painting. Maybe this was worse. It was a really massive canvas of my view from the closet where I had been banished by her, she had forgotten me, and I had seen her, she came in the room six hours later, her two hundred pounds of putrid flesh hauled off the couch where it had lain all day, fed on pork rinds and a cheap cola, shades of Icterine and bile, moving about the room, taking off all her clothes to change for bed, and then getting into the bed and turning off the fluorescent light. It was a frightening painting, I had been frightened, and hungry, and surrounded by giant unwashed underwear and unwanted things—a baseball glove and a bat, I could have beaten her to death with that, a set of knives, a bb gun, they were all there, I could have done it. But I waited years and painted her instead. It had taken me a long time to paint it, it's harder to paint ugliness well, and it would probably take me longer to sell it. I would have given it away free, I didn't want to take it back home, I wanted it to go to someone else. I would leave it there in the park, I thought, as she watched me and tried not to turn away.

So, we had been acquainted for months, and now I thought I could consummate our relationship with a word. I said, and I had to raise my voice for it to reach across the park community to her bench, 'Would you like a cupcake?'

Her smile was a thing of serenity and sweetness. 'I'll get us two,' she said to me, and went over to the cupcake van. She got me peanut butter and chocolate, and red velvet for herself. After eating half of it in one bite, she offered it to me, and took what was left of mine. I wanted to eat the crumb of red velvet stuck to her lip, but her tongue flicked out and took it from my imagination. Her lips were huge, but I knew from long observation that she was not African American. The way she dressed was not anything special, but I had guessed Pakistani, from the fabric of the scarves always around her neck. Oh what a neck, and what bites I had left on it. They were Tyrian Purple, and I may never get it right. I took it down in my notebook anyway. Of course I would paint the bruises on her neck, and the mole on the crease between her thigh and her pubic hair, and all the slick stuff from us both that oozed from her and stained the sheets below her, and I would paint my faded denim shirt with all the paint smudges on it, incongruent among her things, laying on the fine pale blue and beige silk carpet by her bed, we had probably stained that too, when we slipped off the bed and continued our explorations on the floor. Her pubic hair shocked me when I saw it that first time. American women, or the ones I've seen naked anyway, they don't have any. They wax it and take it all off. It's a pity, really, I am not wonderstruck by a naked cunt like I used to be. It's too naked now, looks like a bald cancer victim, or a chicken ass. At best it looks like a young girl's body, and I don't like how that makes me feel, I don't want to do gooey adult things with that. It affects my sex, those naked things, it makes me want to turn away. I stopped doing the things I used to, the first time I saw that wax job, when my then girlfriend came home one day and showed me triumphantly. I couldn't touch it, I couldn't put my mouth on it, I almost couldn't fuck it unless I was behind her, or she had a t-shirt or something on. So Mandy's pubic hair shocked me in a really wonderful way. I think I shocked her by literally falling upon it, that dark matted mass of curls, with my fingers and tongue and cock, I was in pure heaven for a while. I didn't realise how much I had missed such a simple thing. A woman's pubic hair.

Mandy. She followed me home and I parked my van, she said she didn't want it parked outside her house, she didn't want it seen, just in case. I didn't care, but she did. She said she didn't mind the way the van looked, it wasn't that. I told her I really didn't care. I didn't get it, then. I still don't get it. Anyway. She taught me to say her name as we walked to her car. 'Man-dee-rah'. I said it a dozen times and finally got it right. And when I did, she said, 'You can call me Mandy. Easier for your thick American tongue. Easier to say when you are in my bed.' My mouth opened to say something, but I shut up. I knew we would, and she knew we would, but it was she, with the sad smile and sad shyness who had decided if, and when, and where. She didn't decide what or how much, though. She said we could do anything and everything, in fact we must, she said. We must, and so we did. We stopped for bites of food she took out of her fridge and microwaved for me. I was not unfamiliar with it, but I hadn't eaten so many Indian things in one day ever. We had samosas after the first time we fucked. It was very quick and easy that first time, she undressed, I undressed, she lay down on her bed, I went for my condom, she said 'No, really. And don't worry, I haven't had sex with anyone in a long time, and I have AIDS test from a day ago, I'll show you when we are done, and if you're okay, I'm okay with it,' and we did it, just normal and lovely, lots of moaning and pushing, and I came and she did not, but she said we had time, 'We're not on a fast train, that we have to get off at the end of the line,' she said, and I laughed. Samosas, with a hot green sauce. I wanted to get in those curls, and she sat on a beautiful brocade chair with her legs apart while I looked for womanly secrets after such a long time. When I put my tongue on her, after a while she said, 'The chutney burns,' and got off the chair and back on the bed. Here, she said, taking my hard-again cock back inside her. And after a while, I began to burn too, and we laughed. And didn't stop. And took a break for ice water and 'something sweet' she said. She stood naked in front of the open fridge, staring into it absently, while I sat on a stool at the kitchen counter. There was a pile of bills stacked on one side, and I read a strange name on it that wasn't hers. I knew there was a husband somewhere, and children, I knew she was a bit older than me, but it wasn't my business. The fridge was one of those new-fangled things, brushed steel with two little doors, and was somehow not as romantic as the old single doors, with a usually inefficient freezer section up top. I would paint this, I thought, but I would change that fridge to the one in my own kitchen, it would make a better picture. Mandy, naked, with her magnificent areolas lit by the Aureolin yellow of my old single-bulb fridge, looking for something sweet. I wrote 'Cobalt: fridge' in my notebook. That's the less poetic name for Aureolin. Cobalt yellow. I stuck the book on the stack of bills on the table and went to her to fill my hands with her breasts. Her back felt warm against my chest, a warm bronze, and her front was cold from the frigid air. 'Frigidaire!' I said to her excitedly. She didn't get it. 'That's where the name of the brand comes from, frigid air—Frigidaire!' She took out a small glass jar with a plastic lid, it seemed to be full of little matte porous white eggs floating in a cloudy opal-white liquid. This colour is called Cosmic Latte, and, I decided, that would be the name of this painting. I don't actually name paintings, but I named this one in my head at that moment. I reached for my notebook on the counter behind me. She opened the jar and popped one of the little eggs in my mouth. It exploded sugar as I bit down on it. The texture was simply wonderful, but the sugar nearly killed me. She had me up against the counter then, and put the jar behind me. She put her big mouth on mine, and kissed me, very gently, very sweetly, and, very very sadly.

That was all yesterday. Today I'm in this cell, and no one has been in to check on me since they put me in here. I haven't been charged with anything, certainly not murder. I push away the uncomfortable 'not yet' that comes to mind.

I know how they got me, I left my notebook there, it slipped off her bedside table when I knocked the lamp off with my foot, when she was on top of me, she had stopped moving, she was as still as she would be in a painting, her dark hair covering her face, her breasts, those breasts I would never get enough of, I was looking up at them, and then she pushed her hair off her face and leaned over me and kissed me, and moved on me in such a way that I was writhing and kicking, and I kicked the lamp, it fell, and got turned off. We were in darkness, and it thrilled us both somehow, and we jerked and I thrust, and we moaned, and it took us a long time, because we had done it all so much, and then I fell into an exhausted sleep. I woke up once in the night when I heard her moving around in the dark, but then I went back to sleep. I didn't wake till the morning, and that's when I found her, and called 911. She had a plastic bag over her head. I had never seen a dead person, unless you count old Carvalho who lived upstairs from me, I saw him when they carried him out, not him, really, just some toes that stuck out from beneath a mover's blanket, the toes were Tea Rose pink, the blanket was Camel, Mandy was dead. I called 911, I panicked, as all normal people would, I left as quickly as I could, as all people who have lived slightly left of law have, I left my notebook under the bed, or behind the bed, or wherever it fell. They found me within the hour. My name, address, cell number, and a promissory sentence about a ten-dollar reward was on the front page of the notebook.

And that was my last two days. And that's how I came to be sitting in a holding cell, hungry, tired, confused, and at a loss. I smelled strange too, but that could be because my sense of smell goes weird when I am under stress. And surely, I was under stress.

It was four hours later when the policewoman who put me there came in to let me out. She handed me my notebook, said I could leave. No explanation, nothing. They don't owe me one, apparently, they didn't charge me or process me. I went home and showered and ate everything in my fridge. Then I started to paint.

It is almost six months to the day I met Mandy, a woman comes to my little exhibition in the park, looking at the paintings. I have worked on them for all those months. It may be my best work, this, as a collection. It may be because those twenty-three hours with her make me wonder how it will be the rest of my life without her. I only began to understand when I put her in pigments on the rough blankness before me, I began to see her colours on me, my life. My work is beautiful, because it's a memory of her. It's my first day back in the park since the day she died. The pieces are not very large, a very saleable size, didn't need huge commitment to buy, and this woman is looking at the one I don't want to sell. Mandy, wearing my paint-smudged shirt that she never wore, it's open and showing me her breasts that I loved so much in the hours we had together, with her hair down and her jet beads around her neck, I think I got her smile just right, soft on her mouth but sad in the eyes, bruises on her lovely neck left by my fingers and mouth, Tyrian Purple, this woman stared at the painting a long time. Then she said, 'She's beautiful. How much?' I was reluctant to let it go. She saw. She began to withdraw. I needed the money, so I named a high price. She frowned and offered me half. That frown made me almost recognise her. 'Where do I know you from?' I asked her. She said, 'Michael Bronowski, I'll come back tomorrow and give you half what you asked for, and something else to make up for it.' She did come back, it was Sunday morning and the church across the road from the park was full of people. She was in uniform. I knew her immediately then. She gave me the money and an envelope, took her painting, thanked me, and put it in the trunk of the blue and white double-parked on the curb.

I opened the envelope. It was a colour printout of a scanned handwritten page. The long elegantly looped letters were perfectly spaced, and the letter was short, just the one page. I was sitting on the bench she had been sitting on, when she first spoke to me. I read, and my eyes began to flow, even though I never cry. The letters were black on white. It began,

'Will I never be beautiful in anyone's eyes?'

I sold every single one of those paintings on the first day. I heard they are being re-sold for ten times as much as I sold them for. I don't care. I know I ate a good chicken curry for dinner at the Bombay Palace that night. I ordered two samosas for starters. I ate just one. She's probably smiling at my sentimentality. And there's no sadness in her smile.

~

Poison

~

Maia stood behind the makeshift curtain and waited for the old man to unravel his measuring tape. He seemed half blind. His assistant sat just outside the curtain her mother-in-law had put up in the middle of her bedroom, just for that purpose—to keep the assistant from seeing herself and her daughters-in-law in the state of undress that was required in order to be perfectly measured for their new saree blouses. The assistant was pale and barely sprouting a moustache, he seemed bewildered at best. He took down in a large ledger the meticulous and numerous measurements which the old man called out to him, and apparently did not make too many mistakes. Maia was beginning to tire of the whole exercise. She wished her sister-in-law was with her. Her husband, her lovely, large, forceful, manly husband—and she sighed deeply as she thought of his strength, of his sheer overwhelming masculinity and power—was the oldest of three brothers. She got along fine with the middle brother's wife, a plump somewhat silly but good-natured girl with enormous breasts. But it was the youngest sister-in-law, Mina, who was her friend and delight. They whispered and played and cooked and took walks together, they did everything together in fact, but sleep together. Again, Maia sighed, because she thought of her bed, and her husband, and his smell, and the way he walked, and how everyone looked at him with fear and adoration at the same time. Everyone did, the servants, the farm workers, his own brothers, his sisters-in-law, most of all she herself. She did not fear him, not after the first night she spent with him on their wedding day. After that night she only adored him. Before Maia had been married to him, her cousin had visited them once after she had married and gone away, she came back to her maternal village when she was vastly pregnant. She had one afternoon alone with Maia, and she tried to describe in broken words what had transpired on her wedding night, but had become upset and started to cry, so all Maia understood was that something terrible had been done to her by her own husband, and there was pain, and blood, and then the poor girl had tried to avoid him, but it had been the same every night until her period stopped, and then he left her alone. Maia had only this bit of information about the marriage bed. When she saw her husband-to-be for the first time, she was thrilled at the sight of him, his arrogant face, his moustache so black and curled just slightly at the ends, his paan-stained mouth, the way he looked at her, dressed in his silk kurta and twirling his thick gold chain in his long-fingered huge hands. She would have been much more thrilled, though, if she had not heard her cousin's story. She remembered

how she had dared to smile at him from the kitchen door
where she stood for a moment before bringing him and
his family their tea and biscuits. He had looked at her so
kindly, and with such love and delight, that she just knew
nothing could go wrong. And then, that night, after all the
days of ceremonies and eating and drinking were done—and
there was a lot of that because he was the oldest son of a
very rich and powerful family, perhaps the most rich and
powerful in the district, and they had more wheat land and
cows than anyone, and the largest house for sure, so the
expectations for his marriage celebrations were large and had
to be met and surpassed—that night came. Maia sighed again
as the old man measured the precise distance between the
crease where her right breast met her torso and the tip of
her little brown nipple. He barely touched that nipple, but
she was deep in thoughts of her wedding night, and was
thinking of the feeling of her husband's face on that same
breast that was being so carefully measured, of the prickle of
the aggressive stubble that she now knew he had to shave
off twice a day to keep his face smooth, but that day he
had not had the time, so he was careful. In the end it was
she who scrubbed his face on herself, and regretted it the
next day when she poured the warm bath water on herself.
She had her eyes closed, and forgot the measurements. She
knew somewhere in her consciousness that her breast was
being lifted slightly and the old man was probably enjoying
himself, it was a beautiful breast after all, she thought, as
she relived that utter delight of having it in someone's, no,
in her husband's mouth and she had looked down and seen
it, or what was left outside his mouth, a moustache instead

of a nipple, and him, suckling at her like she had seen her older sister suckle her baby. She had laughed, and stroked his long curly hair, and he was surprised. He asked her if she liked it, and she had just laughed again. She must have laughed then, because the old man stopped what he was doing to make her laugh, and she opened her eyes, and was momentarily annoyed, because she did want to daydream and slowly work her thoughts through the whole night, the way he had taken all her clothes off, the way he had lain her down on the cushions, the way he had finally undressed himself and she had seen him, seen it for the first time, what really made him powerful, the way... but she had to stop, because the old tailor was asking her some question.

'What, masterji? I'm sorry I didn't understand.'

'How low do you want it?' he asked again.

Her mother-in-law answered for her from outside the curtain. She was sitting on her bed and crocheting something. She had learned to crochet from some visiting American woman, a professor, a hundred years ago, and she spent a lot of her time with that hooked needle, and produced all sorts of little doilies and doodads that littered every surface of the huge house. It was probably good for her old hands.

'Make it nice and low, she's the oldest, it's nice to show off what Amar goes to bed with.' And she laughed. Maia loved her mother-in-law. She was funny and undemanding, and had some odd ideas about how they all should act, but she never chided them, never made them do things they didn't want to, and was universally sweet to everyone. Her sons thought she let the servants get away with too much, but she said, 'We have so much, what is there to trouble us? We have happiness, and we can afford to give some away.'

'Remember the katori blouse should be open at the back,' she said. 'This Maia has put on a little weight, she is getting bigger on the top. We could have let out all the old blouses, but you know, for this wedding I wanted all new clothes for the girls.'

The wedding this time was for Amar's cousin. His mother had died in childbirth, and the boy had been brought up by his uncle, Amar's father, as if he were his own. And everyone thought of him as the youngest brother. This would be the last wedding for a long time in the big house, and for that reason, there was an air of celebration greater than any of them had ever felt. New clothes were only a small part of it. There were renovations to the house itself which went on all day long, and the road to the house was being fixed, and even public parts of the village were being spruced up. Amar was busy with all that, and the usual farm work, and Maia hardly saw him, and when he did come to bed, he was tired and uninterested. Maybe, she thought, all the new clothes and jewellery and celebrations would remind him of their original delight in each other.

The tailor moved to her left breast. He measured the distance from her shoulder to the nipple tip, from the cleavage to the nipple tip, around her breasts, around her ribs below her breasts, he lifted her arm so he could get some other precise and exquisitely tiny and necessary number for his perfectly fitted blouses. The top of his head brushed the underside of her arm, and she was again in that bed with Amar. Amar. She allowed herself to say his name only in her thoughts. She had refused to close her eyes, and she was eternally glad for it. The sight of him, that huge hunk of flesh that hung heavily between his legs straining, it seemed to her, to stand upright as he knelt in front of her holding it with one of his huge hands, was one of her favourite memories of her husband. Close your eyes, he had said to her, and she would not. He carefully opened her legs and touched her as if he was looking for something. That was the one moment she remembered being embarrassed, she thought she might have peed a little. But he found what he was looking for, and she understood what he was going to do then. She opened her legs wider for him. And as he slowly, carefully put that part of him into that part of her, she opened wider and wider, and felt a searing pain that she wished she could feel again and again, but never did after that first time, and she gasped involuntarily, and he stopped, and asked her if it hurt, and she said yes, yes, and put both her hands on his bare skin and pulled him as hard as she could into her. And then he began to gasp and push and thrust into her again and again, and she could not have enough of that feeling, she did not want him to stop, but he moaned suddenly, and held her head in his hand, crushing her skull and hair in a grip that almost hurt her, and then, after a moan that sounded to her as if his death was upon him, collapsed in a lifeless heap upon her.

Maia sighed yet again as the tailor proceeded around her body. She opened her eyes and looked at him and found him peering at her over his glasses from under her arm. She was sure he had been contemplating her nipple under the loose and pointless garment they wore for measurement.

The garment was made of light muslin, and her mother-in-law insisted they wear it for modesty, but it was exceedingly immodest, probably more than simply being naked. The tailor was old, she explained to her mother-in-law, and she wouldn't have cared, but her mother-in-law only smiled her foxy smile and said something about age having nothing to do with the effect of thoughts on a man's parrot, no matter how old or shrivelled. 'Your father-in-law surprises me still, although it's about once a year and usually after a wedding, when he has seen all you girls and your raw-mango breasts, and imagined everything that is going on in the nuptial bed, and it only lasts a moment or two, so, all things considered, you will wear that thing. I know, it's a pretence, but that's how it is.'

'Can I take a tea break?' Maia asked, and the old matriarch thought it was a good idea. The old man smiled at her, and she said to him, thinking she could use a break from his aged hands groping her, 'You must be tired, masterji, a cup of tea will be good for you too.' He smiled back at her and said, hanging his measuring tape around his neck, 'What a thoughtful daughter-in-law you have, maaji. It is rare these days for these young girls to think of us old people.'

The old woman laughed and said, 'Yes, they are all good girls. And I am not as old as you, masterji, you were old even when I first came to this house.'

Tea was brought, and Maia asked if one of the servants could find Mina. 'Why isn't she being measured with me? It would be so much more fun,' she complained.

'She wasn't feeling well. She was a little sick this morning, when I went to wake her up. So I let her sleep, poor thing.

Amar said he will send for the doctor if she isn't better by tomorrow.'

Maia made a face. That was the only thing she hated about Mina. The only thing. They were like sisters, Mina and Maia, and they confided in each other and relied on each other, and their idyllic life was made even more beautiful by each other's presence. But in the last few months, there was something wrong with Mina, and she was not strong like Maia, she became pale and whiny and took a lot longer to get over the slightest illness, even a cough or a stomach upset, unlike Maia, who couldn't wait to get out of her room and join the family in their daily lives.

'Some people are weak,' her mother-in-law said to her gently. You are like me, Maia. Mina is different, her mental disposition is different. Don't you remember, after her wedding night, how she lay in bed all day, and you, oh you are a strong and bad girl, you were running around like a new-born calf. Let her be, we will finish all your measurements, and next week will be the fittings, and then we can start hers.'

'I'll go and see her when we are done,' Maia said. 'Maybe I can eat my lunch with her.'

'It is your kitchen day today, you can't go eat your lunch with her,' Maaji said, but Maia's disappointment made her relent.

'Oh, alright, but don't sit too close to her. I don't want you catching anything if it is catching. And you can go help with the dishes after lunch. Or if you prefer, you can go make the roti dough as soon as we are done here. How much longer, masterji?'

The tailor looked at his ledger and cuffed his assistant in the head, and missed entirely the first time, both because of his aim, as well as the assistant's deft ducking. He landed the blow on his second attempt.

'These last measurements were for the choli blouse, fool,' he said, but without much heat.

'We will be ten more minutes. I just need the string lengths, we are almost done. Actually, I can get that from all the other measurements I have, she can go.'

Maia put down her teacup and stepped into her mother-in-law's large bathroom to get dressed. She checked her face in case she ran into her husband, and adjusted a few strands so they floated in front of her eyes. She pouted and blew herself a kiss.

'Thank you very much, masterji, ' she said to the old tailor as she was leaving, 'I know you will make the best blouses, and I know we will all look beautiful, won't we, maaji? He is just so good.'

'Yes, yes, it's a good thing I won't need him for much longer. I hope he lasts you girls' lifetime, because I don't see how this fellow is going to learn anything quickly enough to replace him.'

The two men laughed, and the assistant said, 'I am learning very fast, maaji. I will make two of these blouses myself, actually. You already can't tell the difference between mine and masterji's. Isn't it true?'

'Yes, it is,' masterji said, surprising the women. 'But I wanted to say, please have her back in three days for the first fittings, especially for the kameezes.' He turned to Maia who was standing impatiently at the door but not showing it, she was always especially nice to old people. 'You are a very good girl,' he said. 'May God bless you with all the sons your heart desires,' he said. Maia laughed and turned and walked quickly toward the kitchen.

~

The days went by quickly, there was so much for everyone to do. As the wedding day came closer and closer, the activity in the house and outside it became frantic. The event was still a month away, but every day felt as if it was to happen the very next day. Everywhere in the house were workers of all professions—carpenters sat in the courtyard sawing and scraping, on one side making new chairs, on the other side repairing the old furniture from the house. There were upholsterers with yards of velvet and silk, polishers gouging and restoring the grooves in the deeply carved screens and coffee tables, there were the many painters—some with tiny brushes going over the now faded flowering vines which ran along the arms and legs chairs and tables, and some with their huge sloppy brushes and buckets of paint facelifting the walls. Ladders, awls, nails, broken glass, and more such hazards lay everywhere in the house and garden. And modesty was under attack. The women complained of men peering in through windows on the lower and upper floors of the house, and once Maia even found a small boy inside her bathroom after she had squatted to pee. She was momentarily startled, but not so much that she stopped half way and wet her sari. She just shooed him out and asked him to close the door behind him. He was probably more disturbed than she was.

In spite of all the flurry and hurry, the matriarch did not allow their daily activities to be disrupted. They had their meals always at the same time, everyone did their duties, the three brothers went to the farms and to the village meetings as they always did, and Maia found that she saw hardly ever saw her husband except at mealtimes, when he would eat hurriedly and leave. The family meals always took place at the massive dining table. Everyone was expected to be present unless they were at least mortally ill, if not dead, and Maia had heard that the old lady set a place for a year after someone died, so they were not exempt even then. Mina missed one meal, but she was soon back at the table. Maaji insisted on that one thing. The table at mealtimes was a delightful place to be. Maia had always, from the first meal she had there, enjoyed it. She remembered that post-wedding night breakfast as clearly as if it had been that very morning. She sat beside her mother-in-law, her husband sat across from her. Her father-in-law sat at the head of the table, and all the other family members—the sons, their wives, their children—filled the space with sound and arguments and laughter. They were eating parathas that morning, and she was not required to help with anything. She just sat and watched her brand-new husband eat one paratha after another as they came out hot and fresh from the kitchen, stuffed with gobi, mooli, aloo, each with a lump of fresh white butter made from their cows' milk. She watched as he ate with a singleminded devotion to the food, scooping up cold yogurt from his large silver bowl on each piece of paratha , chewing carefully and with obvious appreciation, chewing on the fresh stinging-hot green chillies, stopping only to take a sip from the hot saffron milk next to his thaali. He enjoyed his food, she saw, as much as he had enjoyed being with her the night before. He had awoken three times that night to explore her body and enjoy the fact of her presence, with that same look on his face as he had when he was eating his breakfast. Mina had not yet joined the family then, but Maia had been happy there even before she came. Even if she had been unhappy, she thought, the nights with Amar would have made up for it. She looked across at him that morning, as she had on the morning after her wedding, and watched him eat. He was spooning the dalia into his mouth in a hurry, without looking left or right. He seemed preoccupied. There was no pleasure in his face at all, and Maia was puzzled. This was not like him at all, she thought. It was a pity he was getting nothing but pressure from this wedding. It was so much fun for them all, Mina and Maia, and Shama, the middle sister-in-law, and most of all their mother-in-law, whose swan song this would be. She was determined that everything be perfect, and that included the time of preparation. As soon as the engagement had been announced, there was a buzz in the village and the house. This would be the last big occasion for a long time, probably the last in the old father-in-law's life. He was too feeble to enjoy it even now, maaji had mentioned to Maia that she did not think he would last past that year.

'Amar will really be the head of the house then. He is, even now, but your husband will be the head of the house once his father is gone, and you, my dear daughter, will be in charge of everything. You will do everything that I do now. So you had better pay attention to everything.'

Maia lost her appetite as she watched Amar eat. It was a singularly ugly process. She realised that she missed him terribly. She missed his big laugh when he played with his several nephews and nieces, she missed his voice ringing through the house, how she would thrill with anticipation when she heard it outside her room and waited for him to open the door and throw himself on their big old bed and say, 'I am so tired, Maia, press my feet and everything else and make me ready for you', and she missed his big hands upon her, and his big moans and sighs, and his big... she blushed and looked up to see if he was looking at her and was disappointed to find that he was not, he had finished his meal and his tea and was looking around impatiently. Maaji did not allow anyone to leave the table unless everyone had finished. He had to wait. Maia tried to catch his eye, but he did not even glance at her. She surreptitiously pulled her sari a little to one side, exposing what would have once been delicious to him. She dropped her spoon, and bent sideways to pick it up. When she sat back up she found his eyes looking right into hers. There was a little twitch under his moustache and the barest twinkle in his eyes that made her heart sing and made everything alright in her world. She knew that afternoon's session with old masterji and his silly assistant would go much better than she had anticipated. She got up as soon as the brothers had left the table, and helped the servants tidy up.

Maaji was busy with something. She looked for Mina but could find her nowhere. She had vanished after breakfast, after promising Maia she would help her tidy. Maia swore to herself that she would not give Mina the benefit of her company when it was time for her measurements and fittings, and fumed all the way to her mother-in-law's room for the fitting that afternoon. A maidservant was dispatched with her as a chaperone. The assistant took his place outside the curtain, Maia undressed and redressed herself in the muslin measuring garment, and masterji unravelled his measuring tape. He took a few quick measurements and called them out to the boy outside, and then gave her the blouse he had brought with him. It was a shot silk, blue and green, it shimmered like a peacock's feather. It was hand-stitched, and the seams were unfinished, and there were no hooks or ties on it yet, but it did fit almost perfectly. Masterji was not half as pleased as she was with the work. He said, a bit roughly, to the boy outside, 'Give me the pin box, this is just terrible. Didn't you look at the numbers at all? There are millimetres off on the underarm, and it is looking too puffy on the upper part of the arm too.' So it was the boy's work. Masterji pushed her arm up, and Maia lifted it high so he could examine the seam connecting the sleeve to the body of the blouse. She was glad the waxing ladies had come the previous week, she didn't want to present stubble, even to this old man. As maaji had pointed out, old or not, he was a man, after all.

He was taking the pins out of his mouth and tacking the blouse with them. And Maia was a bit alarmed, considering the tenderness of her flesh and the condition of the old man's eyes. She didn't say anything, though, not wanting to hurt his feelings. He must have sensed her tense, though, because he smiled and said, 'Don't you worry, I would never, never, prick you. I've been doing this all my life, you know, and I have never hurt anyone, not with a pin, nor a needle, nor by my actions or even my words, if I could ever help it.'

Maia was surprised at the emotion in his voice. She said, 'I trust you, masterji, it was just an involuntary thing, I did not mean to imply...'

'I know,' he said, still rolling and pinning, 'I know you are a kind-hearted girl, Maia. But not everyone is like that, you know.' He dropped his voice suddenly, speaking so softly that she was sure even the boy right outside the thin curtain could not hear. 'Sometimes the people closest to you will hurt you, and take away what is rightfully yours, and will destroy your happiness.'

Maia was so unprepared for this line of conversation that she said the first thing that came to her head. 'Did someone do something to hurt you, masterji?'

The old man smiled again. 'Your arm must be tired, put it down for awhile, I will get back to that part in a minute. And, bring it down carefully so that the pins won't hurt you. There.' He said, guiding it down. 'See, even now, you think about me, not yourself. I was not talking about someone hurting me,' he said, 'I am old, and nothing much can hurt me now. But you, you are very young, and your happiness shines from your eyes, and your love is visible in your skin, and people would do you harm,' he said.

Maia thought, he's old and senile. He doesn't know what he is talking about. But she said nothing.

'No,' he went on. 'I come from a long line of tailors. My father was one, and my grandfather too. And we have made clothes for the women of this family for generations.

And there is one story about this family that I must tell you.'

Maia was confused, but intrigued. 'I will make it short, we don't have much time,' he said. 'My grandfather was doing all the clothes for a wedding in this very house once. There were a lot of children's clothes, and a lot of women, and the head of the house, that would be the grandmother of your husband, the mother-in-law of your mother-in-law, said that it would be better if the tailor and his assistants were to come to work here at the house, rather than run back and forth with fabric and blouses from our shop. They did as she said. She was a formidable woman, everyone feared her. She was not like your maaji at all. Her daughters-in-law would never speak to her unless they had to, even her sons avoided being in her presence and averted their eyes when they were. Perhaps that is why maaji is so kind—she knows how it is to be unhappy in her daily life. But, I am getting off the story. The story is simple, Maia. My grandfather found out that one of the sons was having an affair with a woman in a neighbouring village. That village is gone now, it was moved when the big dam was built, some years before you came here. This man, I won't tell you which son it was, because it does not matter, he is dead and gone, was married to a woman much like you. She was beautiful and joyful and loved her husband dearly, and gave him many sons. My grandfather was from the old times, he did not like to meddle in the affairs of others, and we tailors hear and see a lot of things that go on in households. In this case, he was in the house every day, from morning to night, and sometimes he stayed the night too. He was also from an old village, the one near the old temple at the edge of the forest. Do you know what I am talking about?' Maia, fascinated, said no.

'It was the village of the doctor. Vishari, he was called. He was not poisonous, just knew all about the plants and herbs and was the healer of all the villages in this area. So, my grandfather spoke to this man about what he had seen. He was very upset by it, and he knew the girl, the woman, if she found out about her husband's infidelity, would throw herself in the well, or burn herself. He didn't think she deserved that fate, and he had to talk to someone.'

Maia was amazed by this story so far, and she was watching him with her mouth slightly open. She had never heard masterji talk that much in all the time she had known him. He paused then, and held the peacock-hued blouse closed with his fingers, delicately, so he would not touch the velvet skin between her breasts.

'The poisoner told my grandfather what to do. He gave him herbs and powders in a bag. He said to soak the Other Woman's blouse in it for three days, and then dry it in the moonlight. Moonlight, he said, be sure not to leave it out in the sun, or it would not work. And then, the woman had to wear it just a few hours, the poisoner said, and she would stop breathing, and fall into a faint from which she would never recover.'

Maia gasped. 'What a story, masterji, did they kill the poor woman? Your ancestor and the poisoner? Did they kill her?'

'Hush, Maia, don't speak so loud, they'll hear you.' Maia didn't see why it mattered, but she hushed anyhow.

'You are a good girl, Maia. I thought you should know this story.' He would say no more, and would answer no more questions. 'There, the pinning is done, would you like to go and look in the mirror? And I am finished for today, there will be just one final fitting for you now for everything. You can get dressed.'

Maia, puzzled and intrigued, went into the bathroom to look at the blouse. She stood before the huge old mirror and turned this way and that. The blue of the blouse brought out the blue of the veins in her neck and emphasised the delicate transparency of her skin. Maaji was right, this was her colour. She would look stunning in that new saree, with the silver threads on its pallau glistening around her face, with the old silver and sapphire set that maaji had given her when she came to the family. She wanted to try it all on right away, but she knew she would have to wait. She couldn't wait to enter the room in those clothes for the first time and have Amar see her. He would remember that first night again, and he would remember everything they had done and been, and he would be happy and lighthearted from the celebrations, and sentimental from the marriage of his little brother, and he would come to her again that night, and as the newly-wed couple had their first time together, she and her beloved Amar would find joy in their own bed again, she thought. He would untie this very blouse, she thought as she carefully took her arms out of the sleeves so as not to disturb masterji's careful pinning and not to scratch herself. He would see her breasts again, fuller than when he had first held them in his hands, they would fill them this time, those big hands, and he would lie beside her and upon her again, and he would fill her up again, in every way. She wished she could have shown the blouse to Mina, she thought, and resolved to go and find her right away.

She came out in her own clothes and handed the blouse to masterji's assistant. Maaji was in the room, and seemed quite pleased with everything masterji had been telling her.

'Mina was looking for you a minute ago,' she said, and Maia was disappointed that she hadn't knocked on the bathroom door. They had seen each other naked enough times, after all. 'Where is she now?' she asked Maaji. 'She went to the back, she said the cow had calved, and she wanted you to go with her to see. She has probably not even got there yet, if you hurry, you'll catch her. Don't forget, you have to chop the tomatoes for dinner,' she said to Maia's retreating back.

Maia reached the cowshed just in time to go in with Mina.

'Where have you been? I hardly see you, and we live in the same house,' she said.

'Oh, you know, I just don't know what's wrong with me. I keep feeling faint, as if the breath is being squeezed out of me, and then every time I smell food I feel as if I will throw up. I just don't know. I don't feel like doing the chores, I don't want to do anything. I feel sick,' she said, and to Maia's sorrow, her friend's dark and childishly large eyes filled with tears. They went into the shed and looked at the new calf. She was beautiful, a tiny, still slimy little creature trying to stand up straight as her mother licked and nudged her. It made them both smile.

'Have you told maaji? That you don't feel well?' Maia asked, feeling sorry that she had plotted to be mean to Mina. The poor thing, she did love her so, and it must be hard, if the food made her sick, to be at the table for every meal, and to be in the kitchen when it was filled with the smell of cooking. It was no wonder she had looked so sad and distracted as she tried to join the family in their mealtime conversations. But Maia had been so full of her own silly sorrow about Amar neglecting her in their bed that she had not noticed. She felt guilty. She put her hand in Mina's and squeezed. 'Let's go talk to maaji and get the doctor to come over. Let's go right away,' she said, pulling Mina's hand.

They walked back the way they had come, holding hands. Maaji was still in her room talking to masterji and going over some final things. They sat on the huge bed and waited for them to finish.

'Tomorrow, Mina, you have to finish your measurements for the new blouses, or we will have no blouses for you. Am I right, masterji?'

'Yes, maaji,' he said, 'I need to take those measurements soon. Tomorrow will be ideal, but if she is unwell, I can wait a day or two. No more than that though,' he warned.

When he was gone, Maia, with a few words from Mina, described the symptoms to maaji.

'My god, my dear girl, when was your last period?' the old woman asked her, smiling broadly. 'I think that's what is wrong with you. Nothing at all. Just a bellyful of baby is making you ill. I have been so busy with all this that it never struck me. How silly of me! You don't need a doctor, child, just good food, and some rest, and you will be just fine. We will know from masterji's numbers too, you know,' she said, and began to laugh. 'We will wait after the wedding to tell your dear husband, though, alright?'

Maia smiled too, but was filled with melancholy. She was the older sister-in-law, she thought. Why was Mina the one who was pregnant? Mina said she would go and lie down, and left the room. Maaji ran her hand down Maia's back and said, 'I know, Maia, what you are thinking. It was like that with me too, I took so long to get pregnant. Everyone had given up on me, it was three years after my marriage that I finally had Amar, and then, a son every two years, and one daughter, and then a miscarriage, and I thought I had had enough of being pregnant when the American doctor came and secretly cut my tubes.'

'Cut your tubes? Really, maaji?' Maia knew what she was talking about, of course, they would all get their tubes tied after a couple of sons. But in maaji's time, it was unheard of.

'Oh yes, I think if that woman had not come, I would have surely died in the next childbirth, or killed myself, I was so tired of being pregnant. But you don't worry, Maia, your time will come, for sure. These men in this family are makers of sons, and you will have your sons, I know it.'

~

That night Maia waited for Amar to come to their room after dinner. To her surprise and delight, he came in almost immediately after she got in bed. She turned the light back on, and watched as he put his heavy gold chain on the bedside table and went to wash and change. He had smiled at her that morning, and she waited for him. Her breathing was a little rapid, and she laughed at herself for feeling like a young girl. She was a young girl, she reminded herself. She was not yet twenty-two, and she was in her bed waiting for her husband to join her. She had not yet had a child. She was a young girl on the first night of the rest of her life with her husband. She began to wonder what was taking him so long. She began to dream about that beautiful peacock sari again, and then her thoughts went to the strange tale masterji had told her. She just couldn't understand why he would tell her such a thing. And before she could go much further, Amar came out of the bathroom and got into the bed. He turned toward her, and she turned toward him. She looked straight into his eyes, and said, 'Wouldn't you like a son?'

If he was surprised, he didn't show it at all. He smiled at her somewhat indulgently, she thought, and he touched her face, lazily, as if preparing her for what was surely to come next. Her heart began to jump a little, and sure enough, he moved his hand, still lazily, heavily, down her chin and neck and between her breasts, owning that same space that masterji had so carefully avoided touching. Amar suddenly turned on his side and pushed her blouse away, crushing her breast in his huge grip. She closed her eyes involuntarily, loving the sense of what was to come, waiting for it, feeling the slippery heat between her legs.

He came closer to her and opened his mouth to take her lips in his. And suddenly, there it was, an alien smell on him that rushed like ice in her muscles and veins, sending her into a spasm of pain and confusion like she had never felt before. She knew that smell, it was familiar, and yet she knew she had never smelt it before. It was the smell of herself, but riper, richer than herself. It was as if... her whole being rebelled against thinking such a thing, but she had already thought it, pictured it, she knew it. His moustache and hair and mouth smelled of another woman's—another woman's... Maia had no name for that space, that intimate space that was hers, but that belonged to him alone. Her own space seemed to shrivel and die, she felt as if it was not her heart that was broken, but her sex. It was turning bitter and old and was dying as she lay there, she felt her tears gathering in that—in her sex, rather than in her eyes. She lay there as he rolled on her, as he penetrated that poor, hurt place, insulting and torturing it with every thrust, and with every thrust breathing the smell of his infidelity upon her face, and she just lay there, not knowing what to do or say or how to console her broken soul as it burst and bled dry right before her eyes.

He went to sleep, finally, leaving her alone in the darkness that she wished would consume and kill her. She heard through the mists and fog of her sorrow his questioning her, asking her if she was ill, if he had hurt her. She said no, but refused to cry, she just lay there, leaking his fluids from her, leaking her love out with it. She waited till he was asleep and then went into the bathroom. She washed herself, and then splashed cool water on her face and eyes. She caught sight of herself in the mirror, and she was surprised to see that she looked no different than she had in her mother-in-law's bathroom that afternoon, when she had been happy, when she was looking forward to this night. And then she remembered masterji's story. And she understood why he had told it to her. He knew who the woman was, in the other village. He made her blouses, probably. He knew the shape and size of her breasts, and the colour of her nipples, the ones that had been in her husband's mouth. Masterji knew her face, and her name. All Maia knew was her smell, her smell upon Amar's mouth and face.

~

Masterji displayed the silk and velvet blouses and brocade salwars and kameezes one by one to the four women of the house. There were gasps of delight. The clothes were all tried on and they were all perfect. Masterji examined each blouse behind his customary curtain, and nodded approvingly. Maia went in when it was her turn, and put on the now completed peacock blouse. It was stunningly fitted, it could have been painted on her. In spite of herself, she was delighted with it. Masterji came in to look, and was pleased.

'Yes, my boy has done a very good job, after my last pinning. It is really very good.'

'Masterji, I thought about your story,' Maia said quietly to him.

'Story, my dear? It was true, you know. '

'Yes, I know. I know why you told it to me. Do you know, masterji? Who will wear the blouse?'

'Yes, Maia, I know.'

'Do you know how to make this blouse, masterji?'

'Yes, Maia, I know how to make the blouse. It is a family secret, and I received it from my father. I know how to make this blouse. You will not be sad again, Maia.'

From outside the curtain, maaji became impatient. 'What are you doing? Is there something wrong with that blouse, masterji?'

'No, maaji, there is nothing wrong with any blouse I make, it is perfect. Your daughters-in-law will be more beautiful than the bride, you know, I know who will have made her clothes, poor thing, that old fellow in her village is nothing but a cobbler.'

They all laughed, and maaji said, 'You will be making her blouses and salwar kameezes soon enough old man, she will be my daughter soon.'

'And I will make them well.' He gathered up his things and so did his assistant. 'I had better go, maaji,' he said, ' there is just one blouse left for me to make, and hardly any time left to make it.'

~

The morning of the wedding came. The women woke very early, even before the sun was up, before the day revealed itself, a brilliant winter's day full of pale sunshine. A perfect day for a wedding, Maia thought. They all took long baths, and got ready for the ceremonies. There would be singing and dancing that day, and food, and long naps in the afternoon, and singing and dancing at night, and food again, and Amar would not disappear into the village, it was his family's wedding after all, and he was the oldest, and he would have to be present, and maybe he would not go to where he went. Maia could not bear to think about it, and yet, she could not bear to stop thinking about it. She imagined him in some small house in the village, naked on some thin blanket with a young girl, or maybe she was someone else's wife, but Maia doubted it. He would not share a woman with another man. No, this had to be a young unmarried girl. Maia tortured herself with images of a faceless woman in a well-made blouse and nothing else, all she could think about was how her husband could get the smell of that woman on his face. Did her put his face so close to the source of that smell, she thought, did he put his face there, in her sex? She imagined them together until her pain turned to desire, until she ached for him worse than she ever had before. She wanted to see them together, not just imagine them, and she wanted to kill the woman as she lay there with her legs apart, she wanted to behead her, burn her, burn that smell with her. She wondered where masterji was, and if everything he told her was real. She began to think it was all a fantasy, his story. Absurd, she thought. A tailor could not kill a person with a garment, however well made. She would wait until the wedding was over, and then she would talk to her husband, and explain her pain and misery and her love for him. She would show him the source of her love and her pain, she would do anything he asked of her, she had always been ready to. And how could he then refuse her, how could he go back to the other woman, when she told him how much she loved him and how she could not bear the smell of her on his face?

The night of the actual wedding, she took great care to bathe and dress. All the women gathered in maaji's room, helping each other with sarees and jewellery. Even Shama looked radiant, all in purple, her fat face creased in a constant smile. She thought everyone was beautiful and laughed and gasped and complimented them all endlessly. Maia thought what a sweet person she was. Maaji took the sapphire set out of her safe and handed it to Maia. The huge blue velvet box was heavy, and Maia opened it. She put on the peacock earrings and the heavy intricate necklace that sat like a silver cascade on her skin. The blouse had just enough lift to receive the tiny droplets of blue onto the tops of her breasts. She turned to show maaji. There was a silence. She was the most beautiful woman in the room, and everyone knew it.

'Oh, Maia,' was all Mina could say. She was dressed in a deep garnet sari, and wore the rather traditional ruby and pearl colours, but they worked for her suntouched skin and black eyes. They went out together into the main hall. Maia wanted Amar to see her. She dropped Mina's hand and went to look for him in the crowd. She saw him standing among a group of men, and knew she should not go up to him. She waited by the door, willing him to look at her. He turned suddenly, and his eyes fell directly on her. His whole body stilled, and he did not take his eyes off her for a few moments. Then he put his glass down on a table and strode toward her. He stood as close to her as was decent in public, and said, 'My Maia.'

Two hours went by in a blur for her. She was as happy as she could ever hope to be, even happier than she was when she was first married, even happier than she would be when they found out she was pregnant. She could not be with him at all, he was with the men, and she with the women. But he would glance at her again and again, and she knew that this was the beginning for them. She knew that there would be no other woman who would ever lay her smell upon her man, no other woman who would disturb her dreams or her imagination. Her happiness was complete when she saw Mina, a little sick from all the revelry, and remembered, after being concerned at first, why her sister-in-law was sick. As maaji had said, there was nothing at all wrong with her, she only had her belly full of baby. The maidservant took Mina's hand and led her gently to her room, she could not take any more of the chattering and the smell of the food and flowers and incense all around her and the wail of the shehnai that would not stop.

Maia was standing next to Amar and her mother-in-law, looking at the newly married couple when the servant girl came screaming down the path from the house. They could not hear her words until she was right next to them, there was too much noise. The poor girl was weeping openly.

'She stopped breathing, maaji, maaji, please come quickly, quickly, hurry, there is something very wrong with her. She fainted and has stopped breathing, please help her, maaji...'

Maia heard the words clearly. They poisoned her soul.

~

Inside

~

As I flowed with the energy to a single point between Sarangi's legs, as I jumped with the short breaths jumping in her throat, as I was introduced to the feel of Amoran's muscular ass barely yielding to the insistent pressure of her palms, as I opened with her legs opening more and more and more and I was lifted with her begging hips begging for the nicely hard cock to please take its rightful place in the slippery core of her longing, I knew I was not needed there anymore, and I could leave, and neither the man in that exquisite moment before the commission nor Sarangi in her agony of anticipation would feel my departure.

In twenty-three generations, I was the first male to be born with this particular tuhn. Every other tuhn was variable over gender. Girl and boy babies were, for example, equally likely to have the invisibility tuhn, or the shape-changing one, or even strength or flying. But travel, ah, that was a female tuhn. Or so we all thought, so we all *knew*, until

I was born. And that first time, when I reached the lovely age of nine, was when my mother realised that I was not a dell, as such rare children were called. I was thought to have been born without a tuhn, without one of the abilities running through our vast and varied and old family now spread over countries and continents. Until I was nine, none of the abilities had manifested in me. No one thought that I would be endowed with travel, which normally showed itself at nine, because I was born with a penis and testicles. Penis and testicles and travel had simply never occurred together in a single entity. So they all assumed, for the first nine years of my life, that I was a dell—an empty child. Empty of a seventh sense, which was really an ability, not a sense, but that's what they were called. The seven seventh senses.

And then at nine, my sense was found out, in quite an ordinary way really. My mother was beating carpets in the yard. It was springtime, and the snow in the foothills of the mountains of our home was in thaw. The carpets smelled musty from being on the floors of smoky and overheated rooms shut away from the crisp freshness of the air outside. So she was beating the carpets, and I, swaddled in layers and layers of wool and fur, so bulked up and heavy that I could do nothing but watch her, eventually fell asleep. I remember my last thought was, I wish I could be the mountain goat I spotted in the rubble and rocks right behind my mother. My mother later told us, and she has told us this story so often since that no one wants or needs to hear it anymore, that as she beat the carpets and puffs of dust flew out of them, a little baby goat came bounding down the hill at her. She turned and looked because she heard it. It stopped right in front of her, and looked into her eyes, with its yellow eyes and square pupils. Then it butted the carpet, again and again, in a little game. She said shoo to it many times, and threatened it with the carpet beater, but it wouldn't leave. It just ran around her, and butted the carpet, and bleated in a funny baby-goat voice. She decided to ignore it, and after a while it wandered away. I woke up soon after, and told her, 'Mamia, I dreamed I was a mountain goat, and I came down the mountain to play with you, but you shook that beater at me!' She thought I must have been awake and watching the whole thing, but she knew I wasn't, because I looked as I always looked when I had woken up from a nap—my eyes were bloody red, and I was rubbing them with my fists. She looked at me for a few moments and then dropped her beater and grabbed me by my upper arm. She paid no attention to my protestations, she just dragged me into the house shouting for my father and older siblings. There were five of them, and no one materialised. My father was inside the house, sitting on his favourite—no, his own—chair, knitting a scarf.

'What is it?' he asked her.

'He was travelling,' she told him, and said nothing more. Then they both stared at me without saying anything. They seemed relieved, but I sensed a great sadness pass through them, and to each other. I was right about that, I did not know why they were so sad until I was so much older. At that moment, thinking back, I was probably confused, at least. But that was the beginning of normalcy in my life. Until that day, I was a beloved but poor sibling, and I was treated well, even better than the rest of the children. I wanted to be whacked on the side of the head by my father as he did to my brothers, or yelled at by my mother. But never till I was nine. They were always kind and gentle to me. And instead of inviting my siblings' hatred and derision, which I would have welcomed, I got from them too, kindness and gentleness. It all came from pity for the poor impoverished, incomplete dell. And then, at nine, I travelled into the goat as I slept, and I was released. Released from the life of a dell, of course, but also released from myself. I was free now, to inhabit whom I wanted, when I wanted. I spent a lot of time in animals, in those early years. My mother forbade me from leaving without a meal. She said my body, laying there in my room without me, would become weak, or even die, if I had not eaten. So I would eat a huge breakfast, and then drink the vile potion all travellers had to drink before a journey, and leave. I had to be home for dinner, we all did. So I didn't go very far, as a child. I ran in the mountains in a goat, I jumped in rabbits a lot until the day I flew in a hawk, and he scooped down and ate one of them. I didn't go near the rabbits again. I asked my mother what would happen if I was in a rabbit when it became food. She said I would feel the pain of the rabbit, but I would be transferred, either to the hawk, or straight back home. It would be unpleasant, but not harmful let alone fatal. One day I roamed the mountains with a larger goat when I discovered mating. As I mounted the female and entered that wonderful hot goat vagina, I was entranced. What a beautiful thing was this! I began to inhabit my sisters when they bathed. I was right to do so. As they soaped themselves and played with their breasts and nipples, sometimes they put the soap there, between their legs, and rubbed and rubbed until they had the most delicious spasms run through them. My oldest sister would actually push the whole soap inside herself and then stroke her clitoris with her fingers. Her orgasms were magnificent grinding succulent creations, as the flesh of her cunt rippled and clutched at the soap inside. I loved being in her. I loved being in my brothers too. I found their work exhilarating, and inhabited them most often when they were out chopping firewood, or gathering up our flock of sheep and corralling them in for the night, or when one of them went up on the roof that always needed fixing. I was lucky enough to be there one day when he looked down into the bathhouse where the soap routine was in progress, and there was nothing he could do but take off his glove and give himself a little relief from the horrendous erection that appeared at the first sight of his own naked sister. I felt a sourness and anger rise within him afterward, but then I asserted myself in him, and thought very hard, it's not your fault, it just happened. And I felt his face smile, and his shoulders shrug ruefully, and I went back home. That was the day that I understood that I could change how someone felt from the inside. I was sixteen then. I wanted to speak to my mother about it, but she asked me first.

'Have you only travelled and pleasured yourself, or have you found your strom yet?'

'Strom? Mamia, do you mean like when I feel or think then... '

'Yes, so you have found it. Tell me about it.'

'I think I can change the course of a person's thoughts or feelings, Mamia. If I want it very hard. But I feel very tired when I am back,' I told her.

She smiled. 'I will bring you the leaves,' she said.

My post-breakfast potions became viler and harder to drink, but this my mother was firm about. No potion, no travel, she said. She had ways to stop me, but I didn't ask what they were. I went where I pleased, in the early years. I did what I wanted. I was gone for days sometimes, and sometimes even weeks. When I returned, I was sometimes unable to get off my bed and walk downstairs to eat, and my mother installed some sort of sensing plant in my bed, its roots grew down to the floors below. Small brass bells all over the house would trip and shiver when the plant signalled my return, and she would come flying up the stairs with more vile juices to revive my softened muscles and bones. I understood the importance of those potions then. She said I would find my body dead one day if I didn't prepare it for my long absences. Sometimes I came back too early, and I would experience the strange sensations of a body overrun with weedy juices and living organisms that scurried around in my muscles and veins reproducing at a microcosmic level the motions and actions and responses of muscle and bone and tendon and fibre as if I ran and walked and ate and lived. My body had to stay motionless while I was gone, but motionless is a relative term, my mother explained, and it was only vitally important that my outline did not change. So I drank the potions diligently, and travelled wherever I pleased, until one day my mother called me into the horse shed where she was mucking out the stalls. The horses were gone, my father and brothers had taken them somewhere into the villages below to bring us supplies, and to deliver the meat and milk we didn't need for ourselves. She was so strong, my mother. She could do the hardest jobs with ease. She never tired, it seemed to me. She worked from the moment she woke up, which was early in the morning, until she finally sat down to the dinner my father cooked, and they told me, my father and brothers and sisters, that she worked right through all her pregnancies, and went right back to it all a day or two after she had given birth. I watched her for a little while. I was like my father, small in stature, small hands and feet, even my head was small when compared with other children. This should have been a sign of my tuhn, and would have, had I been a girl. We travellers were all small. I watched her, my mother, large, strong, sweeping and lifting and there was no sign of her labour on her face at all. She spoke to me easily and quietly, and she told me what she wanted me to do.

'Tamur is only five years old,' she said. 'He is not set in his ways. You know who I mean?' I didn't. 'The butcher's youngest boy, down in the blue village.' I did know who she meant. I had been down to that village with my sister, she had a lot going on with the butcher's oldest boy. I knew, because I had been sampling the butcher's oldest boy myself when I found myself in the taste of my sister's dark nipples, and in the sense of my face all over the velvety slopes of her breasts. The butcher's oldest boy did something that I loved being part of—the ridge run. There were several of the young men in the villages who did this crazy thing, but he was best at it. The literally breakneck speed was exhilarating, and tasting the edge of fear that came with that unstoppable run was one of the best feelings I had ever shared. So I stayed with him as he ran downhill through the ridge, as his legs pumped hard and he fought to keep himself upright while hurtling down that impossible angle, I stayed with him when he slowed to a stop on the flat at the end of the hill, and I stayed with him on his slow walk home with the other boys, and before I knew what he was up to, he slipped into a small barn-like structure next to his own house, and together we were on those breasts of my sister. My sister was invisible, so it was all the more delightful, and the butcher's boy and I, in his hands and his mouth, sensed her everywhere but could not see her. She was naked, and she must have walked naked through the village to get there, and the thought made him smile inside and hard as can be outside, and that was the first time I felt a slippery salivating mouth on the head and foreskin of a man, a sense of teeth on the ridge, and it was me that made him choke my sister and smear her invisible face, because my thoughts went coursing through his nerves, and I shattered his control. They both began to laugh, and it was beautiful when he slipped his fingers in her mouth and then I felt his fingertips searching for the unseen curls of my sister's soap-clean bubbly pinkness where he could bury his hand and draw out her moaning pleasure. The butcher's boy, I knew him well.

'What are you thinking?' my mother asked me, 'you haven't heard what I was telling you. Do I start the story again?'

'Yes,' I said, And I didn't say I was lost in my own sister's invisible skin, oh that skin, I would wrap that all around me and sleep forever in that skin. I stopped right there. I didn't want my mother to have to repeat the story a third time.

'The butcher's little boy,' she said. 'I shouldn't say this, but that man was too old when he had the child before this one. This one should never have been born. Imagine, his son is younger than his grandson. Stupid meathead. He's a butcher. It's not unexpected. And I suppose now that he has that young wife he can't resist her. Anyway. The little fellow is a bit slow. He is shy and slow, and the other children trouble him and even hurt him sometimes. I want you to help him.' I didn't know what she meant. How could I help a little boy who was slow and troubled by other children? My mother had a plan, though. This plan was the first of many such plans. Years of my life were sacrificed to her philanthropic plans. Not that I was the only one. All of my siblings had to use their tuhn to help people around us. My brother was always being dispatched to fly up to roofs to fix them, and my other brother, even stronger than Mamia, spent his days fetching and carrying and moving peoples' houses and ferrying sick animals and people to the doctor on is back. My sisters too, spent a lot of time feeling for and finding the root of a sickness or a sadness, and then healing it. It was my turn now, to be useful to our mountain community, and I had no real choice but to do so. I knew that this was how our family had survived the fear and violence through ages. We made ourselves beloved and indispensable. And we were still here when others had been reviled, exiled, staked, burned for being what they were. Many hid, we didn't. We were beloved and indispensable.

We spoke about the plan over the next several days, and every day, along with my father's delicious dinners of soups and root vegetables and wheat porridges, my mother gave me big cups of thick viscous drinks. They were worse than ever, dark and exuding a green steam that burned my nostrils as I sucked down. I began to understand what this plan entailed. I would be sent to the village where the little boy lived, to watch him and learn his ways. And then, I would have to be in him, for as long as it took. I didn't know what she meant by 'as long as it took', my mother. When the time came, I became one with the little boy as he slept, a few hours before he woke up in the morning. I didn't know it then, but this would become my way. I liked the feeling of slipping into a sleeping person. There was no resistance, and of course they never knew I was there, even when I insinuated myself into their thoughts and actions, even when I took over and thought and acted for them, in spite of them. But still, I liked slipping in while they slept, like the thief I was. I slipped into their dreams. I walked and ran and danced with them. I touched frogs and ran after dogs. And I understood my own oddness when I lived within that little boy. Tamur. Every night when he went to his corner of the house to sleep, Tamur played with his fingers and toes and lips, and finally, right before he fell asleep, he wriggled and jiggled his little penis and squeezed the skin on it and twisted and annoyed it till it was a stiff little fellow under his itchy wool blanket. And then he fell asleep, and I felt it slowly lose blood and tension and fall asleep too. I hadn't done this when I was his age. I still didn't. But then I didn't have the time, I thought, I was always off in someone else's dreams and desires and abandoning myself with their reckless abandon on rooftops and hillsides and underwater and in the high cold air, in sleeping old men and mountain wolves and my brothers and hawks with yellow blood-smeared beaks. I didn't do what this boy did, or my brothers did, or my sisters, I got no sense of delight from my own silky, hairless skin nor visceral carnal spasms from rubbing against my palm or my mattress or my sister's breasts. I thought my own lonely thoughts as I watched the dreams of the little boy, of other children's laughter and derision as they left him and ran out of a room to play together. Over the next months, I would help Tamur. I would lighten his heavy tongue, I would hold it up for him when his words weighed it down into the curve of his jaw, I would stick it out at ugly boys, I would lift his lips and form a smile when that schoolteacher I could sense in his mind came into the classroom and looked toward him, I would lift his hand for him and share his mother's delicious meal with the other little boy in the margins of his class, I would even, after two months of living within him, speak to a girl who came in with her mother to his father's shop, and I would slap a bullying boy for hurting his new little friend. And when I finally left him two months hence, Tamur was different. When I left him, I left a bit of me in him, a bit of what Mamia wanted for him. Boldness I took from a butterfly, I left with him.

And then there were so many little boys and girls, shy ones, and sweet and fearful ones. And sometimes Mamia sent me to bullies too, and harsh creatures, and I learned to subdue and restrain, and left behind the memory of the joy of gentleness.

There was Habeer, he was all strength and anger, and something ran inside him that he could not control, and did not want to. He waited for the women at the stream where they washed our clothes, and bathed sometimes, and I would feel a terrible pounding in his head area and the vein ran straight to his pelvis, blood and anger wound their way there, pushing his purple cock into a heated spoke that taunted him and he and I felt its eye look at us from inside and out with fire. He would tear it out of his clothes and rake it with his rough calluses and hurt and ravage it with a bloody friction till it burst out streams of choked frustration, and he would cry out, and the women all heard him and knew he was there. They ignored him, and I tried to think inside him about soft things and the sounds of wings and the love of my mother and the soup of my father, but his fire eye spoke louder than I. I stayed with him, though I hated being there with his thoughts, they were of the pain of others, of tearing and gouging and biting female flesh. But I stayed with him, I did not want to fail. And then one day, there was only the one woman at the river, and I could not stop him when he ran down to her and ripped off her clothes. I wanted to be in her instead of him, to numb her perhaps to the pain I knew she felt, but I could not leave him, and I tried not to rush into his anger and weakness and brutality, but it sucked me in. He pumped his ugliness against her, and as he did, I ran myself all around his black and jagged mind, looking for something. I found a little corner of sadness. And I concentrated on it. I made it glow, I made it grow and grow and grow in him until he released the poor woman. Habeer sat on the edge of the water and began to cry, weeping and weeping as I pushed the sadness forward and upward in his consciousness. As I left him, I told Mamia I knew, I must have known what he would do. But I was exhausted too, and I left him. As I lay on my bed and reassembled myself they found him washed up on the other side, his lungs full of water.

And then Mamia sent me to my most important task. Sarangi was sixteen, she said, and if she did not speak to a man soon, there was no hope for her. Sarangi was the daughter of my mother's friend. I had known her since I was born, because we were born the same day, she and I. She was a sister of mine, and a daughter of my mother. I had to do right by her. And so, there I was, after a year of being and living and doing Sarangi, she was with Amoran. We had done everything right, she and I. We had spoken, softly, we had looked at him, we had taken long walks with him, and let him touch her hands and lips with his lips. We had moaned at his caress and laughed at his stories, we had given him glimpses of curve and whiffs of wetness and once, just once, I moved her hand along his forearm like a slight wind, and then surprised him with a hard pressure, letting him know how it was inside her. He went to her father the next day to beg for her to be his wife, he could not think anymore about anything but her skin against his.

And so that night, Sarangi lay on Amoran's bed. I waited. This was when I would know what I know now—that I love the moment of unity. Perhaps I loved it more than the man or the woman did, because I felt it so differently than they did. But not yet, then, I didn't know it yet. I waited. She was quiet, and so was he. I felt her quiver a little and almost say 'please' but she didn't. She was soaked with want.

He was pulsating with it. But still, they held back. These two seemed to understand the importance of the moment, the beauty of the first contact between their cores. And they didn't know it, but it was my first time too, with a man and a woman, and I was grateful that he held back. Later, much later, when I knew this moment well, and I had been in this moment many times, I found out that the core of man and woman is not their heart or soul or even the mind. It was this, the volcano. The cock and the cunt. The hawk and its nest. The origin of life. Later, I lost interest completely when it came to the point after entry. Now, I leave them to their thrust and parry and moan and clutch, on and on until one or both give up the dance. Fuck and come don't interest me anymore. But that day, inside Sarangi, I did not know anything yet. I had never felt it before. I had never been there, when a virgin lost her virginity, willingly and sweetly and achingly. With Sarangi, even though I knew she didn't need me anymore, and I could go back home to my own tired body, I waited. And then, when Sarangi, and I, didn't quite expect it, Amoran did it. All three of us howled at the moon, as all of him slid slowly and intently in, and she opened, and then closed around him like a mouth around its own tongue. I had just wanted to be there for a moment I had worked for, that I had made possible. And I was so very glad I did.

What my parents had thought was because of my premature birth, was suddenly clear to them, that day when they knew what I was. This tuhn explained my diminutive size, and the size of my every part. Their sadness came from the fact that anyone, male or female, born with this remarkable and most precious of all tuhn, was not really a male or a female. We are sexless. The females have the outward appearance of a female, but none of those delicious orifices and crevasses that real females have, none which actually experience the succulence and interference that real females do. They had no vaginas of vulvas or cervixes or uteri. Now we know what the males are like. We, or I, if I am the only one of my kind, have a kind of penis, and even little sacs. But I have never had an erection, and so, I will never be surrounded by the hot vaginal flesh I have felt again and again in my travels, and I will never pulse and pound and plead and surrender my flesh or my non-existent sperm. We cannot make children. It doesn't matter to me—I have felt the pleasure and pain of every creature in its own creation, and man and woman in their sex, whether making new selves, or in the expression of their rage, jealousy, power, shame, loneliness, and lust. Though they never knew it, people gave me more than I could ever give them. There were times, like Sarangi, when I have been inside love.

~

Slight Return

~

Suman was tired when she went to bed, with the kind of tiredness that wouldn't allow her to fall asleep. It was a soul-tiredness along with the physical exhaustion. Pictures and conversations shifted and followed each other randomly through her thoughts, some pleasant and most unpleasant. She felt unable to get up and get a glass of water from the kitchen, though her throat felt like paper. Her work, sometimes she thought it would kill her. Maybe not actually, though even that was a possibility, but certainly her feelings. She had learned over years and years of doing this job, how to still herself, how to keep the vomit and tears inside. When she had just started, she was close to quitting within the first month. It was Madhu who convinced her that she could do it, and that she was needed, and that she was very good at it, and that it would get much better as time went on. Still, sometimes she wished she had not listened to him. There were days when she witnessed moments she knew were moments that made all the world better, and then she was grateful to have been there. Like last week, when they had found a nine-year-old girl in the houses at Kamathipura, and returned her to her family. Suman was there on a routine visit with the doctor, checking on vaccines, distributing cartons of condoms, just checking on things. One of the women whispered that there had been a girl stolen from the railway station, and that she was very, very small. The family were so very grateful to have her back. They had neither sold her nor were involved in any way, she had simply wandered off at the station, been picked up by the wrongest person possible, and there were so many of these in the city, especially in places like the big railway stations and bus hubs, waiting for just such opportunities, when poor families had no recourse but to keep going wherever they were going. They were so lucky that this agent of the devil had not found a client to sell the child to, he had been greedy, he knew the price of a virgin-child, and she had been intact and unharmed when they found her. Suman had many friends there. Women and transgendered sex workers, the kinnar community, the doctors in the clinics in the area, and even some of the policemen in the station at the end of Kamathipura. She had many dealings with them, because of her job. There was medical help, psychological counselling, education. That was at the beginning. Eventually, after years of visiting the same places, she got to know people there, and they got to know her. Sometimes she would think of one of them when she saw something at the market, or when she was out shopping with Tara, her own sixteen-year-old, and she would buy it, and take it to them. Not as a favour, but as a normal gesture. Of friendship. And they understood that she saw them as people, not degenerates, nor, as some of the other social workers in her organisation did, inferior creatures whom they would lift out of poverty and the miserable lives they lived. Suman simply saw them as they were, people who were not in the best circumstances humanity could offer. To her they were just people, not of any race or gender, just people. People who found sorrow and joy in their lives, whatever they were. She remembered the sweet tears of one of the HIV-positive women, who after a difficult pregnancy and a C-section paid for by her organisation, was handed a little girl who was uninfected. The mother had no idea how long she herself would live, or what future awaited that girl, but none of that interfered with the primal feeling a creature has when it sees a newborn calf, or kitten, or child. Her eyes shone, and Suman had to wipe away her own tears. But then there were those times, like that last Monday. The case involved a three-year-old, nothing but a baby, who had been brought to the hospital brutalised and bloody. The hospital authorities registered a rape case with the police. They did not expect the child to live. Suman accompanied four policemen to the slum where the parents of the poor child lived. After barely fifteen minutes they arrested a neighbour. He was a middle-aged man, he worked close by, and had offered to watch the child while the parents went on an errand. The four policemen could not contain their disgust and sexual horror, and all they could do was take it out on the man. They beat him near to death, in her presence. Suman did not even attempt to stop them, she knew she could not have anyway, but she had just stood there along with all the other neighbours and parents of the child, her fists clenched, jaw clenched, heart clenched, and wished she could do it too, kick and beat and hurt that man, rip out his eyes and slice off his genitals.

She was so tired. She lay heavy in her bed. She thought she would ask Madhu for a couple of weeks off. And go to Panchgani or Mahabaleshwar, or maybe even further, south somewhere in Kerala, to take time to look beyond the buildings and people so close to her face in the city, encroaching on her being, they were managing to get in, because she was weak, her emotional muscle was weak. It was getting hard to stay sane, to find joy in anything. She had been warned to take care of herself, when she first trained for this job. She knew had to give her eyes a rest, her body and mind rest. Tara could go and stay with her father and his new wife, she liked them both well enough, and they lived close enough to school that her life would not be disrupted at all. Suman was grateful for Tara. She knew, of course, that she had a lot to do with the way Tara had dealt with her parent's divorce. Suman had explained it to her gently and over a long period of time. It had been four years, but those four years were delicate ones in a girl's life, and now, at sixteen, Tara was a cheerful, popular, and lovely girl, who did reasonably well at school. She did a lot better at art and drama than maths and science, but these days it didn't matter so much. Tara could do what she pleased. She had a rich father, and a caring mother, both of whom had learned from their mistakes and would not force her into a marriage like they had been by their parents. Suman, not for the first time, smiled when she remembered her own naiveté and childishness when she had married Tara's father. She thought they would love each other and live happily ever after, among their three beautiful children, two boys and a girl. She got pregnant immediately, probably from the very first encounter, and then everything went downhill fast. He didn't like her much, and although physically she didn't mind him, she didn't like him at all as a person. He was brusque with colleagues, rude to servants, and did not have friends, only business acquaintances. Physically he was in good shape, he could have been attractive had he been a nicer person, but Suman was not so interested in sex that she would show any emotion or physical reaction when he turned to her in the night, pushing her nightgown up, gently enough, kissing her, or trying to, and then quickly getting on top of her with his usually short-lived erection, thankfully for her. She didn't say or do much at all, and she felt nothing much. It didn't hurt or feel unpleasant in any serious way, and nor did she enjoy it. She couldn't understand what there was to enjoy in this act. She preferred visits to the gynaecologist, at least he was friendly and chatted with her about cricket and the latest movies while he spread her legs and penetrated her with a warm object. He was gentle, and he did it for her good, not his pleasure. She knew, of course, that many people did enjoy that sex activity mutually, even her own best friend, who laughed at her and said, 'One day, Suman, someone will have the right key for your lock. And then we'll see.' We'll see indeed, she thought.

She gave up the struggle to sleep and opened her eyes. She looked at the time, it was a little past one o'clock. Her mouth still felt dry, in fact she was having trouble swallowing. She sighed, and even that breath rasped at the back of her throat. She thought of these sighs as something old people did, her grandmother used to do it, sigh long and deep in the middle of doing something, reading the newspaper, or knitting. It was a sound of being overwhelmed by weltschmerz, when everything had become too heavy, life itself had become too heavy, and the sigh would somehow shift that weight. She used to think then, that when she sighed like that, she would know she was old. She did feel old now, she was almost forty after all, but she also understood where that breath came from. She was right about the weariness if not the age. She pushed the sheet off her feet. Then she sat up and turned so she was sitting facing the window with her feet on the floor. She knew she had to get up and get a glass of water. She knew she would have to go down to the kitchen to get it, she just didn't like drinking water from the bathroom tap. This was the one thing she missed about being married. He ex-husband lived in an apartment, and it was brand-new, and all on one level, not like this old house, beautiful, and with an actual garden, but just too big for her and Tara to live in alone, and falling apart in ways that she could not fix, nor afford to have fixed. Maybe her friend was right, maybe there would be someone who would have the key to unlock her, and would move in and fix the place, she thought. Madhu, bless him, offered to send his people. Madhu worked more with construction workers and labourers so he did know a lot of people who could have come and fixed things, but she refused. Mainly because the idea of having workers crawling around the house on weekends was just too much for her. Not that she didn't work weekends when she had to, but still. Some Saturdays that year she had actually stayed home all day and cooked and eaten and spent all day with Tara. Maybe this weekend, she thought. Maybe she would really put in for leave.

She stood up, and quietly, so as not to make the house creak and wake Tara, she put on a robe, and softly opened the door. She was puzzled and momentarily blinded by the light, and wondered if she was mistaken about the time, and if it really was morning, but her eyes adjusted. It took a long time for her brain to adjust to what she was seeing, though. Suman knew whom she was seeing, of course. But it took so long to make the connections, that she didn't feel the shock or revulsion she might have had she understood the scene before her sooner. She had not seen Tara naked in a long time, was her first thought. Not since she used to bathe her. Suman had to think a moment. Tara must have been six, she thought, or seven, no more than that. She remembered some time around that age Tara had said to her while Suman was washing her hair, 'Mamu, I can do it myself now! I'm old enough.' Suman had smiled and left the bathroom, but insisted that the door be left unlocked. She didn't have those breasts she had now, gentle slopes, no creases on them, one nipple dark and erect like a small temple on a mountain peak, and the other one, oh god, Suman thought, the other one is covered by a hand, and she was immensely relieved because she knew whose hand it was, it was just Tara's boyfriend. Suman shocked herself then. Here was her sixteen-year-old daughter on the sofa of their living room, entirely naked, not even her panties on, and naked with a man, and giggling, and she was relieved. She leaned against the old banister and looked down, and wondered what was wrong with her. She knew she should have been very angry, she should have gone down those stairs in a cold fury and asked Biren to get out, and she should have told Tara, the shameless whore, to put her clothes on. And then she should have wept and berated her all night, and demanded apologies and promises that such a thing would never happen again. And then she heard Tara giggle again, that same childhood giggle, she had giggled like that when she hadn't learned to speak yet, and she still did. It was her most basic expression of delight in the world and herself. It had always made Suman smile, that sound, and when she heard it now, it did not make her smile, but it did not allow her to step out of the shadows and destroy her daughter's delight. Tara was not a whore, and there was no way Suman would ever call her that. She was ashamed for even having thought such a thing. Not only because she knew Tara, but because she knew what a whore was—it was a man or a woman with no choices. It was a person locked into a life that no one deserved, and yet so very many lived. Tara would be old compared to some of the children Suman had seen in the brothels, and on the streets. She would have lost her virginity a long time ago, to some fat businessman from another city who had paid for it in a suitcase-full of cash, which Tara would never see any of.

Suman stopped that thought process immediately. She did not want to go there. She had often compared her own life to those of others she worked with. A single mother with a good job and her own house, a grown-up daughter, a spoiled girl when compared with those girls, but also not, when compared with her cousins on her father's side. Suman smiled to herself in the dark. Those fat Hindi-movie obsessed girls, they were certainly more spoiled when compared to her lovely Tara. She stared at the two children below her. Tara still giggled as Biren stuck out his tongue and licked her nipple.

Then he began to lick her face, like a little puppy, her eyes, and forehead, and ears and mouth, and Tara's little breathy giggles carried up the stairs. Tara put her hands in his long dark straight hair as it fell heavily like black water over his shoulders and brushed her shoulders. And then the boy moved down her body as Suman watched, frozen to the floor and to her own thoughts as they unfolded with the rhythm of the two children below. She let them run where they would.

She had never ever been, in her memory at least, entirely naked in the presence of another human being. She would be so uncomfortable, she thought. She had always wondered about that, when she saw it in movies. People not only were comfortable in their nakedness, but even in doing personal things, bathing, even sitting on the toilet with another person present in the room. She never could. She could not even go to the bathroom in school during break, when there were other girls around, even if they were outside the stall. She could not imagine herself like this, naked, with the light on, all of her exposed and vulnerable to someone else's eyes. She could not imagine wanting to see anyone naked like that either, especially not a man, with his peculiar bodily features. All right, his penis and testicles. But then she was seeing her daughter, and the boy she was with, and they were entirely naked, and they were so beautiful, like two animals in a forest together, just playing with each other. She saw Tara's arm thrown over her head, and his hand came up and wove his fingers into hers, and then they were kissing each other, on the mouth, like in a movie, Suman could see Tara's other hand in his hair, and his head moving. And then Tara said something to him, and he sat up. That was when Suman saw the torn condom packets on the floor beside them. There were four that she could see. She sighed, again relief. How odd, she thought, this was of course not the first time they had done this. They were completely comfortable with each other, and it was not only not the first time, it was not even the first time in that night. So it was not just play then, it was actual sex, the boy had been inside her. Many times. Suman felt the slightest wisp of fear and uncertainty then. She was confused. She was the mother of this girl. What was she supposed to do now? Now that she hadn't done the right thing of screaming and throwing a huge fit and making both children ashamed and angry and hateful of her and perhaps even each other, what should she do? What was the right thing? She wondered what her mother would have done. Her mother. She would probably have begun to cry and wail. Then and there. And then gone running to her husband. And he would have come into the room just as the boy ran away, and he would have stood in the doorway for a while, with his most thunderous face on, building on the terror that would have gripped Suman's heart, shrivelling forever all the delicate lusts that boy had planted there. And then her father would have raised his hand high and hit her across the face. And he would never have spoken to her ever again. And in that moment, Suman understood her older sister, and her sudden departure from the house, and her marriage to Manoj, which was never spoken of in the house, and her happiness, which was never spoken of either. No, Suman would not do what her mother had done, because Tara's father was not there for her to run to, and if he had been there, Tara would probably not be naked in her living room with her lovely Nepali boyfriend. She would have gone as far as kissing him in at a movie where they had gone with a group of friends, she would have told her parents they were all girlfriends of course, or they would have held hands at a school trip at most. But this? This would not have happened if her mother and father had still been together.

Here was her girl, her responsibility, now actually climbing upon the boy. Suman glimpsed a flamboyantly vertical penis for a moment before her daughter straddled him, gently lowering herself upon him, placing her hands against his chest, and still giggling as he moaned and called her name. Tara shushed him, saying he would wake her mother, and placed one of her hands on his mouth. He put his hands on her naked bottom, one on each side. His hands on her bottom—that was a part of the body just not meant for touching. Suman herself wore long shirts, or kurtas, and sarees, things that covered her own bottom entirely. It was meant for—other things. She watched Biren's hands move, his fingers begin to slide inwards, to a place Suman was so embarrassed by that she could feel her face glow, and she reached up and touched her own cheeks. They felt hot. She wondered if while her daughter discovered her body and found so much pleasure in it, she herself was hurtling toward an early menopause. The thought made her deeply sad. She couldn't fathom why. She should be pleased, she thought, that she would be rid of the bleeding and cramps and chafing from the sanitary napkins. And she didn't like the idea of nakedness, let alone sex, so why would it feel so sad to contemplate menopause? Biren had a tight grip on Tara's bottom, and he was moving her up and down, slowly, and she was beginning to make little sounds like a kitten, and still giggling, and moving faster and faster and faster. Suman could not take her eyes off. She felt helpless and sorry and felt her breasts move in her nightgown, and felt her tears begin to flow, and still she stood, frozen there, as her daughter, delighted and happy, soon triumphantly announced her pleasure to her boyfriend, 'I came before you! Again! Come on!'

And he laughed, and hauled her over like a light sack, and went at her like a young puppy, growling and mauling her, till finally he did too, and they both lay there for a time, and then, to Suman's complete amusement, began to talk about a history project that was due the next day, and then got up and dressed. They then opened their school bags and laid out books on the floor. Biren stuffed all the condom wrappers into the zipper of his bag.

Suman took a breath, and went slowly down the stairs for her glass of water.

'I hope it's going well,' she said to the two children, startling them. She smiled at them as she went back upstairs with her glass.

As she lay in bed, she thought about Madhu. She wondered how she hadn't noticed before that his beard was much more salt than pepper now; like her, he must be tired from all the horrors and sadness and misery he got to see during the course of his long dedicated career of social work. He started before there was even any funding. As she fell asleep she promised herself she would invite him to dinner. Her waking thoughts slid seamlessly into dreaming. She thought, he might be able to fix the stairs with his key.

~

Taxidermy

~

There are lives that must be close to dead boring. Taxidermists' lives, oral hygienists' lives, whores' lives. It's how you think about it, or how you do it, after all, that makes it dull or not. Anything could be boring and anything could be interesting. Doing the same thing over and over again for a whole lifetime makes you good at it. Imagine that—a taxidermist, out of all the things in the whole wide world, good at that one thing. Stuffing dead animals. And to become good at it, she would have to do it over and over again. Before the taxidermy there's dressing the dead animal. It's called dressing, but it's really not. It's undressing: sharpen the blades, skin the animal, keep as much of the fur or hair off the meat, clean, clean, skin, skin, the animal hangs there, dead, keep the meat and fat off the skin, remove the head, take the skin off the head, wrap the creature neatly to send to the taxidermist. That's why the skin is so important. And then the taxidermist begins her job, one she has done again and again so she does it well, she makes the dead animal look alive. What does a taxidermist good at her job do? She makes a dead animal look as he might have when he was alive. The little wolf turns his head toward a sound in the bushes, the stag walks with head held high, the pet tabby lays in his basket as he used to. The sleepers are easy to do, much easier than the ones who are supposed to be awake. The sleeping dead ones do have to look good in repose, but a dead animal looks better, more realistic as a sleeping one than a walking one. So the taxidermist says. The oral hygienist, that's another story. She has to clean dental interstices and surfaces—these become vast cliff faces to her, and she goes at them with the equivalent of pick and ball peen, of earth-moving machinery and granite polishers. She thinks about what's all been in this mouth, what's all sticking between the teeth of even the most religious flosser. She tries not to be distracted by that giant cross rising and falling with the freckled breasts of her client, a woman who goes to church every Sunday, whose husband brings her to the dentist's office every three months and waits outside reading old issues of old golf magazines as his wife's teeth and gums are attended to. The hygienist finds and carefully extracts a pubic hair of his trapped between the jagged edge of an impacted wisdom tooth and the woman's reddened gum, she tried to cough it up for half a day, and it was still sitting there, one trailing end tickling her throat. The hygienist scrapes off his dead sperm from under his wife's gumline as he reads tips to a better swing. No, the oral hygienist doesn't think about what's in the mouth, just what will be in her own mouth once she gets out of there, the dinner that we will have together, she and I and our taxidermist. Thinking about the Goan shrimp and the buttery hot rolls she plans to order causes her belly to speaks in a low rowl. The client with her mouth open and eyes closed has to have heard, but she makes no sign. The teeth are beautiful, and better looked after than most the hygienist has seen. But she does sometimes wonder how much of this woman's sex life involves her mouth. She did tell me all this at dinner, I didn't make it up.

Doing something over and over burns grooves into the brain, and shapes the muscles and tendons and bones into the action. They learn it, the whole body learns it. It gets better and better at it. It becomes the action, whether it be caping a dead stag or cleaning tobacco stains off teeth, or moving just the right way to end an encounter quickly with a reasonably satisfactory ejaculation, giving the patron his money's worth. The body learns with the brain, and the person becomes that action, those actions.

Why do we listen to the same song over and over and over again? To get better at listening to it? In a way, yes. To fix the emotion felt at that first listening, maybe, to deepen and strengthen it, like a crease made by feeling the same anger or irritation over and over again. So does doing the same job over and over again soothe us? Like listening to that song? Like caping a stag, or sliding mouth over penile ridge in a motion that is so familiar to the muscles and tendons doing it that the mind can disengage, do its own thing, move to other places and sensations, liberated. I've been told by a friend that she thinks about crochet patterns while performing very pleasurable and very long and very expensive blow jobs. She told me how much she charges, and many of her clients have told me in words and sighs how pleasurable she is. She is also a very skilled crochet artist. She's really an artist at it. She makes pieces of lace that also make her a lot of money, cod pieces, bras, socks, even cashmere scarves.

Or does doing the same thing over and over irritate us and leave creases in our psyche? Some habits age us on the inside, just as they do on the outside. These wrinkles, and creases, and maybe the pain in my knees, is the result of so many habits I have allowed myself over the years. I thought about this a great deal when I chose to live the way I live. I did not want to grow old in quite the same ways as other people I saw around me. I noticed aging since I was a little girl. I saw old aunts and their sagging walk, it caused their breasts to touch their chests. I decided that mine never would, way back then. I walked with my chest held high, and insisted that my nipples point out and up and away from the ground. They still do. I did not allow myself bad habits, or tried not to allow them in, though I do know some slipped into the years of my life. I floss my teeth, often and well. I would not let plaque form like a sediment hardening between my gum and enamel, loosening the tooth and pushing it into the ground one day, my teeth would go with me, the oral hygienist has been familiar with my teeth, she has picked out her own pubic curls from around my gums, and the taxidermist would find them in my head when I was sent to her, caped and undressed. But then, in order to break the habit of the plaque, I formed a flossing habit. I had to learn early on how to separate good habits, desirable ones, from bad ones, the ones that would cause me to wrinkle, or sag, or form a crease in my psyche.

I listened to every kind of music, even Beethoven, and read every kind of book, from Chaucer to Xaviera Hollander, I tried to commune with every kind of person, men, women, masculine women and feminine men, men who preferred women and men who preferred men and women who preferred women and women who preferred men, oral hygienists, and yes, taxidermists. Well one anyway. I found ways to entice them all. I cooked well, I could talk about everything and everyone, and things new and old, I could wrap my tongue around a penis as well as I could stick it deep into a vagina, I could convince anyone at all that sex with me would be wonderful, and I made good on my promises. Doing things over and over made me good at what I did. I did them differently with different people, but my part was my part, and I had practice at it, and I did it well. I got to know every part of a body when I was very young. I started with my own, and I had no favourites when it came to choosing what I'd rather touch. There was no particular progression to my travels around my own skin and limbs and holes and moles, I just loved touching all of me, and all of me was happy to be touched. So when I touched another person for the first time in a way that was not quite accidental or unintentional or platonic, I followed the formats of my own habits, or lack of them. I wandered from fingers to wrist and belly button to lip and hips to knees to hairline and back. And I learned, and I even formed habits. I let myself. So, I know how to touch. My fingertips know, collarbones love my tongue, I love to let my ass feel the warm curve of a belly and the tickle of a bush or the insistence of an erection as much as tasting a tongue or an earlobe. I know, there is an expectation, an endpoint. It makes me annoyed, this impatience and need to rush from look to orgasm in sixty seconds. Habits, all. Bad ones. People forget, we don't always eat to survive, and we don't always copulate to procreate. There are things we need, looks, touches, moments, that have nothing immediate to do with survival. People would die without touch, but not as quickly or obviously as without food. And without sex, the whole race would die. But sometimes there's no need to think about all that. Sometimes we can just be, and touch, and allow ourselves to feel.

Women are of course better at giving up their habit. I had an advantage with them, especially those who said they were not really like this, they preferred men for this kind of thing. So when they were spread out on my sheets or soaking in my bathtub in a froth of anticipation, they had already broken a habit. It was easier for me then to linger on some particular unique feature—a small pout, the sweet bulge of a post-pregnancy belly, especially symmetric toes, flat breasts with huge nipples, I could spend an hour on each nipple, and if the woman tried to end it herself, then I stopped what I was doing and obliged, I had the techniques and the fingers and tongue and all manner of lovely silicone and plastic penile replicas that would fit where she wanted, large ones and tiny ones and really huge ones I could slip in and keep there as I bit and sucked her clitoris, I was as good as a practised taxidermist, I could bring her to the intersection of life and death so slowly and for such moments as she didn't care really if she lived or died after that. I never was with any one too often, I never sucked a person, man or woman, enough times to create a habit, either for them or for me. Life is too short to form habits of that sort. I derived my own pleasures too, of course, from these men and women. And nor were they ever just bodies to me. I knew who they were, what they did, what their habits were, and their practices, and their favourite foods and drinks, and I never discarded anyone. I just didn't make them a habit. I didn't let it get to a point where a person, however much sweat and fluids I had exchanged with them, could ask me when the next time would be, or, more important, could presume to think that they were the only one in my life. No person became a habit. It would never be that I did someone so often that I became good at that one person, and that one person became good at me, that we became each other's psychic crease or physical wrinkle. No person, though I loved many of them, or really all of them, became so much of a habit that I could do them with my hands and mouth and vaginal muscles and let my mind wander and do its own thing. The habit went as far as only myself. I knew how to move my hips, how to run my fingers, how to jerk my wrists, how to clench my ass, but not the lay of a particular body, not length or girth or depth or agility, not spread of thighs nor capability of cunt nor heft of cock nor strength of back or bicep. Those I had to find out by finding out. Those I had to explore, and set aquiver, one way or another.

So there we were, three nights ago, my taxidermist, my oral hygienist, my escort service owner. I say mine not

because I own them, but because they were more than once
bedmates, and would be again, but also, they were my friends.
We had dinner together sometimes, and everyone always had
stories. The taxidermist was the best, oddly enough. She was
all about touch, textures and smells of death. There was
something about that. Something about someone who talked
about those things she saw and felt so deeply. Something
about feelings, physical feelings and emotions brought on by
dead things. She had received a baby raccoon that morning,
and she described to us its nose, which she had to remove
and replace with a leather nose she had made herself, but
which she said was too big for the little face, and his paws
and claws and mini raccoon tail, but she had made him
perfect, she said, or tried to preserve his perfection. She
wanted to show him to us, and by the time we got to
the end of our excellent dinner, she was drunk enough to
insist. I didn't think she could drive herself home anyway,
and since her home was upstairs from her workshop, we
said we would go look at the raccoon.

She let us in through the back door. I had been there
before, all of us had. There was a smell in her place. It
wasn't something negative or unpleasant even, but it was the
smell of her place, and, to me, it was the smell of her. I
associated it with her. The first time I met her, there was
a faint version of that smell on her clothes, a little stronger
on her hands and skin, and, it even tinged the smell of her,
down between her legs. In her place it was much stronger.
I loved it, actually, the smell and the feeling there. A small
fox stood proudly on her table, he was clearly visible from
the door because the streetlight shone on him. And that was

just the beginning. When we turned on the light, we were surrounded by small animals. They were everywhere, at every level. She did not do birds, only small furry animals, and she did not do people's pets. So there were unthreatening woodland creatures, the largest was a baby bear who stood with his back against my leg. My skirt was short, and his brown fur felt a little bristly against my skin. We were not in the main studio yet. In there, there were no completed animals. It was very cold in there, and two giant freezers took up some of the large space. I had looked into everything in that amazing space, including those freezers. Always something new and dead in there. And I had been in her apartment upstairs as well.

She showed us her baby raccoon, it was a fine little creature. But it was the way she had posed it that was so her, that reminded us all why we all loved her so. It sat there and looked for all the world like a lost little soul, it looked like it was waiting for its mother to come home. I looked around, and everyone was tired and a bit low after the high of the wine and company. The others soon left and I thought I'd leave too, once I'd seen our genius taxidermist up to her bed. She wanted to stay there, and finish the raccoon. I needed to use her bathroom, which was upstairs in her apartment, so I went up the stairs at the front of the studio. I opened the door and walked through the living room into her bedroom. It was a beautiful bedroom. A friend had given her two magnificent stags that hung on the walls on both sides of an old and very simple rosewood four-poster, a zebra skin with the head intact lay on the floor in front of the bed. I walked into the bathroom and peed. I came out, and gazed at the stags again. And then, finally, I noticed a person in the bed. I said nothing, and began to go softly out, glad that I hadn't turned on the light, when he, and yes, it was a he, turned on the bedside lamp and spoke to my retreating back.

'Hey, come to bed, I'm hungry.' My hair was a different colour from hers, my body was a very different shape. He must have known I wasn't her. I smiled to myself. She was downstairs working. If I knew her, she would have forgotten by now that I was upstairs in her house. She had probably forgotten a long time ago that this man was in her bed. Whatever he was hungry for, I thought, he could eat off me. I turned around and walked toward him. I was right about him knowing I wasn't her, there was no surprise on his face at all. He held open his blanket for me, and I climbed in. He immediately and without preamble crawled down inside the blanket and found my black cotton panties. He rubbed up against them a bit, and I liked the feel of stubble against my own. And this was the one time, maybe the only time when I pulled the man up on top of me, and I let him know my expectation, and he laughed. 'Okay,' he said, 'if that's what you want, that's what you get'. And for the first time in my life, I surrendered to the simple pleasure of being fucked by a man who was happy to fuck me. We didn't kiss, we didn't play, I didn't know him, I didn't care, I didn't try to please him, I wouldn't have known how if I had intended to, and I didn't intend to, it was an unexpected moment which had just thrust itself into my life, and I, joyfully and happily opened my legs and accepted it. We moved and pounded and he asked politely if he could come inside me, and I said yes, and he asked if he could please come now, and I said no so he didn't, and I laughed and let go, screaming and clutching and clenching as I never had before, and then when I was quiet he asked again, politely if he could, because, he said, he couldn't wait much more, and before I could answer, he did, and then, quiet too, he looked into my eyes and kissed me. And I heard my taxidermist from the door say, 'I see you met him. Didn't take you long. I haven't had a chance with him yet, and I've known him all my life.' I looked at her, and she wasn't unhappy or angry or sad. 'He's my cousin,' she said, 'we know each other too well to even want to fuck, don't worry,' she said.

She came into the bed and lay down next to me, feeling between my legs gently before falling asleep.

That was then. That was who I was then. And this now. This is me now, waiting by the phone. Three days have passed, and I wonder where he is and why he hasn't called me. I had the waxing lady come over. I had the manicure, the pedicure, I had every inch of me waxed. I was stubbly the last three times we had sex, the only three times we had sex. It was the next morning when we found ourselves still in the bed we had met in. And again before I left to find some fresh clothes in my own wardrobe. I listen to the radio as I write, and discover that the Polish accent slapped upon English could induce me to murder the speaker, she must stop, or I will scream. There are many phone calls, none I want to answer. Everyone but Taxi-taxidermy calls me. The day goes by. I do nothing. I eat nothing. I take two showers. I play with my hair. I water some plants. I think about habit. I think about what I can do well. I can make women feel good in bed and out of it. I can make men feel good in bed and out of it. I can make myself feel good in bed and out of it. And I am good at not forming habits. I have friends and lovers and people to eat with and people to walk with and people to sleep or stay awake with. And all I want now is the cousin of my taxidermist lover, and he's gone.

I know he's gone, because I know that's how he is. I know him as well as I know myself. And I know he won't be calling me because that's what I would do, I wouldn't call me either. He wouldn't make a habit of me. He didn't want to find out how it would be if I was a habit of his. I would become the groove in his psyche, the wrinkle on the skin of his perfect face, the same old same old who knew how to do him and whom he knew how to do. I knew he wouldn't call me, and maybe I would never see that face or feel that cock or hear that laugh in my ear and against my neck again, because he didn't like habits either. I'd met my match, you could say. I'd met my mate. Except, we couldn't do that, he and I.

~

Goblin Market

~

Lizzie woke very early and lay in bed, she waited for the sun to rise enough over the buildings to reach her window. They were very old, those buildings, and the brickwork glowed as the sun hit them. The forest lay quiet and malevolent behind the city, only the trough of a running quicksilver stream kept the trees from walking in and taking over the streets and shops and homes and markets of the place she grew up in. As a child, she didn't walk under the trees, her mother told her not to, and she never did. There were dark things there, living among those trees, and even the trees themselves had grown tall and gnarled from drinking the murky waters of some subterranean stream, and were not to be trusted.

Lizzie looked at her sister sleeping beside her. Laura did not always listen to their mother. When they played with the other children, she, of all the children, would always be the one to run into the forest after a ball, she would hide there when they played hide-and seek, and no one else dared go in after her to find her. She had been hearing those voices of the forest, calling and calling to her since she was a little girl. Lizzie watched her sleeping, a fitful and restive sleep. Fear and exhaustion stained the pale and modest translucence of her skin, and her torn and swollen lips still quivered in what must be dark expanses of experience too close to yet be called memory. Lizzie propped herself up on her elbow to look at her sister, and ran her eyes slowly up from her sister's ankles, trying to be calm, some moments almost managing to quell her anger and tears. She could see her sister's toes touching the shoreline they had sculpted into the bedsheet during the hot night, one in restlessness and the other surely in pain. The toenails had splintered and Lizzie had wrapped them in gauze, they had seeped blood through the night and now looked like rough brown pebbles. Bite marks from greedy teeth ran up her sister's shins, they looked like an inept hem-stitch against the bloodless lactescent skin, done in a contrasting burgundy thread. An aura of congealed blood beneath the skin puffed up each little stitch. Deep fingerprints smudged the calves and the insides of the knees, there were so many of those dark marks on the plump skin of the closed thighs that Lizzie thought of some dappled sea creature when she saw them. Laura murmured slightly, and Lizzie shifted her eyes to her sister's tiny face. She couldn't look at the face for longer than a few moments before the sour and bitter began to rise in her throat, and she turned her eyes away, and closed them. A late beam of sunshine finally landed on the pillow, and she opened her eyes. Laura's hands were pushed beneath the pillow, and Lizzie felt tears, like hot grit in her eyelids. She let them run, out one eye and into the other, and then into her hair. She felt the dampness collecting in her scalp. She thought of her sister's hands hidden beneath the pillow. When they healed, Lizzie thought, there would be no lines, nothing on them that would leave fingerprints. Lizzie had salved and bandaged the soggy inside-out fingers and palms, and her sister had made not a sound through what must have been acid pain.

Laura wore no sleepshirt, her only clothing was a pair of silk shorts to keep the most broken parts of her covered, parts which had only, till that time, been touched with the lightest hand, to wash perhaps, or to bestow a caress upon, though Lizzie doubted her sister touched herself in the way she herself did, and now those parts of her sister's already fragile body were torn and used, over and over, a blood and blue pulp of ecstasy and pain.

Lizzie touched her sister's murmuring mouth, first with a fingertip. Then she leaned over her and licked her with a warm wet loving tongue. Laura's lips felt hot and dry, and opened slightly. Lizzie pushed her tongue into her sister's mouth, opening it a little more. She felt her sister's tongue flick against hers, and she was still a moment, not wanting her to awake and turn away. She lay there a while, and felt a strange suction, as her sister began to bite and suck her tongue, gently at first, and then harder and harder, like a child sucking a mother's tit, in hunger. The hunger became frantic, and Lizzie let her keep sucking. Laura began to open up her thighs, still sucking and still asleep. Her hands began to reach for something, and Lizzie knew what it was. She removed her mouth from Laura's and sat up. Laura did not open her eyes, but moaned through her open mouth, in pain, the pain of a desire so foul that Lizzie knew she must help her. She placed her hands on her sister's thighs and pushed them gently apart. The silk fell to one side, and Lizzie looked at the bruised, bloody swollen bud and the dark hole below it, a squashed fig. She knew her fingers were too rough to touch it. She bent her head down and stroked with her tongue. Laura moaned, softly, and opened herself into her sister's mouth with her fingers. Lizzie knew she was in pain, but she seemed to want the pain, and to what must follow the pain. She had been tortured and thrust and spewed into again and again and again by fingers and tongues and penises of goblin bodies and the vicious fruit and vegetables grown in their evil tangled gardens, and the juices of those vile creatures and their gorgeous peaches and lemons had drenched Laura's little cunt and mind alike, and she wanted nothing but the pain and torture at the goblin men's hands. She did not want her sister's gentle tongue lapping at her wounds with care and love, she wanted to be possessed by the little goblins, and by their obscenely large fingers and toes and penises, that they had thrust into her in every way, two and three and four at a time, leering, laughing, crushing her, while those who couldn't reach her or enter her thrust themselves into the over-ripe fruit, or thrust the fruit into themselves and one another. Lizzie knew Laura wanted to be back among them. She had seen what they did to her sister, their smells and cries and screams and their testicles, giant and bursting with the seeds that grew those peaches, the ones she smashed into her face and into her cunt, Laura could not resist the smell of the fruit, and the goblins licking them off her, off her breasts, biting and sucking and grabbing her, and then off her cunt, they gathered around it like creatures at a watering hole, lapping, sucking, squealing and pushing each other, fighting for the juices that flowed from her.

Lizzie had shuddered with cold and misery and fear, as she watched and heard her sister shudder and moan and cry with the evil ecstasy the goblin men brought to her, and brought her to, again and again. She wished for a moment she hadn't come looking for her, but then she knew she wanted her beloved Laura back, she was her companion and her life, and she knew she had to find her, and bring her back, and she knew they would have children of their own one day. She would bring her back for herself, and for the young man across the street who watched for her every day. So she had stepped into the line of dark trees, and followed the sound of the dark water under her feet, and come to the clearing of the goblin market. She had marvelled at first sight of those fruits, she had never seen the like in their own markets. The peaches were bigger than her breasts, and even bigger than her head, and the berries, laid out in clusters on golden trays, begged to be popped into her mouth, and the bananas were perfection, not a black spot on any of them.

But then she heard her sister's moan, and all the greed fell away from her, replaced by another kind of feeling. She felt her own berry nipples against her shirt, begging to be touched and squeezed, her own belly rise and fall with the rapid breaths of ugly desire as she watched her sister succumb to the goblin men, she knew that if she so much as touched herself she would be transported into the world of her sister, all sensation and no consciousness. Her thighs ached, and the blueberry under her dress was ripe to bursting, but she did not slip her fingers down, she did not touch the nectar she could smell, lest she was heard, and dragged in, willingly then, to the midst of the glen where the goblins and her sister spilled seed and skin and juice and pulp, and rose and fell in pain and intense and filthy joy. She was so close, and so full to bursting, and she could not tear her eyes away from that clearing, looking this way and that, first at the goblin men, greenish and yellowish in their waxy skins, naked as the day is bright, their fat penises like their perfect bananas, some hanging between their spindly legs and some standing hugely against their fuzzy bellies, but not for long, for they stroked the shafts rapidly and grinned and laughed as they sprayed each other, or they jumped upon her sister and got busy burying in her and bouncing upon her, between her mango breasts, between the melon cheeks of her sweet behind, inside that precious space that she had saved so long for love. Lizzie watched her sister's face. She had never seen such agony or delight upon it in all their years. Laura writhed and stuck out her tongue for the goblins to suck, she opened her mouth and took any part of the little distorted men into it, and the sweet little plum mouth Lizzie had kissed so gently and so often was now gorging upon peaches and berries of every hue and shape and size, and the limp and hard green and yellow and dark and white protrusions of the goblin men, their ears, their lips, their tongues. Lizzie watched as the juice of the fruit and the goblins covered her sister's face and her body like a salve upon which they slid ever more gleefully upon her. Laura's screams and moans mingled with theirs, and she was so full of goblin fruit and goblin juice that Lizzie thought at that moment that she should let her sister go, that she could never cleanse her of them, she should walk away and never return there. And in her grief she thrust her own finger into her pit, her hand brushed her mound and touched her hard and erect hood, and she let the waves flow all over her, biting her lip as hard as she could to stop a sound from escaping, and never taking her eyes off her sister's face, so beautiful even with her mouth stretched around a penis and a purple plum. She shuddered and shuddered and thought the long moment of her sad delight would never end, and she thrust and thrust her finger deep, and slammed her palm into her mound, looking and looking at her sister's wide open thighs, making the moment longer than she thought possible. She longed for hideous goblin men to feast upon her too, she imagined the leering mouths and prancing penises inside all of her too. But it was too soon, and thankfully over, her solitary rapture. She wiped her hand on her skirt and felt the bile rising in her throat. She stood up carefully and quietly, and turned and ran with shaky legs and shaky heart, all the way home.

She waited for the sound of her sister's footstep and knock upon their door. Laura returned, late in the night, bruised and torn, and soaked in a foul sap. Lizzie bathed and soothed and bandaged her and put her to bed, but she knew Laura was sick, the signs were all on her. They both knew now, what their mother spoke of, what all the townspeople warned of, what lived beyond the stream, inside the trees.

The next day, Laura, in a pitiful state, begged that Lizzie take her to the edge of the forest. Lizzie knew that she must. They walked slowly there, Laura was so weak. The old lady in the fruit and vegetable shop below their home watched them. Lizzie said nothing to her, she avoided looking at her. At the forest's edge, Laura called and called plaintively to into the trees, begging for the goblin men and their peaches and pears and berries and grapes. She yearned and burned, I must have the fruit, she told Lizzie, or I will surely die, and if I do not, I do not wish to live. Lizzie believed her. She looked pale and could hardly walk, but still, she wanted to go deeper into the forest to the goblins, to lay with them and eat their fruit. Lizzie knew they were done with her. They had taken her sister and eaten and drunk her until there was hardly any of her left. But Laura had to have those peaches, and those cherries, and the wild seeded strawberries. Lizzie knew she would have to go back there, and find the goblin men, and bring her sister the fruit, if she was to have her whole again.

And so, that winter's morning, Lizzie rose carefully from her bed and drew the curtains across the windows so her sister would not be disturbed by the brightness of the cold morning light. She went softly to the bathroom and brushed her teeth as she ran the bathwater. She climbed in the copper tub and filled it with the potions of lemons and verbena, and stepped into the water. She coldly and carefully sponged every part of herself, making sure she smelled of nothing but the scent from the bottles, making sure there was none of her own scent left. She took care to rub the sponge behind her ears and on her neck and the nape of it, below her hair, and behind her knees and inside her elbows, and of course she cleaned between her thighs, from the front to the back, again and again. When she was sure she was scrubbed and squeaky, she stepped out of the now tepid water and dried herself. She scented herself again with lemon and verbena. She brushed her hair and put on a silk dress over her silk panties. She put on her stockings and boots, and kissed her sister goodbye. Laura did not stir. She was dreaming of the goblin men, and she would keep on dreaming of them unless Lizzie did what she had to do.

Lizzie ran across the street to avoid the old lady in the fruit shop, but the old lady saw her, and shouted after her, asking where Lizzie was going in such a hurry. Lizzie told her. The forest, she told her. To buy goblin fruit. The old lady called her back across the street, and something in her voice made Lizzie go to her. The old lady gave her a small cherry. Eat this, she said, and hold the pit in your mouth, she said, it will help you keep your mouth shut. Do not eat their fruit, she said, and you will return to save your sister. Lizzie put the cherry in her mouth. It was tart and drew her mouth together so she could hardly speak to thank the old woman. The old woman nodded and told her again, do not eat their fruit, Lizzie, or you will be lost like your sister. Do not eat their fruit. You will be able to speak, when you reach the forest, but the cherry pit will keep you from being tempted by their fruit. Then the old lady pressed a coin hard into her palm, and closed her fingers over it. Your sister bought the fruit with a lock of her hair, she told Lizzie. Do not let them take any part of you. Give them this coin, it is from the new world. Where there are no goblin men. It will undo them. It will make them fade from the world. Lizzie ran across the road and across the stream and crossed the tree line a second time into the darkness of the forest.

She heard the goblins calling to her, laughing and leering. She stood where she was, and they soon swarmed all around her, their magical golden fruits on platters and in baskets, their eyes and mouths hungry for her delicious firm fresh breast flesh and the perfectly rounded downy cheeks of her behind and the blueberry between her soft thighs, sitting like a surprise inside a peach. She didn't move, she just stood there. They wouldn't come closer though. They wouldn't touch her. What can you give us, for our fruit, they asked her, what can you pay us with, for our plump gooseberries and our dark wild cherries, and these grapes, they are from golden vines, what can you show us, for a taste of our bananas? They began to squeeze the fruit and let the juice run out so she could smell it, and they peeled the bananas and pushed their fingers into the figs and plums, wriggling them deep inside the fruit so it made her squirm. But they wouldn't come closer. She ran her fingers through her hair, holding it out so it caught the slanted light that barely made it through the thick canopy of the trees. They laughed, we have your sister's hair, they said, we don't need any more of that. What else have you got, to buy our fruit? She sighed, an exaggerated sigh, and moved her hand over her shirt. A little mulberry nipple appeared under the silk, and they watched, and waited for more. She opened the pearl buttons, one by one by one, and opened the shirt completely, and pushed her breasts at them. They were silent, and sighed too, and some dropped their platters and stroked their penises and sucked their fingers. She cupped and stroked her breasts, her nipples and freckled skin turned blue in the cool air. She sucked her fingers, imitating them, and the goblin men all laughed and leered and began to dance and thrust their penises at her. What more do you have, to buy our strawberries and loganberries and cranberries and gooseberries? We have plums, juicy as your sister's cunt, and pomegranates too, don't you want some, Lizzie? They asked, taunting her, poking their tongues out at her, long and slimy from fruit nectar, and again, she shivered, and felt herself want their hideous fruit smashed all over her. The old lady's cherry felt sour in her mouth, and the pit hard between her teeth, and she lay down in the moss under the giant trees. She pulled her silk panties to one side, and opened her thighs as wide as she could, and she knew they were all looking in, they wanted to consume her. That's what their fruit is made of, she thought—the juices of all my sisters from all the ages who bought the goblin lies with a lock of hair. The fruit was so moist, so precious, so plump and delicious, because it was made from all the juices and all the young beauty and innocence and sweet need and first awakening of so many girls like her own sweet Laura. She was angry then. She pulled apart the lips of her cunt, and showed them the nectar of her girlhood. She knew they would smell it, she knew they wanted to harvest it, to suck it and lick it and take it from her. She knew they could take nothing from her unless she ate their fruit.

They swarmed close to her. They began to squirt the fruit at her, and they stood over her and rubbed themselves and squirted that on her as well, and then they came closer and began to push the fruit at her mouth. You can have it, Lizzie, you are sweet as honeydew and prettier than a strawberry field, eat our fruit, Lizzie, you have never tasted the like, and no men have such, eat our fruit, they begged her now. They rubbed it on her, and themselves, and rubbed themselves on her too, until she was covered with a slime of goblin and fruit, until her clothes and her hair and her breasts and skin and cunt and face were sticky with it, but not a drop went in her mouth. They coaxed and pleaded and entreated her, but she would not open her mouth. And then they grew angry, and began to grumble and sneer and snarl and spew foul words at her, and the fruit lost its shine and bloom, and fell rotting from the platters. Lizzie knew she had won. She stood up, and they growled and keened and shook their hideous goblin penises at her, and showed her their hairy behinds, some threatened her with fists and eyes and teeth. As she turned to walk away, she remembered the coin, and threw it at them. A big yellow-eyed goblin man caught it and looked at it. And before her eyes, his eyes grew wide, his penis fell slack, he screamed a thin and hollow scream of fear and dropped the coin. She heard much scrabbling and clawing as she turned her back on them for the last time, refusing to run though she desperately wanted to, run and run home to Laura, without turning back. But she walked, did brave Lizzie, across the treeline, into the light, across the flowing quicksilver stream to the street where she lived. The old lady smiled at her as she passed by. She opened the door and went to her sleeping sister.

Laura smelled the evil goblin smell and fell upon her sister with surprising strength, licking and touching and sucking all the goblin slime, swallowing every bit of it she could find. Lizzie just lay back in her bed and let her sister gorge herself. Laura had all of it, from her sister's face, her breasts, her belly, she chewed and sucked her clothes, she squeezed her sister's hair, to get all the goblin juice she could. Then she smelled some more, and spread apart her sister's tired thighs and sucked and licked till Lizzie was fainting and sighing and moaning from sadness and delight, and until there was nothing more left. Then Laura got off her sister, her stomach heaved, and she spewed the contents of her belly, and her whole soul, a green glutinous malignance onto the floor beside the bed. Her face turned white, and she fell back on the bed, and slept a long deep sleep, while Lizzie scrubbed and washed the floor, the sheets, and her sister in her delirium, before she bathed herself for the second time that day, and scented herself in vanilla.

Hours and hours passed, and Lizzie watched her sister sleep, watched as colour slowly returned to her face, and her eyes opened. I had a terrible dream, my darling Lizzie, she said, and I dreamed you saved my life. Lizzie smiled at her sister with all the love she felt in her heart. Yes, my darling sister, it was just a bad dream, and there will never be another like it, and there's the old lady's grandson from the shop across the street, calling you.

~

Christina Rosetti's poem entranced and horrified me when I first read it. I was repelled by the goblins, and the sisters as well, but I was a child, I didn't understand why. Goblin Market was featured in Playboy in the '70s, illustrated in the way I imagined the poem. I was relieved that I wasn't the only pervert who read it the way I did. With this story, the result of years of fascination, I'm done with this Goblin Market. I won't have bad dreams about it anymore—I leave those to my readers.

Scars

~

My room is sunny and warm today. I was up at five, as always, I scrubbed my dentures and combed my hair, put on a clean white shirt, a pair of khaki trousers, and my socks and shoes. I went for a walk in the grounds. I watched the light from the sun hit the tops of the trees and then the whole face of my old stone apartment building. I had driven past the gates of this place a few times when I had to see a client in the village close by, and I knew I wanted to live here when the time came. I made plans. I chose my apartment five years before I actually moved in, though there was someone living there. I know it's morbid, but I had to wait, I lived for a year in a different apartment, till the occupier of my preferred apartment passed on. Maybe there is someone waiting for me to die too, so they can have my rooms. But they will have to wait a while yet. I am strong and I look after myself carefully.

I feel not that different than I did six years ago, when I was seventy. The body is a strange place. It changes so slowly, and living in it, one adjusts and accommodates and accustoms and accepts, as it ages and gives up. There must have been one day when my knees didn't bend as they used to the day before, and I changed my walk accordingly, and another day when my left wrist didn't have the strength it had the day before, and I switched my coffee to my other hand, or put it down while reading the paper. And there must have been a day when my hard-ons stopped being hard. I remember walking differently ten years ago than I do now, I did not have the old man shuffle I have now that is gentler on the knees, and I remember holding my coffee in my hand while I read my paper. And I remember being hard as a fat salami, slipping into Shaila easily, and again and again and again. We pleased each other so much. And when she was gone, I remember thinking about her long after, though I have not in a long time, about her skin and her hair, and the way she smelled, the same the day she died as she did when I first met her. When they mowed the immense lawn, that smell that drifted into the air and into my room, that reminded me of her. It was so fresh. I thought about her as she was in all the forms I had known her. She was the nasty young girl I fell in love with, with her dark-as-thundercloud eyebrows, she was rough and demanding. And yet, in our marriage bed, for fifty years, she was quiet and soft and never raised her voice, neither in anger nor in delight. She was the tough mother who fought tooth and nail with her three daughters all her life, she was never happy with their choices, of careers, of partners, of clothes, and with the youngest, even her haircut. Our youngest is my favourite. She was a mistake, of course. And she may have been the result of my very last hard hard-on. I was fifty-five, Shaila was forty-seven. It was early in the morning, and she was up and about in our bedroom, making a racket though I was asleep. She slammed the bathroom door, and I finally yelled at her. She was surprised, and she apologised, but said I should have been up. That made me even angrier. That was probably the only time in our decades-long marriage that Shaila and I consummated a quarrel. I found myself unbearably hard, and I must admit, I was a little rough that day. I think she liked it, when I held her wrists above her head and forced her legs apart. It was a wonderful morning, and afterward she smiled at me slyly and left the room. She looked beautiful that day. And when I eventually got out of bed and went out, I saw she had made me a fried egg and a nicely brown toast, and a cup of coffee, though by then I was not allowed to eat eggs or drink coffee. And then we found out Shaila was pregnant, and this daughter of ours, Joya, was all the anger and sparkle of the emotions that created her. She is the only one who lives close enough to come and see me now, and she does, at least once a week, often she and her partner of twenty years stop and have a drink with me on their way from work. They own a bookstore in the village, specialising in gay and lesbian literature. I suppose, no, I know, her sexual orientation was one of the reasons Shaila did not get along with her youngest daughter. How classic, and how silly. But my wife couldn't help her own upbringing, I suppose. Her parents were orthodox Hindus, although they had lived in Canada most of their lives, they had stayed isolated, and ensconced within their own little community. It wasn't that little, as I soon found out. When I returned from my fifth tour in Iraq, she took me to one of their weddings. I found out how big the community was. I was also relieved to see enough mixed-race couples there to think she would eventually marry me.

I haven't thought about all this for such a long time. I always thought some of the people in the complex spoke too much about the good or bad old times, and didn't focus on the present, didn't live in the moment of their lives enough. So I spend my time perhaps focusing too much on the present. I read, I spend a lot of time on the internet, I walk through the woods and paths all over the grounds listening to Bach concertos I download the night before. I go for my physiotherapy appointments, and sometimes, I cook in the small efficiency kitchen which is really meant only for making coffee or tea. They didn't like us cooking meals there, people were likely to hurt themselves. I usually go to the happily named and happy place they call the morning room. The sun streams in through the French doors running the length of the whole building. This room was one of the reasons I had wanted to live in this particular facility.

The breakfast they brought me was as sunny and warm as the day. A fried egg, the unbroken yellow jiggling slightly like Tamara's breasts as she bent to take my tray off her laden trolley. An array of toasts and a small jar of golden honey. Apple juice in a clear tall glass. Sunny and warm. I said good morning to all the early-risers around me, and concentrated on my breakfast. I broke the yolk with a rough point of toast, and it slid gently out emptying from the crater and crawling onto the plate, a yellow oil. I lifted the whole thing onto the second slice of toast and ate it slowly and carefully with a knife and fork.

Later that day, I went in for my physio appointment. I was surprised to see no one there at all. The young man who attends to me, Irfan, was nowhere to be seen, and Amber, the receptionist, was not there either. I wondered for a moment if I had made a mistake with the date. It was unlikely if not impossible, I didn't make mistakes of that sort, and the calendar on the desk confirmed it. I walked around for a while and watched the geese on the lawn outside leaving turds as big as a small dog's, the gardeners complain about it incessantly. They call them feathered rats, the loonies, the symbol of the country.

Not much later, a young woman came bounding into the room. She was tough and muscular-looking, her hair was cut very short, and she had a perfectly shaped head. She had a single gold star in each ear, and tattoos all over her arms. It was a single vine actually, that started somewhere inside her clothes and came out and wound around before disappearing into her black low-necked t-shirt, on the left of her cleavage. She was very vivid-looking, and had very white crooked teeth when she grinned at me and apologised for being late. I followed her into the physio room, and she asked me to lie down on the low padded table, and consulted my chart.

'Just the knees today,' she said. She pushed my pants up to take a look, and gasped. I had forgotten about those old scars. I laughed, and said, 'They are very old. Older than you, probably.'

She still looked a little disturbed. 'Do you have more?'

'Oh yes,' I said, ' I was five times in Iraq. I have plenty more.' She didn't know what I meant by Iraq, of course. It was way before her time. Forgotten war.

'Let's finish your exercises, won't take long. I'd like to walk a while with you, to see if we can't get you to stop dragging your feet.' This surprised me. I am seventy-six years old, I thought, why would anyone care if I shuffled till I shuffled off the planet? But I was pleased too. As I huffed and puffed through leg-lifts I found out that she was new, and she was there to stay. Irfan was gone, and would not be back. Her interest in the treatment of geriatrics as people who would live forever, and not stopping at just palliative care, was what got her this job. From what I understood, she planned to strengthen my knees and legs as if I was going to need them for the next two decades. Why not, I thought.

When the session was done, she picked up a short fleece jacket which she put on over her sporty looking clothes, and walked out with me. We walked a little, and she kept stopping to let me walk ahead of her, to observe my walk from behind, and then ran ahead and watched me approach. We talked about this and that, and I told her about Joya. She laughed when I called her 'my lesbian daughter'.

'Why do I need to know that?' she said, and I laughed too. 'Are you trying to set us up?'

And that's when I understood my immediate trust and affection for her. I never can tell when someone is gay or lesbian, and nor does it interest me much. As I always tried to tell Shaila, if I didn't want someone sexually, why did I care what their leanings were? Shaila never understood. The other thing she didn't understand was that I was always quite happy to be sexually attracted to a woman who did happen to prefer the company of other women, because I had no intention of being unfaithful to my wife anyway. I could fantasise about whoever I wanted, lesbian or not, because to me they were just as available as non-lesbians. Not.

Abby, that was the name of my new friend, was asking me about my scars. We sat one of the many benches along the path. I pulled up my pants again and showed her the ones she had seen before. I explained that those, as well as the ones on the other leg, were from a small but nasty home-made explosive, and had taken me a long time to recover from. The wounds were not deep, and nor did they affect muscle and bone, but they took a long time to heal, because of the extensive burning and scrapes and tiny puncture wounds from whatever they had put in the bomb. I said I had others, but I would have to undress to show her, and there might be objections.

'I have scars too, ' she said thoughtfully. 'I'll show you mine, if you show me yours,' and I am certain I was not mistaken that there was a hint of laughter in the corners of her beautiful eyes. I am old, yes, but still a man, and memories of feelings still linger hauntingly in my loins, and in my heart, of romance and the sweetness of a woman's skin, and the way her bones push against the skin at the hips, and how the muscle is deep in the flesh of her behind, covered by a lovely layer of chubby, touchable fat. My own thoughts did not disturb me, they were mine, and they kept me alive. And thoughts of the kind I was having that day did not come to me often, and if they did, I did not let them linger long. I asked if she wanted to come to my apartment and have a cup of tea.

'Something stronger?' she said, and I said I didn't have anything. She said she would be at my place at seven, with a bottle of wine and 'some goodies'. I offered to contribute, and she took a twenty from me saying, 'I wouldn't, but I'm still paying off student loans.' I thought about saying she was like my daughter, but this didn't seem appropriate in the context of the date we had just made.

My doorbell rang at seven precisely, and I was surprised. I hadn't thought she would show. Even so, I had spent the day cleaning and tidying my already clean and neat space. When everything including me was satisfactorily sharp and bright, I went to the flower shop on the premises and bought a pot of the cyclamen they sold there. They sold flowers and grasses grown on the grounds, and I liked that they were not farm-produced roses.

I opened the door. Abby was radiant. She smelled of what I call cyberperfumes that I have never liked till now. From now on it would be my favourite scent. I was always infuriated by the little inserts in Shaila's and my daughters' magazines. Shaila would tear them out and put them in her underwear drawer, and all her bras would smell of the stuff, and no amount of requests or tantrums on my part would convince her that I hated it.

Abby poured us wine, and arranged all the goodies on my coffee table in little red paper plates she had brought with her. There were olives and two cheeses, a mango chutney that she said 'goes divinely with the Camembert', a dark thinly-sliced mini loaf of bread, hummus, pita chips, vegetable pakodas, and best of all, hot tandoori chicken wings with a yogurt dip. Before we settled down to eat and drink, she asked if she might turn on the tv, so she could watch the American football playoff game while we talked. I didn't mind at all. And then she gave me a receipt for the food and drink—my twenty had only paid for some of the wine. I offered her more, but she wouldn't take any. Eventually, the conversation did actually turn to scars. I showed her mine. She looked at them all closely, and touched them, and asked me questions about each one. She saw the ones on my knees again, and the one on my left rib, where something from another explosion had penetrated my left lung and I had thought my end had surely come.

For every scar I showed her, she showed me one of hers. It started as a joke, she remembered and repeated what she had said to me earlier that day. When she was looking at a small jagged chop on my finger, she held up her own finger and said, 'Look, I have one just like that.' It was just like mine. She had been cooking for a girlfriend, now ex. She was making a lamb curry, and the knife had slipped on the fat as she cut the meat into cubes. It was a happy memory, she said, because once this girlfriend drove her to the emergency room and had her stitched, they went out to pizza and came back and went to bed, and didn't get out for days except to eat or use the bathroom. I was curious, of course, about what they did, but I didn't ask. It could wait. She showed me another scar, which looked like a sharp rounded object had been inserted into one side of her arm and out the other. She had been out flying kites with her baby brother. She slipped and fell, and a piece of metal on the field went straight through her flesh. It looked horrendous, but just didn't hurt that much, so she bit her lip and told her brother, who was in shock, that it was just fine. And they walked the four miles home, and her father yanked out the metal with a pair of pliers and a lot of numbing foam he kept for the animals. She had grown up on one of those organic, ethical meat farms which came up after the oil sanctions. They were marvellous places, I had been lived and worked in a couple. They had wind turbines and solar panels and all kinds of new technology thrown into the old-style family farms. The way it should have been in the first place. Her third scar was a long scratch running up her torso. She pulled up her dress all the way to the lower edge of her moulded black bra. I liked seeing bits of her naked skin, rather than all of it all at once. And I got to see that vine tattoo running here and there running in and out of her clothes. This scar was from a wild cat, she said. She and her brother had climbed into a tree thinking it was one of the farm cats. It was not. It was a feral tabby, it was cornered, and Abby was part of its successful escape route. Again, she bled, and again, it was a good memory.

'What a way,' I said to her, 'to find out about a person. Through their scars.' She smiled at me, and raised her glass. 'Yours are scars of death. You have scars from people who tried to kill you, or ones you tried to kill. They are scars of violence. Mine are not. Mine are good scars, aren't they?'

She was right. They were good ones. Mine, not so much. And I hadn't even shown her my best one yet. As if she knew what I was thinking, she said, 'What's the worst scar you have?'

It was on the back of my head. I showed her. She gasped, as she had when she saw my knees. It was not easily visible, and I had not seen it myself in a long time, but I do know it was a spectacular wound which had left its spectacular mark on my head. The skull itself had been damaged, so when my hair is parted, you can see that vertical cleavage of the bone. I had seen it in mirrors, and in photographs, and in x-rays, and even in CT scans. And I had felt it when it happened of course, and then with my fingers through my life. As scars go, it is big and ugly and impressive.

'What happened?' she said. And I told the story once again, as I had in years gone by, because no one had seen it, nor asked me for many years now, maybe even decades.

'There was this boy, Achmed. He was very young, maybe not even fourteen. He used to hang around our pit, the compound where all the allied soldiers lived. He would come and sell us things, porn videotapes, postcards of Baghdad before the fall, souvenirs looted from museums, old, old things, you know, Mesopotamian old things. He was a friend of everyone on the base. He was funny and smart, and we talked about bringing him back here, as a political refugee. One of the guys even talked about adopting him.' Abby sipped her wine, and looked at me intently. I looked back, and in the glow of the football game on my tv, I saw her, as old as my youngest daughter, but not my daughter at all, and I saw her heart-shaped face and her perfect skull, and her little breasts and muscular arms, and I looked back into her eyes, and I felt happy. I went back almost five decades to tell her about those events, I wanted to tell her the story from back there, not from the last time I had told it.

'There were many such kids, and dogs and cats too, we as soldiers, away from home, arrogant, occupiers, we fell in love with every living thing. There was one guy in particular, Anders. American. He really loved this kid. He loved him like he was his own kid. He gave him stuff all the time, he went to his house, he met his parents. He hung around with him in all his free time, though that meant being outside, unsafe. I remember there was one time when Achmed was missing for a week, and Anders went half nuts. He spent all his off time looking for him, and then finally he went to look for him. The kid was fine, just helping out at home with his father's business, whatever that was.

Anyway. One morning I walked out of the gates, and he was there, as usual, with his things strung all about him, this big smile on his little face. I walked straight up to him, and he kept his eyes on mine, smiling and smiling. Anders was there too. And suddenly Achmed opened up his shirt, and I just dove to the ground and made a small ball of myself, screaming at Anders to hit the ground, he had a bomb vest strapped to him. I fell, and Achmed fell on top of me. I was knocked unconscious by the pain, but I cannot remember it, but that's not because it was so long ago, I could not remember the pain even when I woke up a week later from the coma they put me in. I didn't understand at all what happened. And then Anders came to see me in the hospital. He told me what had happened.'

Abby took another sip of her wine, waiting for me to continue. I didn't say anything for a few minutes, I ate a chicken wing, and took a sip of my wine too. Poor Anders, he shipped home soon after he visited me. I got Christmas cards from him every year till he died a few years ago. That day, he had the look of a boy whose dog had died. I didn't know when I had that thought on that hospital bed, but that is exactly what had happened.

'Tell me!' Abby said, 'I'm waiting for the rest of the story.'

'Anders told me what happened to my head. I dived hard onto a piece of metal, a hub cap part or something that was embedded on the ground. I tripped on my dive, spun, and hit it with the side of my head. It embedded in my head. What was puzzling was that I remembered Achmed falling on top of me. I remembered an explosion. I said so to Anders. He nodded. I will never forget his words. 'I shot him in his heart,' he said to me. And then he put his head in his hands and cried and cried. The guys told me later that he had not cried at all until then. He had saved our lives, Achmed had a small amount of explosive, but it would have killed us both. Anders shot him before he could detonate it. The funny thing is, I was the coincidental person there. So he must have targeted Anders. Who loved him. Strange. Never understood it. Maybe someone got to Achmed, because we trusted him. Maybe they threatened to kill him, or someone close to him. That's what I told Anders. I hope it was true.'

Abby had tears, I could see them. She looked down, and they didn't actually fall from her eyes, but I could see them.

'For that story, I will show you my best scar,' she said.

And she put her glass down, and stood up. Then she unbuttoned her dress, and took it off and draped it on the back of the couch. Then she took off her panties and lay down. And then she did something so unexpected that I was stunned into silence, and actually thought to myself, 'I'm too old for this.' I tried not to look at her lovely trim thighs, the muscles in her belly, the piercing in her bellybutton, and, finally, I think there were piercings in other parts of her too, glinting in the small highly decorative pubic hair. I followed the vine as it disappeared behind her. She spread her legs very wide, and the vine reappeared inside her thigh. She pointed. 'Come here and look,' she said, 'this is my best scar'. I looked. There was a thin red line where her finger was placed. 'It's called an episiotomy.' She said, smiling. 'My baby was early, and they thought her soft skull would be damaged by the contractions of labour.'

'Yes, I said, I know what that is. Again, yours is a scar of life, with a happy memory. Is it a happy memory?'

'Oh yes, it is. Sapphire is five years old. My partner and I decided I would have the first one, and she would have the second, and it would be from the same father, so the children are siblings.' She had told this story before, I guessed. She didn't get up and put her clothes on. 'What's the point, now you've seen me naked?' she said, so we just sat on the couch, she in her amazing black bra, and me in my shirt and khakis. We drank wine, and we watched the game. Her team, the Detroit Lions, lost as expected.

I am old, as I said, and erections are few and far between, and sometimes only I know they are erections, because I feel them far inside the shadows of my mind and heart and body. Abby's light illuminated those shadows. I think she could see this one, but she didn't say anything. I lifted my glass to her when she said it was time for her to go home. 'May your scars always be good ones, Abby,' I said.

'I'll see you tomorrow,' she said, and put her panties back on.

~

Flight

~

The cathedral is thrust six hundred feet out of the ground
as though in an instant by forces of the earth. Built
painstakingly stone over stone, century after century, it seems
as a young mountain peak, angry and defiant, piercing the
sky darkly even on bright summer days though it is neither
angry nor young, but insolent and anchored. The hawk
was invisible on the brittle silhouette of a northern spire.
He looked down at the people floating in and out and
around his home on a stream of time. He had lived there
long, he knew the change of the seasons by the smell of
the river and the coming and leaving of the small animals
and birds he lived on. His memory was a continuum. He
knew what his mother had known, what his brothers and
sister had known, what his children would know. That the
city grew leaves of ice in the long winter, that parakeets
flew over the river in the summer, that dogs barked on

barges which floated down to the sea, that people cried in their aeries at night, that mice came out into the cobbled streets to look for sustenance, and so he would not be hungry.

The sun rose warm and torpid that day, took its time to traverse the sky. The girl came every day, sometimes with the woman, she sat on a bench under the trees, she ate, she sometimes went inside the cathedral, and then they left, walking fast toward the bridge. He could see her all the way to the great train station where frantic pigeons lived, and then, every day, she left his line of sight, and he did not know if he would ever see her again, but he did, that day. The girl was not like the others. She moved her hands, like wings, her fingers like the tips of his own wings. She turned her head, like he did, she looked at everything. When crowds of children ran screaming right behind her, she did not turn to look. She did not flinch when the sirens burst into the air. He cried out to her, in short notes and long, keening straight down to her. She looked up. There was someone or something there, she felt it. She had always felt it. She didn't remember the first day they came to this place, it was just part of her life. When she was a baby, her mother would push her there in a stroller. She remembered it. When she was gone, her grandfather would walk there with her, his hand around hers. And when he was gone too, and she was old enough, she came there, not every day, but often, by one street or another depending on where she was, over the bridge sometimes, she liked that best. She smiled at the permanently flying tail of the king's horse on the statue, the silly urban climbers with their nylon ropes, she loved running her fingers over the padlocks lovers had locked onto the wire fence between the railway track and the footpath. She, and her love hadn't locked their love there and thrown away the key. She didn't think that was why he was gone, she knew the reason why. Now she brought the old aunt to the Cathedral, but really, she came for herself, to feel the presence of time. Time was more than now, in this place. More than before and after and today and tomorrow. It was nothing unnatural or supernatural, that she felt. Just a presence, an acknowledgement of her presence by something other than all the eyes of all the people who did not watch her, or even see her. She was outside their world. She had always known that, since she was born, she had known that. I am mud, she felt, part of the mud, sludge, lies of the earth, and she looked up at the shiny hawks that flew above her sometimes alighting to swoop up some creature of the world so he would be shiny and grow wings in us all. Maybe, she sometimes felt, it was the hawks watching her. There was always a hawk. If she looked carefully, if she felt for him, she felt him, and then she knew where to look so she could see him. She could feel them. She always had. She felt them calling to her. Maybe, she thought, they were looking for another of their own, maybe she was just in the way, and got a message that was not intended for her, and maybe she just received it in her loneliness, everyone else was so busy with what they did with each other. She saw him, almost lost in the uneven edges of the spire. If he hadn't moved in readiness to fly she would not have seen him. His shape separated from the darkness of the stone and took off into the light summer sky, growing larger not smaller, as he coasted down and settled on the bare branches of the tree right in front of her. He looked right at her with his cat eyes, turning this way and that and he opened his wings slightly to balance on the branch he had known was too weak to support his weight, but he wanted to look at her. She looked back at him, and he could see her clear eyes, a winter sky, she saw things far away, and things very small, and she could see him, and he could see her, so he ruffled his wings again, just to preen, just to show her the bars on his tail, the unbroken curve of his beak, he turned his head this way and that giving her both sides of his fine head, his tawny eyes. Then he took off from the tree, straight up to his northern spire, wings in full span, tips spread out, he knew she was watching him, he was keening as he rose, he knew she didn't actually hear him, but that she did feel him. The old woman was tired and wanted to leave, so they walked to their train. There were vendors crowding the square almost to their doorstep by the time they got home. When they had left, very early in the morning, people were just driving up, some unpacking and laying out their white asparagus and silver mackerel. Now they crowded every foot of the market square, and women in scarves covering their hair and ears walked behind dark men with dark eyebrows and moustaches, stopping to maul tomatoes and to taste pastes of chickpeas and garlic and aubergines and almonds, critical and careful and aggressive and very busy. They all moved their mouths, and lips, incessantly, as people did. As she once had, only she did not remember it, not as an act anyway, just a distant shadow, the imprint of a wet leaf on the concrete, long blown away. She bought a huge slice of apple cake from a woman who had known her mother, to eat as she looked out of her window at the cathedral. She knew her aunt was telling her not to, something about becoming fat and about no man wanting her and about not having babies, but she didn't look at the old woman. They bought a piece of pork, to put in the soup, and then walked up the stairs. The aunt opened her door and went in, not bothering to say goodbye, or thank you, or anything at all. She had never expected it, and was surprised at herself for noticing the lack of acknowledgement. She went two more flights up to her own rooms, in the attic, with dormer windows and slightly sloped ceilings, and a view of the only thing she wanted to see.

She had no tv or radio, just her father's books, and the paintings on the walls, and the windows, and the remains of a life she had had with a man once, before he tired of her silence and left. They were sweet once, when they first met, when they first fell in love. They were sweet when he was fascinated by the difference between her and other women. When he liked himself for his own kindness and charity. When they were enclosed in silence and sensation. They communicated in ways other than sound. She awoke because she smelled the coffee he made. She didn't open her eyes, he kissed her when he brought in two cups, she smelled that he hadn't brushed his teeth yet, and she smelled the coffee on him, and then, some days, if it was early enough, they would lie together, fingertip to fingertip, they would look at each other's faces, which were beloved, which they thought always would be, beloved. But it was not to be so. He said, gesturing, his eyes dry while hers flooded over, that he could not bear it anymore, that it was not enough that she cooked his meals and washed his clothes and cleaned his toilet and waited for him when to come home, to take his coat from him and kiss his lips and nose and face cold from the long bicycle ride on icy streets, it was not enough that they lived together and loved together, that they lay on a blanket on the summer grass along the riverside, that they ran all the way home when the blanket became too public for what they had to do next, and even after the run home, their desire was still rising when she knelt before him and crushed his fluttery soft curls against her cheeks as she gorged on his dense penile flesh, she would stop at the moment before he surrendered to her so she could have him elsewhere too, so they would feel, for the few moments they both could bear before they sighed away their final consciousness, the gorgeous sliding, the inhale and exhale of him in her, no, none of it was enough. It was the silence, he said, and she knew he was shouting when he said it. His skin darkened, a pancake on a hot pan, veins crawled anxiously on his forehead, his open mouth discarded their life in front of her, the words dropped heavily, and broke, and bled around her, and screamed to be gathered up and comforted, but she did not hear them. She never had. He clenched his hands behind his back when he saw her looking at them, as she tried to read his lips and gestures, and she knew then that there would be no more words spoken between them. She said nothing, neither with her hands nor with her eyes or face, and he stopped speaking, and he left. He didn't take everything that day, but he never came back for anything, and one day, when the winter came back, she stopped waiting for him.

His warm robe she used in the winter, his razor in the summer, when she would wear a cool dress and lay in the grass by the river on the blanket they had shared, watching the parakeets and the barges for hours until it was near dark. She wondered, as she ate her cake, if the hawk could see her in the window. She wondered, if she walked all the way home instead of taking the train, if he would follow her, and sit on her window sill, or share his fresh killed mouse with her. She brushed her teeth and lay in her bed, and even from there, she could see the distant spire, and she imagined she could see him, soaring in the still blue summer sky, making the stars come and go as he covered them with his wings. The image was still in her eyes as she slipped quietly from conscious into sweeter realms, from the city streets in daylight to the night sky, and the smell of grass and leaves and the touch of wings on her face.

It was still dark. She looked up at the spires she had looked at every day of her short, silent life. She stood there a while, and then saw him, her hawk. He sat on the lowest part of the scaffolding, swinging slightly in the mild breeze. He turned his head and opened his beak, and she felt a vibration. She felt him calling to her. She closed her eyes so she could see nothing, only feel, and see what he was showing her. She felt his wings, she felt the air through them, she saw what he saw, as he rose, higher and higher and higher, past the gargoyles and the saints and the flying buttresses, past the low clouds till there was no dimension to anything anymore. And below her the church, just a small green cross, laying on the face of the earth.

Down on the ground, she felt her feet, and she leaned against the dark abraded stone. The scaffolding was right beside her, and she held the cold metal to support herself. She was dizzy, a little dazed, as if she had really flown too high too fast. And she soon recovered, but there he was again, the hawk, calling to her. She saw him, again on the scaffolding she was holding. They were connected by the metal, and she could feel him so clearly, as if he was inside her head. She took off her shoes and her socks and put her bag beside them too, and with the firm grip of her bare hands and feet, she began to climb up to him. She saw his golden eyes come closer, he did not move, just sat there, unafraid, as she climbed. And when she was close enough to touch him, when she could see the shafts of his feathers, he lifted off his perch and sank a little before opening his wings wide, so the pale pearl sky shone through them, and went a little higher. She followed him. And so they climbed, together, to the point where she could go no further, and she stood on the narrow wood laid there for someone who would stand there and clean the stone of its darkness, inch by inch, always seeing only the stone before their eyes, never the whole church, all at once.

He was there, at her shoulder, this hawk of hers. And they both stepped into the air together, the girl and her hawk. He called to her, and she answered him, as she trusted the air beneath her feet, he called to her as he went down, short-winged and fast after her, and he stopped his drop and floated, but she did not recover her span, she did not come up with him.

He called to her, and she answered. Once.

He called to her again, but she said no more.

The people of the city slept, its lonely heard the hawk's cry. A man in his bed stopped in mid-stroke, he called to his lover, she lay in another bed with another man across the river, he could not but momentarily end his eternal longing for her, beating it into temporary submission each night, an injured creature biting the dust. The woman heard the hawk, and she heard her lover's anguish in the cry, and she answered, the lonely whisper of a prisoner in an old iron bed, velvet drapes, her wedding ring on the table beside her. The baker heard the hawk, as he pounded his dough in the dark hours between night and day, and he called too, for the sun to rise, for morning to take him from the heat of the ovens and labour. And the little boy heard him, as he tumbled in the grass, upside down in the early morning grass, and he looked, upside down at the sky, and he saw the hawk, red-tailed in the rising sun, and he laughed, and all was right with the world.

~

The Fifth Tale of Malekh

~

In 1936, my great-great-grandfather on my mother's side, a man who several photographs in possession of my family show to be a strong and handsome young man, was among those who followed T.E. Lawrence to capture Damascus from the Ottomans. Yes, that Lawrence. Of Arabia. I like to think that they drank tea together, or at least they shook hands one cold morning in the desert. That piece of my family history, however irrelevant to this story, is one I can never resist telling.

During his stay with the British army in Arabia, this same ancestor of mine was once assigned to guard a distinguished British antiquarian who had been sent to Palestine ostensibly to safeguard precious materials. As we know, safeguarding these from the natives meant taking them away to be put in museums in Britain where they would be better appreciated than by the people whose ancestors had created them. According to my own ancestor's journal, which was not really intended to be a journal but rather a ledger of his accounts, my great- great-grandfather spent several months hanging around outside small libraries, schools, and once or twice at a British led archaeological dig. On one such assignment, it is not clear from his journal which, he came across a book. Being bored out of his wits by the heat and lack of action, he borrowed it. I am certain, being a man of great conscience, he had every intention of returning the book when he was finished reading it. But time and war took its toll, and when he returned to his wife and his liberated country, it was without his left arm which he left in pieces in the desert, first shot and then amputated because the gangrene set in, but with the book, which has now come into my possession since the death of my mother. The book is large, and heavy, with a deep indigo purple-dyed leather cover embossed in silver letters, Tales of Malekh, and nothing else. The pages are old, of course, but perhaps from loving use, and much reading, and the touch of human hands and eyes, the book is not a brittle antique, but rather, an old friendly book, wherein the pages are supple and turn easily, with the smell of foods and leaves of the places it has been. With this book, which I could not have read, I inherited my grandfather's translations of all the stories, in his own order. This is one of the stories, along with his introduction.

The fifth tale of Malekh tells the story of how the King, Malekh, whom this entire book is about, was conceived. I translated this story first, because I read it first. I kept as close to the original as I could, I thought carefully and long before making my choices among words, and I maintained the time and place to the best of my ability. I hope, if anyone reads this, they will forgive me if a turn of phrase or a word here or there is not to their liking, for I am a soldier, and not trained in words. But it is such a beautiful and strange tale, rich with detail and layered with the voices of many storytellers, and as there are not many who speak this language anymore, nor are there any other copies of this book that I know of, that I felt compelled to undertake the task of translating it, so I could share it.

~

The third full moon of the year is the day of the mother. On this day, every man and woman and child in the country kneels before a mother. If a person is an orphan, he will then kneel before a neighbour, or the sister of a father or the wife of a brother. If a person is very old, for him there is a daughter or daughter-in-law or granddaughter who is a mother. And when we have a queen, and our queen becomes a mother, she will come out to the window of her room, and people in the city of the king will come to kneel before this mother, the mother of our next queen or king. On this day we give thanks to our own mothers through the one we kneel before, for our small life in this wide and neverending world.

All the people kneel, but not our king. For he, among all men and women, is born from no woman. No woman bore him within her womb. No woman parted her thighs and brought forth the feet and body of the king. This day of the year, no one glimpsed the face of our king. He did not leave his rooms, the guard outside his door let no one in, even if the gravest of troubles came that day. No one knew what he did that one day of the year, but our master neither saw anyone nor even spoke to anyone through the door, nor did anyone see or hear him until the moment of the midnight bell and the end of the day. Then he would come out, and begin the day from where he left the one before that one, as if the day of the mother never happened at all.

This king was a good one, he made no war, and he asked nothing of his country but that we work the land as best we could, and we help those who had less than we did, even if they be from another country. When a flood came to our neighbours, our king sent succour and men to help build their lives again. The people of that land to our north had their own king, who had debauched himself in his palace even as the people died, who had taken the best young men of his city as lovers and playthings, and did nothing to help those at the fringes of his country who had been left without land, home, and even family by the floodwaters. When the waters and the troubles abated, and all was well, some men from the floodlands went to the capital city to find work, so they could quicker rebuild the wealth they had lost. There they conspired and devised a plan, and they took their depraved and cruel king hostage in his own house. There they bound him, and there castrated him. Then they cast him, weeping and bleeding, out into the forest, and that is where travellers from our country found him. He was in a state so terrible that they risked a sleeping draft which could have killed him, because they could not stand his piteous screams as they travelled through the peaceful land. They brought him to Malekh, our king.

Now Malekh knew this man was no devil, he had not the power for that. But our king knew him to be creature from the lower levels of the world. And yet, he was a king, and Malekh could not allow that a king be dealt with in such a way as he had been. If people heard that a king had been attacked, not by another king, but by fishermen and basketmakers, if they heard that a king was castrated and uncrowned, and if they heard that those who did this were neither punished nor even questioned, then every king everywhere in our world and worlds above and below would never be safe again. So Malekh took his fifty best guardsmen, and two of his councillors, myself and his cousin Sasskia, oh how I loved her, and rode to the distant capital city of that country. He was not stopped, but was welcomed, he had been the saviour of those in need and trouble, in flood and famine. But when he came to the palace, he asked that the men be brought before him who had dethroned their king. Six men came out proudly, for they were proud of what they had done. They had defeated and mutilated and driven away one who deserved much worse than what they did to him. They believed they had done right. Malekh said immediately that they must kneel before him, and they must be punished. The men were consternated at first, and then angered. But this was the king Malekh who had helped him in their time of dire need, even when their own king would not. So they tried to reason with him.

'Did he not deserve it, lord Malekh?' they asked him. 'Did he not offend his people and disdain their suffering? Was he not a raper and ruiner of our finest young men? Did he not deserve to die? We only exiled him, we did not kill the fiend,' they said.

Malekh understood them, and they were reasonable, but he was there with a different reasoning. 'Yes,' he said to the men, 'he deserved all the things you did to him. But you do not have the power and right to harm the body of a king, unless ordered to do so by a king. And in that you were wrong, and for that, brave men though you are, you will have to pay.'

One of the men was strange and scarred, and he said nothing while his companions fell to pleading for their lives. I saw Sasskia watching him. Oh how I loved her, with her face like gentle rain. Malekh held up his hand, quieting the men. 'I will not take your life, for you did not take the king's life. And your king would have produced no heir, so I will not punish you for ending his line. But you will give one year of your life for each blow you laid upon his kingly person.'

'To whom shall we give these years, Malekh?' they asked him, grateful now, and loving my master again.

And to that he answered, 'To me, I am your king now.' And that was how he acquired the country to the north, and that was how he came to find out about the origin of his own life.

Our king spent one season in that north country. He sampled the food and the wine they made, and he lived in his new palace, it was like nothing he had in his own country. This one was all gold and silks and comfort and pleasures, and Malekh saw why the castrated king was so hated. Women came to his room each night, young women, virgins, to offer themselves to our king. He allowed them to sleep in his bed, but he did not touch them, nor did he allow them to touch him. Though his body desired the sweet skin and bone and mouth and thighs of these lovely dark northern creatures such as he had never seen in our land, he did nothing but look at them. There would be a time, he knew, when he would taste every pleasure of mind and body. That time had not yet come.

And I, though I slept alone each night, all the days I was with my beloved Sasskia, oh how I loved her. I was never more than a few feet from her glowing body, I could look upon her anytime I had the urge, and knowing I could, I denied myself, and when I could bear it no more, all I had to do was lift my eyes, and there she would be, by the side of the king, her cousin. She was a sister to him, her father and mother, after all were his father and mother. They had brought him to manhood and kinghood, since he had no father or mother of his own.

Malekh tired of the country soon, of the unfamiliar palace, its fountains, dancers, courtiers and cooks, the constant revelry tired him. He longed for the harsh wind of his home, and he longed to sit with his own courtiers, serious men and women all, he longed for their considered advice and quiet humour. He wished to be home again, among children and people who lived real lives, not pleasure days rolling one into another with no conversation, and no meaning. I was told that in the last king's time, they did not even retire to their bed chambers when the urge to copulate came upon them, they would do it right there, in the main palace hall, and wash themselves in the fountain after. The king himself desired young men, and he could be found, many times a day, dismissing petitioners while his harem took turns to suckle on his seedless phallus. I was glad he was in the custody of my master.

I myself was not to return home until I had diminished the opulence and stamped out the decadence of this palace and its occupants. It was his palace now, my lord Malekh's, and he wished that it bear no mark of the excesses of its previous occupant. Our company began to prepare for their journey home. Imagine my joy when I was told that Sasskia, the joy of all my organs, was to stay there with me.

The day before they were to depart, the quiet scarred man from among the six conspirators came to seek audience with my master, he said he must speak with him alone. Malekh spoke to no one alone. So when the man came to have his meeting, Sasskia was in the chamber looking over the palace food ledger, and I sat with the king. Guards stood inside and outside the door. The man knelt, and the king told him he could speak.

The man seemed afraid, but he took a few deep breaths, and said, 'I know your mother, my lord Malekh.' I would have ordered the guards to have him removed, but my master raised his hand just a little, he wanted to hear what the man had to say.

'It is a long story,' he said, and the king sent for our evening meal, and ordered the man to dine with us. We ate while he told his story, and the king, in his usual calm and stoic way, listened. I watched Sasskia, my sweetheart, eat, she put tiny morsels of food in her mouth, and chewed many times before she swallowed. I watched the food descend down her throat, and wished I could go down with it. I had never before felt the need to touch her, and the thought surprised me. But I forgot, as I listened to the scarred man's tale.

'From my boyhood, my father wished me to be a captain. I was an army apprentice from a very young age, he gave me to them as soon as they would take me. The army was my family and my friends, my brothers and sisters and home. My work was to sharpen and polish the swords and spears, clean the soldiers' boots, wash the floors of the armoury, and service the men. The hardest work was when they came back from a skirmish or a campaign, and we would be assigned to the quarters of the brotherhood, or armoury duty. The armoury was harder work. Soaking and scraping the blood and mud off everything till it shone, or laundry, which meant washing the war off their clothes. We would boil everything in vats of soap and water, stirring them with sticks, scalding our forearms as we did it, then pouring out the sludge and doing it again, and again, till the water ran clear. I preferred personal duty, and I think most of the boys did, but they did not like to admit it. The soldiers were tired from the war and the tedium and the travel, and they had no aggression or viciousness left in them anymore. They chose among us, and it did not matter who chose us to serve them, because they were all the same, tired young men, some wounded, all in need of touch and gentleness. I served one man, Jamu. He always chose me, and I knew how to treat him and how to please him.'

The king, and Sasskia and I listened. The details of his story were well known to us. The customs are the same in our own country. The origins are the same, we were one country once, before the separation wars, and now were again. Our captains were not free to go home when they returned to the capital from battle. They were to remain in the palace complex where they would recover their bodies and their spirits. It was believed that if soldiers were allowed to go home to their families, their mothers and wives would, with intention and without, supplant the feelings of brotherhood they had for their fellow fighters. Family would draw them back into the fold, and there they would weaken in resolve and in body, and our army would diminish. Mothers would remind their sons that they carried the seed of the family tree. Wives would fill them with love as they emptied their sacks night after night, and cause them to forget their training, their purpose, their duty to the king and to the land. We had women in our army. They too, were housed in their own quarters, and were attended to in every way by the girl apprentices. They were not sent to their homes to be married and filled with children. The man's story was about all soldiers. We knew the details, but the king did not interrupt him.

'These captains lived naked for fifteen days. Their battle clothes were dispatched to the laundries. They were watched night and day, waking and sleeping by healers and body masters. They were fed foods to cool and cure and calm them. They were not denied any comforts, nor were any desires left unfulfilled. I saw their meals, and they were made from the finest food available in the land, and I saw the masseuses caress them with golden oils, kneading and pleading their bones and sinews to strength. I saw the healers bring these grown men to weeping pleasure with their clever hands. I, along with my fellow apprentices worshipped the soldiers' bodies, we consumed their manly effluence, or received it in our own bodies when the men chose to use us thus. We were honoured, we knew that with their pleasure we received also their strength. I was an apprentice then, but I also knew this life as a soldier, later.' The scarfaced must have been a captain then, if he had been in the quarters as a soldier.

When the war wounds in their minds and bodies were repaired, when they were no longer in need of help and healing, only then were the captains sent home. And then, even after they had filled their mothers' hearts with joyful reunion and their wives' or husbands' with love and flesh, none could stop them from returning. It was a strange thing, but it always worked.

The soldier now spoke softly, and his meal lay untouched on his plate.

'My soldier was a lonely captain, he did not have a home to go to. He lived in the capital, and he was the last to leave the quarters of the brotherhood when the time came and their clean clothes were brought back. I was good to him, I knew his body well, and no matter how broken it was when he brought it back to me, I made him well again. I was not a healer, but I made him happy, and I gave him comfort. When we got word that the soldiers were returning, I waited for him to walk through those gates, into the compound and into the bath I prepared for him. I even knew what herbs he preferred for scenting the waters, and how hot he preferred it. I knew he would need my hands on his manhood, I knew he liked to be brought upright in the water, and I knew he liked to look upon himself and know that he was whole, and he was still a man. Many who returned became incapable of this. Many could not be coerced or pleasured into prominence, and it was the apprentice who would tell the healers, and then it was their duty to restore such a man. And now I come to the story of your life, my lord Malekh.'

I looked at my lord. He ate his meal steadily and quietly,

looking up at the storyteller, nodding sometimes, but there was no sign that he was disturbed. The man continued with his story after a drinking a glass of hot water.

'Your father was a captain in the army. He was my Captain Jamu's closest friend. They rode together, they fought together, they ate together, they protected one another, and they had both saved each other's lives and bodies on many occasions in many wars. Then came the war to the west, when the king wished to make the coast ours. It was of great value, for trade and power, the coastal king was old and dying, and he had no heir. He wished to cede his lands to our king before his death, but his cousins and uncles and nephews, and one niece in particular, wanted to rule after him. The war was brutal. All wars are brutal, but this one took many lives and many limbs and eyes and hearts. We won the land, as you know, it is yours now, Malekh. But we lost so very much, in that war. I nearly lost my master Jamu, but he did return, some shadow of him, some part of him. Enough that we made him himself again, eventually. As for your father, he returned too, but without his manhood. His apprentice, the healers, the medicine men, they all tried everything they could, but his heat would not rise. Even in his sleep, it remained like a slug slung upon his thigh, and no dream would rouse it. The healers said there was no injury to the organ. They said the injury was to his mind. They gave him herb to smoke. He wandered the quarters and the gardens for days, speaking to the dogs and the birds and the fruit in the trees, but when he came out of the herbsense and his apprentice massaged him with oils and bathed him in scented waters to arouse him, there was nothing.

One morning, as I combed the tangles from my master's hair, all the healers gathered to talk. Every known remedy to reverse your father's impotence had been tried and had failed. There was a silence then, and nobody spoke. I began to whisper a question to my master, and he reached behind him and squeezed my thigh to quiet me. Then, into the snoring of the sleeping captains and the breathing of the waking ones, the youngest and most inexperienced healer spoke, 'We must bring the witch.'

Among loud and horrified protestations their elder spoke, firmly, but his voice was high with fear. 'Yes, he speaks the obvious. We must bring the witch.' The silence settled upon them again, and no one said another word.

I asked my master Jamu why such an apprehension. He said the witch had been summoned before. She had always succeeded in curing the men of their ailment. Always. But she left a part of herself within them. She always took her price. She was a witch, after all. A sorceress, a child of an unknown goddess. She was a danger to all. And there was one other thing: no woman was allowed into the quarters of the brotherhood. This violation weakened us all, and it damaged us all in our manhood. But we had no choice, it seemed. Your father had to be cured.'

As we listened, we knew that there was no lie in his story thus far. Everything was exactly as he told it, the rituals, the wars, the alliances. Our healers never let a soldier carry his impotence from a war through his life, they did what they could to cure him. My beloved Sasskia's father, the paternal uncle of my lord Malekh, had brought up the king from a very young age. His kingdom was lost, but he took it back from the blue queen of the coast. He returned her in pieces to the ocean where she was born. It was all true what he told us.

My lord Malekh listened intently now, lost in the tale, and my beloved Sasskia, her plate licked clean, was asleep on the cushions. Her eyelids fluttered as she breathed, and her naked feet were close to my fingertips. I wriggled them, like creatures who would leave me and run up her toes and ankles and calves. The man spoke, removing me from those thoughts. I was grateful. My thoughts were unbecoming in the presence of the king.

'The night of the witch had come. We had cleaned the quarters all that day, apprentices were sent away into the gardens. I was the last one to leave. It was dusk, I was alone. I knew a place on the roof where I could look into the chamber where the witch would meet the captain. I looked all around and made certain there was no one following me, then I climbed up the wall. I found the captain's apprentice already there in my spot, but he just put his finger to his mouth and made place for me. We pressed into a small flat gap where two parts of the roof met. We looked down into the quarters. There was no one there. We could smell the burning herb we had lit, and the smell of the burning oil from the lamps. There was a glow in the room. We waited, silent.

Both of us must have fallen asleep, for when we awoke it was to the sound of a man's voice, low and heavy with desire. Below us we saw a strange scene. The king was chained upright to the wall, we could see his wrists strain and his shoulders joints wrench backward in their sockets as he pulled himself toward her. And we saw her in the gloom of the lamplight, the witch, she lay on a bed, naked as the king was, naked as the stars, her breasts flattened like two moons upon her chest, she had her hand on one as she pressed and caressed it, and the other, the nipple, surrounded by a smaller moon, she flicked with a tongue that was as long as a cat's tail, and twitched like one too. Her other hand was on her mound, I could see strands of blue through her fingers as she opened and closed her thighs. The captain strained and groaned, and my fellow apprentice and I felt our spit form within our mouths and our seed gather in our bellies and we began to writhe upon the hard roof and rub against each other. But the captain, with all his groaning and all his need, there was no hardness upon him that was visible to us. It was a slug still, hanging like a dead lamb upon a butcher's hook. He begged and she laughed, her joy and pleasure never ending, she moaned and she showed him where he could be and what he could do, and where he could enter her and how he could own her, if only, she said, you lift your spirit and your sword, young captain, you could cut me in half and send me to heaven with it. But he would not, and he could not. 'Untie him,' she screamed at the healers. 'You have all witnessed my power, your manhood is spent upon the floor, you have seen what I can do, now untie him, the poor wretch. His poor phallus is defeated by his mind, and war has had its way with him. But you have seen my power. I will have him yet, your captain. I will have him when he is king. And as they untied the captain, she took the hilt of his sword and swallowed it with her nether mouth, pushing it slowly deeper and deeper. Then, as the captain was free and fell upon her, she disappeared, and the sword lay there beside him. He picked it up, groaning and crying, and smelled and licked and rubbed it upon himself. 'I will have that ruby cunt,' he said, 'I will have her one day'.

And then as the days passed the captain became strong again, and he led the men to war again, and he came back home one day and became king, as the witch had foreseen. But my master Captain Jamu said the king was still not a man. The king never slept at night, Jamu said, he only stared into the dark, he walked in the forest looking for the witch, he saw nothing but the bloodruby that he would one day sink his manhood into. He was lost, this father of yours, my lord Malekh, though he showed no one his weakness but his brother-in-arms, my master Jamu.

I was not an apprentice anymore when the big war came. You know the one I speak of. Your uncle, the sleeping lady's father, became king when this war was over. But that day, after nine months of fighting, we were finished. We were driven into the palace which you have seen, we were surrounded on all sides by our enemies, and we huddled in the innermost chambers, waiting for our end to come. Our king, your father, my lord Malekh, stood by the window and watched as his guards fought to keep the enemy out, but they came like a tidal wave upon us, and we all knew there was no hope, and that we were at the end of our time. At this time, at the end of his small life in the wide and neverending world, the king turned to Jamu, his friend and brother for so many years, and said to him, 'I would give my life happily, Jamu, if only I had my ruby woman once. If only I had not lost my manhood, Jamu, if I had lain with her once in my life, I would die without a regret now.' And he began to weep, and lament. And then the palace, in the breadth of noon, turned suddenly dark and gloomy, and the smell of the herb suffocated and elevated us all, and then the doors that fifty soldiers held closed flew open and she walked through them, and said, 'I am here, King, show me your sword, and cut me with it.' And she embraced the king and kissed his face and beard and took her hooded robe apart and revealed to him her blue nakedness and the ruby light between her thighs. 'Here it is, King, the pathway to your immortality.' He gasped as she grasped him, he was as hard as a pomegranate and as full as a desert lemon, and she wrapped her thighs around him light as a feather and buried him inside her ruby tomb. 'I cured you, King, but I wanted you for this, at this moment, of my choosing. Your death is upon you, King, lose your kinghood in me,' she commanded him. We could hear the metal upon metal and the slicing of flesh and the hammer on bone and the cries of the dying come closer and closer, and the king, he laid his witch upon the table never once coming apart from her, and he thrust, and he thrust, and the doors burst open and the warrior queen of the coast strode into the chamber, bloody and torn and still the king thrust and thrust, his eyes open and fixed upon his witch, and the queen stood for a moment and looked at the king and saw his phallus, godlike and swordlike, and smiled, and raised her sword above him, and still the king thrust into his beloved witch, who said, 'The moment is come, your death is upon you O King, relieve yourself of your seed, and let me carry it for you till your heir comes forth.' And with her words she screamed from pleasure and from pain, and he, he made his final thrusts, pouring into her his love, his seed, his very life. The queen of the coast sliced off his head as he smiled his final smile, as he said, for the last time, 'I am your king.'

His brother-in-arms and his lifelong friend picked up the head of his king, and held it up for us all to see. The pleasure was still upon it, of the witch's ruby cunt.'

I turned to look at my lord Malekh, the man had spoken of the mother and father of the king in words which would have him killed. But Malekh made no move and said nothing. Of course I knew why, it was because the man had not as yet told us the story, and we did not know that the king and the witch were the father and the mother of the king Malekh. Sasskia my beloved lay asleep, still.

'The queen of the coast let us all live, she did not care to kill her own subjects, she said. And she was our queen for just a year before the father of the lady Sasskia, your uncle my lord Malekh, came and took the kingdom. And it was the day of his coronation as king of the three countries of the west and the east and the coast that the witch came back to the city with a baby and the dead king's seal.

I was one of the captains of the land, and I was there, for the coronation of the king. She did not kneel before your uncle, lord Malekh. She stood, hooded and cloaked before him, and said, 'He is lovely of course, he is perfect, of course, but I do not want him. Those who will love him and grow him into a human being, remember that he is the son of a king, but also of a woman. So tell him not only who his father was, but also who his mother was. I will not be his mother, who teaches him the superiority of men and the weakness of the enemy. I will not be cow to this calf, and whore to his father. I am a traveller of time, I have spacemoons to cure, this is but a human child. He will live and he will die. I will not be his mother, but I cured his father's dead kinghood, and I received his father's seed, and I gave to him this life. Tell him he is Malekh. The line between the stars.'

And this is why I tell you the story, my lord Malekh, which no one else told you. You are a king, and your mother is a great witch, living in the real world of a thousand worlds, not this one, where we dream and live our little lives. You are not just a human child, my lord, you have the power of a witch within you. I kneel before you, and I beg your forgiveness for any dark words I may have uttered in the telling of this story. I only wanted you to know, and I only wanted you to know it as I saw it, My lord Malekh, the line between the stars.'

Sasskia awoke when Malekh laughed full and loud, and told the man to stand up from where he knelt, with his head at the king's feet. She stretched her legs and her feet touched my fingertips.

~

On the third full moon of the year, the day of the mother, our king came out with my Sasskia, pregnant with my child, her arm upon his arm. He knelt before her and said, 'I thank you, mother, for giving me a time and a place in this wide and neverending world.'

~

Fall

~

Srinivas sat on the black leather sofa next to his best friend's wife. He did not turn his head or move. He was not aware of his silence or stillness, because he could hear his blood pouring through his veins and slamming into his heart like the Niagara river on the rocks below. His thoughts had stopped entirely, deafened by his physical reaction to what Jenna had just said. He swallowed, because his tongue felt thick and his throat began to close. He closed his eyes, and the sound of his heart threatened him inside the darkness of his head, and he quickly opened them again. He felt her sitting next to him still, but he did not turn to look at her in the gloom of the fading day. He fell into a hole of memory, of pain and longing, skins began to peel off haphazardly as he plunged. Yesterday, at Niagara, her hair, cascading, tumbling out of the black wool cap onto her shoulders, her green eyes squinted against the cold, her skin, he wanted to reach out and touch it, he knew it would be cold under his hot fingers, but he just held his cup of mocha as she took his picture with his back to the falls, the wind cutting through them, a few huddled Koreans, trees with no leaves standing naked, the falls frozen in bits, like him, beginning to seize as the winter of his loneliness took hold, the drive there, the colours muted by snow, speaking to him in whispers, so he had to watch and listen, the hawks everywhere, palely marked, like giant moths against a bright grey sky, lakes, the Welland canal, cold outside, warm inside the car, Jenna driving beside him, again taking him somewhere to show him something in some corner of the world, her hair, her mouth, how long, he had known her, so long before today, before yesterday, how long, through his life, his own long partnership, the persistence of his longing, like a burn on his retina, though he could live and see his life and the world, it had always been with him, since the first moment he saw her.

That was then, twenty-five years ago, he was twenty-two years old, his friend had come home, to show his new wife to his beloved country. Srinivas, running down the stairs of his parents' house when he heard his mother calling Ravi was here, and he saw her, Jenna, and his breath had stopped, and he had never quite caught it again since. Green eyes looking up and him, a huge smile on her happy face, her glorious hair, her delight, and the beginning and end of his. He laughed at himself that night laying in his bed after they had spent the day together, because what else could he do, after falling in love with his best friend's wife, what else was there to do but laugh. That was probably the last time he laughed about it. He thought, they would leave, go back home to their life in the cold north, he would go back to the mad heat of Mumbai, his job, he would dream of her again, for sure, but that would be that, and time, a week, would rub out his infatuation. There would be some of it left of course, she was too lovely to be forgotten, and he would always know her, of course, because she was Ravi's wife, and Ravi would always be in his life, and they would even be good friends some day, Jenna and Srinivas, he thought. In the shower that night, he conjured up what he had seen of her body, a smudge of skin between bra strap and dress, a classic look inside the front of her dress at the swells of her breasts, it was her hair, he had never seen anything that colour, which flashed in his imagination even as the hot water washed away the remains of his infatuation. And that was the last time he had allowed himself to think of her in that way, he felt a kind of uncomfortable betrayal, and he didn't do it again.

But then the job brought him to Los Angeles, and then Atlanta, and Ravi and Jenna, and then Ravi and Jenna and Megan were one flight away in Toronto, and there it was again. Seeing her again, a not-so-old, not-so faded picture repainted in vibrant new colours so they glowed, more glimpses into her eyes, her life, her dress, drives through Ontario wine country, Ravi asleep in the back seat, just him and Jenna talking, laughing, she touched his hand sometimes as she said something, his skin blistered, her hair in the wind when they hiked through a gorge north of Atlanta, he caught her once when she slipped, late evening, after a noon of wine, many friends, old college friends from five years at Hostel 4, wives, some from back home, some from this new country, him, Srinivas, then still single, and the only single man there, she took a false step in her pale green high-heeled shoes, began to fall forward, he caught her, by the waist, and her face was close to his, his face was in her hair, and he took a deep breath, the first in years. She turned and smiled at him and thanked him, and he almost forgot to let go of her, Jenna, and he knew why he didn't think of her when he had the little two week layovers with various women, or even when he jerked off in the shower, he knew why he avoided thoughts of her, because they were feelings of her, because she was his dearest friend's wife, because she was Jenna, because he loved her.

'Fuck me, Srinivas'

Had she really said that? Or was it just a part of a fantasy which had sat in him unopened and untouched for two decades, and was breaking out now in spite of his best efforts? Ravi had gone on an unscheduled trip, and there he was, with Jenna and Megan, sixteen, who had grown into a smart, talkative teenager, always on her way out, always texting on her fancy phone, three whole days in a huge house which was beginning to close in. He had woken early, let the cat out, made himself coffee, chatted and eaten toast with Megan before her ride to school honked loudly outside, sent out emails, he had an exhibition coming up, and he had to liaise with transporters and packers for his rather huge pieces. It was funny how his art was beginning to make him more money than his job these past few years, his five years at engineering college were reaching the end of their usefulness finally. By the time Jenna came down from her and Ravi's bedroom it was almost ten, and she was very happy that he had made himself at home, and even happier to curl up on the couch with the cup of coffee he handed her. And the rest of their day had been spent mostly on the couch, she sat at one end and he at the other, both with their laptops, talking occasionally, eating a snack every so often, drinking coffee till it was all gone. At dinner time he said he would cook, and he did, he stir fried shrimp he found in the freezer with a chopped-up habanero, and cilantro, and segments of cucumber and bits of pecan, and he served it to them both on brown rice. She was amazed and delighted. She finished the whole plate, she had two glasses of wine, he knew she loved her pinkish Zinfandels which he found unpalatable, but loved that she drank it, a silly pink wine. She put the glass down, she put her empty plate on the coffee table, she turned toward him, her arm on the back of the couch almost touching him. Then she leaned toward him and kissed him on his mouth. And his blood began to pound in his head. And he was not sure what he did and didn't hear after that.

He thought about the six-year relationship he had ended just before this visit. It had not been a bad relationship at all, except for her incessant insecurity, her constant need to know where he was and with whom and why. Classic, really. And if he had loved her, he would have even put up with it, built a sense of security in her. Sara. But he hadn't. He just hadn't loved her enough. Or at all. His mother was disappointed when he had told her it was over. She had thought there would be marriage, and hoped there would be children. She thought he had left it too long, they should have married much sooner. But Sara had a job, a career she didn't want to interrupt with marriage and children, yet. Well, it was too late. And wherever his thoughts went in the past, they came back here, to the couch, to Jenna, to what he would do or would not do, he knew this was the beginning of a new hell. He knew it.

He turned to look at her finally. Jenna's hair, that he wanted so much to push his hands and face into, and her green eyes, he would look into them when he did what she asked him to, there was such pleading in those eyes that it shocked him. She smiled. 'Sex is easy, isn't it, Srini? We can go to your room, please, and stay in bed all day and all night and all tomorrow, and then we can go on with life, what's changed? Except we'll both be a bit happier?' What was he going to say, he wondered. Even if Ravi had not been his friend, even if he had not spent his childhood, his college years, his youth with him, still, still, this was his house, his hospitality, his trust, his woman, his wife, and Srinivas began to realise the extent of this landscape of his new home, his new acreage in hell. She leaned closer to him, her mouth, Jenna's mouth, making small, perfect kisses around his mouth, little breaths brushing his mouth, she trailed tiny kisses down his neck, his descent a trajectory of a Dylan song, darker, more beautiful, all the old desire, the final layers of him peeling off, his control vanishing, his morality, his friendship, his right and wrong in pieces, gone all to dust.

'Jenna,' he said. 'No.'

She drew back, in anger. He opened his mouth, and she put her hand on it. 'I heard you. You said no. There is nothing else to say. I've heard it before. I wasn't asking you to love me, Srinivas. Just to want me a little. To be a man. To lie with me.' A smile, then, and her voice became soft, and cold, he had never heard it like that before, 'Lie with me.

Funny. A Freudian slip. I meant to say lay with me. But if you lay with me, you'll have to lie with me too. He doesn't give a damn who I sleep with Srini, why should he? He hasn't said yes to me in years. And you are like brothers, all you men. No? No what? No, you won't kiss me? Why? Is my mouth all wrong for you? Won't it fit on yours? Won't fit on your cock, Srinivas? Why, don't you think I can please you? Am I too old? Forty-three too old? No what?'

Srinivas took a breath quickly. He loved her, and he couldn't fuck her. He answered her, honestly. 'No, I can't fuck you Jenna. No, not because you are not the most beautiful woman I have ever known, not because I haven't thought about nothing but you these twenty years since the first day I saw your face, not even because Ravi is my friend and I won't disrespect him, Jenna. Though all this is true, I won't fuck you, because I love you. I know how it will be, my love. I know how we will be together, I know how you look at me, and how I look at you, I know we will touch and all our moments will be perfect, I know we will fit together my love, I know we will breathe together, and sleep together and our fuck will be love and sweetness, my love, Jenna, my love. All this I know is true. But it isn't why I won't fuck you. I won't, because I won't go home tomorrow after this day and night with you, and sit in my room after this, day after day, night after night, week after week, year after year, wishing for you because I have known you, and wanting you, and dying from this love. I can't.'

And he put his fingers in her hair, and he pulled her close to him, and he kissed her, and she kissed him, deep and long, and deeper, and longer, and he began to pull away, and she wouldn't let him go, she put her arm around his neck, she slipped below him, she put her legs around his waist, she moaned his name, she said, 'Oh please, please...'

And he held her arms, and separated them from each other. She sat up, and arranged herself, pushing her hair away from her face. 'It's fine, I get it,' she said. And he heard bitterness. And his sorrow showed in the shine in his eyes, but she was angry. 'You said no. And you won't do it. You think of yourself. And your future misery. And your friend. And your honour. And mine. And betrayal? You think you will betray your friend? And what? I'm his property, that you cannot use? Like driving his car? What if you drove his car? Or fucked his wife? And anyway, I'm not his car. I'm me. If I want to fuck you, that's what I want. It has nothing to do with him. Or you.' She was clenching her fists, and her jaw was hard together and she spoke through her teeth, almost hissing, full of poisonous anger that he knew had nothing to do with him, or his no. But he had to listen to her, and see this through, whatever it was.

'No. You say. No. Why? Why can't we just do it? And forget it till some other time? Do you want me to beg? I will, if you want. I know you want me, Srinivas, and you know right now I want you. You know I've thought about it a lot, I know you have too, and now we can do this. We are adults, Srini, I need someone who loves me, who is my friend, to do me this favour. Will you not do it?'

He was lost. He had stumbled onto something he was not prepared for. He knew what it was, but he could not name it. She was in a state of passion so beautiful that he would have had her there, in that moment, on that couch, and why not, her mouth was so soft, her breasts, she had no bra on, her nipples, he could see them, her legs, strong around his body a few moments ago, he hard and ready and willing, why not, he thought. But he knew this thing she was feeling. Her whole body quivered with a desire, and a need, this woman, angry for having to ask, he knew what this was. Her desire, deep and desperate, it was not for him. She wanted to be held, and touched, and wanted, and she wanted to be told she was wanted, by look and words and touch and frantic orgasms, over and over. And he knew it would be that way, with them. But her desire, it held him back even more than fear for his life without her. Her desire was for herself, for her, she wanted to know herself, find herself, unlock herself.

He was puzzled as he watched her, standing there, her anger fading, she was not even aware of her tears wetting her cheeks. How could this be, he thought. Twenty years, since she was a young girl he had known her. She was without a doubt beautiful. By any standard, by any stretch. She was beautiful, and motherhood and age had made her more beautiful. There were lines around her mouth and eyes that he adored, she wasn't a slim young girl anymore, but the sixteen years since she had Megan had put curves on her, and he stopped himself there. His long years of hunger licked up into him, and he was glad when she said she had to take some clothes to Megan in school because she was spending the weekend at a friend's. He said he would tidy up and take a shower. 'I'll be about an hour,' she said, 'I may have to drive all the girls, and I'll pick up a couple of steaks and wine for dinner. You can grill, can't you?'

'In the snow?' Srinivas asked her, a bit confused. 'No, on the indoor grill, I'll show you.' She said, and she picked up her bag and keys and left, and he didn't sense much anger trailing her. He picked up the coffee cups and newspapers and tidied up a bit. He went to his room and took out fresh undies and a t-shirt. He looked around for a towel but didn't see one. He wondered if he should wait for her or go upstairs and find one. He had been upstairs before, he had sat with Ravi and drunk beer in the den and watched football while she slept in their bedroom across the hall. There was no reason why he shouldn't go up and find a towel. He went. There was no towel in the den or hallway, and, as he had known he would have to, he went into the bedroom. It was as he remembered it, a dark green Rajasthani quilt covered the bed, a desk stood at the window, an open notebook drew him there immediately. He bent to look. He realised that he knew her handwriting because she had written to him, every Christmas, every Diwali, she was the one who wrote in a pretty card and signed for herself and Ravi. He stood there, wondering how much he really knew about her.

'I'll read it to you,' he heard her voice from the door. He turned, and was embarrassed, and angry with himself, and tried to tell her he had not read, nor intended to read. But he said nothing, there was no point.

'Sit,' she said, 'I'll read what I wrote last night.' He didn't sit. He wanted to leave the room. He just stood there, looking at her hair, and the return of her anger. She said again, 'Sit, Srinivas. I want you to understand why I said what I said, why I want what I want, and why I am so angry.'

'Can't we go downstairs?' he asked her, smiling a little. She smiled too, and said, 'Oh all right, go. I'll come down in a minute, I have to pee. Srinivas, what were you doing in my bedroom anyway?'

'I wanted a towel, would you bring me one please?'

He went downstairs and got a glass of water. He considered for a moment that he could have said yes, and would have spent the afternoon, and now the evening, and all night in the arms of the woman he had wanted for two decades. He wished he could crush his conscience, and crush her, in his grip, in his arms. He took a few shaky breaths, and sipped his water. She came to the kitchen, and sat at one of the barstools across from him. She had her book, she opened it up in front of her.

'Marinate the steaks, that way you will have your back to me while I speak to you,' she said. But he sat down in front of her with a bottle of wine and a glass, just one. She looked at the page. And then she really began to read from it.

'I fantasise about rejection the way other people fantasise about pain. What else can I do now, when that's all I have ever had?' She stopped. She looked at him. 'Just come to my bed, or let me come to yours. It's been so very long, since someone said yes to me, Srini. Be the one.'

He got up and went around to where she sat, her tears had begun again. He put his arms around her and she leaned back against him. He put his face in her hair, Jenna's hair, and he knew, there was no going back. He had tried, in some small way, and he had failed. He gave up, and gave in, and she felt it. She stood up, and put her arms around him. The moment he looked at her, like that, all his love was there, between them, all of it, from the years and years before, thawed, and boiling over. He took her hand and took her to his bed. There was a moment of uncertainty. For them both. Her need to feel drowned it all. She led him, into her darkness.

~

Jenna walked into the guest room of her house with her husband's best friend. She closed her eyes a moment. Srinivas. She had said words to him she had never said to any man, ever. She did not know how else to ask. Four years had gone by, since she stopped. Stopped what? When they had married, Ravi and she, she had been so very very happy. She saw photos of herself at the wedding, the party in Hyderabad, the party in Toronto, where all her sisters and brothers and mother and father and uncles and aunts and cousins came. Young and full of anticipation of the sweetness to come. That night, they stayed at her parents' place, and everyone slept all over the house, but they had the guest bedroom, and she was thrilled. Of course they had slept together, for two whole years, but this was their wedding night. She undressed and slipped into the bed and curled up against him, already feeling wet and warm, anticipation. He kissed her, and she thought it would be the loveliest sex they had ever had. And then he turned her a little, so she was facing away from him, and put his leg over her, and said, 'Sleep well.' She was too stunned to say anymore, but she was tired, and soon fell asleep. And then there was sex of course, and some of it was sweet, and there was Megan, and there was school, and her own PhD, and his father's sickness, and then she was just not the main thing, not even to herself. And then, every time they met Srinivas, and every time she turned to look at him and found his eyes on her, with such a look in them as she never saw on Ravi's face, a clear and transparent ache for her, she would open up, she would remember that she was a beautiful and sexy woman. She would believe what the mirror sometimes showed her, a toss of wild loose red curls, slanty green eyes, a face that was older than young, but not as old as old, waiting for a man's urgent touch, sweet touch, loving touch, aggressive touch, demanding touch, because he wanted her. Srinivas wanted her. Ravi had said no in so many ways. He was tired, he was late, his parents were in the next room, his head hurt, he was busy, he had to wake up early the next day, he didn't feel like it. And one day, she stopped asking. If she had said to him, 'Ravi, please just fuck me,' she wondered, if he would have, if he would have understood the urgency she felt, and the danger that she was almost lost to him. But she never did ask that way. So now here she was, in their guest bedroom, in their own house, she had said to this man, who had wanted her so long, whom she knew she would hurt, whom she would use and destroy, 'Srinivas, fuck me. Sex is easy, we can do this.'

She took her dress off over her head, she unhooked her bra, she dropped it to the ground, her breasts dropped slightly, but he stepped toward her and put both his hands on them, and he bent down and kissed her. Then he just looked at her face, and there was an amazement, wonder in his face as he did, childlike and quiet, he brought her to lie on the bed. He pulled a blanket over them, and kissed and kissed her and said, over and over, 'You are so beautiful, Jenna, and I have wanted you so much, my love, my life,' he kissed her, all of her, he forgot no part, he neglected no little inch of her skin and her being. Not her face, her crazy green eyes, not her breasts, not her back, which he lay on, not her hair, which he had lost himself in, and not the sweet little strip of red curls he found under her green panties. Those he kissed, and reached inside with his tongue, and she held his hands, and raised her hips to him, and suddenly pulled him all the way up.

'Look at me,' she said. 'It's been so long, and it's so sweet, and I don't want to feel this alone,' she said, pushing his hands down, and his fingers, with hers, inside her, where his tongue had just been. She looked deep into his eyes, and as they sunk their fingers deeper and deeper inside her, together, he saw it in her eyes, her orgasm, long before he felt those little and then huge contractions as she finally moaned, and said 'Kiss me, my love.'

~

He took an early flight home. He had a message from her on his cell phone when he touched down in Atlanta. And later an email, with an attachment. He opened it up. He stood holding a cup of Tim Horton's hot cocoa. He smiled sadly into the camera. It was the sad smile of a clear conscience. The Niagara river plunged down behind him, as it had done forever before, and would do forever after him.

~